She could ba
"He said he'd ... ... n
pieces if I inv...

"Oh, Shannon." He ... her shoulder.

The immense sympathy in those two words overwhelmed her. She didn't know if she should lean into him or run away. "Thank you for helping her and fixing everything."

"I followed you to help you," he said, a lick of impatience in his voice. "You need to report this."

"If I do and they hurt my baby, it will be my fault. I can't live with that."

"What's really going on?"

"I don't know much more than you do." She didn't realize she was crying again, or that Daniel had her wrapped in his arms until the fabric under her cheek was damp.

"Will you trust me?" Daniel asked when she quieted.

It seemed she already did.

* * *

Be sure to check out the next books in this miniseries:

Escape Club Heroes—Off-duty justice, full-time love

* * *

**If you're on Twitter, tell us what you think of Harlequin Romantic Suspense!
#harlequinromsuspense**

Dear Reader,

Welcome back to Philadelphia, Pennsylvania, home of the Escape Club! This riverside hot spot for music lovers has also become known as a safe haven for people with problems that slip through the cracks of typical law-enforcement channels.

Daniel Jennings is facing a turning point. Will he take on more responsibility with his family's construction company or stick with his passion of serving the community as a firefighter? It's good to have options, but what he needs is some objective guidance.

An employee of Jennings Construction, Shannon Nolan, is facing a nightmare. When her young son is kidnapped while she's at work, her relationship with her boss, Daniel, gets complicated. Yet soon it's clear she'll never see her son again without help from Daniel and his connections at the Escape Club.

Spending time with these characters became an intriguing and lovely study in what family means to each of us. I loved Shannon's tenacity to carve out an ideal life with her son despite a deadly threat and Dan's resolve to break through her stubborn, protective layers. I hope you'll enjoy their journey and that soon these characters will feel like family to you, too.

Live the adventure,

Regan Black

PROTECTING HER SECRET SON

Regan Black

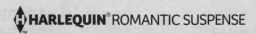
HARLEQUIN® ROMANTIC SUSPENSE

Recycling programs
for this product may
not exist in your area.

ISBN-13: 978-0-373-40235-9

Protecting Her Secret Son

Copyright © 2017 by Regan Black

Printed in U.S.A.

Regan Black, a *USA TODAY* bestselling author, writes award-winning, action-packed novels featuring kick-butt heroines and the sexy heroes who fall in love with them. Raised in the Midwest and California, she and her family, along with their adopted greyhound, two arrogant cats and a quirky finch, reside in the South Carolina Lowcountry, where the rich blend of legend, romance and history fuels her imagination.

Books by Regan Black

Harlequin Romantic Suspense

Escape Club Heroes

Safe in His Sight
A Stranger She Can Trust
Protecting Her Secret Son

Harlequin Intrigue

Colby Agency: Family Secrets (with Debra Webb)

Gunning for the Groom
Heavy Artillery Husband

The Specialists: Heroes Next Door (with Debra Webb)

The Hunk Next Door
Heart of a Hero
To Honor and To Protect
Her Undercover Defender

Visit the Author Profile page at
Harlequin.com for more titles.

For my grandmother.
Her love, belief and wisdom carried me
every day of her life.
She epitomized courage, determination and
motherhood and never turned down an opportunity
to make her family or the world a better place.

Chapter 1

Shannon Nolan loved this stage of a building project, the spark and buzz in the air when the crew rode the rush of adrenaline as they neared another finish line. Dipping her brush in the small cup of paint, she glided another coat of glossy gray over the wide wood trim around the doors and windows. Her boss's eye for design was almost as good as his eye for detail. It only spurred her on knowing that, when she was done here, she'd be assigned to the pro bono project the company had taken on last month.

Another perk of working for Jennings Construction, she thought. Beyond the steady work, good pay and great supervisors that made it easier on her as a single mom, the company kept a finger on the pulse of the community and frequently stepped in to help. The way she understood this project, a charity group had reached out to her boss, Daniel Jennings, and his father, the company owner, for help remodeling a home to make it more accessible for a police officer injured in the line of duty. She couldn't wait to get over there and pitch in.

"That's coming along, Shannon."

Speak of the devil, she thought, smiling to herself. She carefully finished painting the section before turning to greet Daniel. Since he was a Philadelphia firefighter, the construction work was his secondary interest, although he could easily make an excellent living based on his construction skills. With his black hair, dark blue eyes and fit body, he probably made hearts race whether he was in his turnout gear or the Jennings T-shirt, jeans and loaded tool belt he wore now.

"We appreciate you coming in on a Saturday," he said.

"No problem." She stepped back to check her work. "The extra hours this week are a big help to me."

He was paying her time and a half. The extra pay would be a welcome boost heading into the holidays. In her mind, she already had the money divided between her son's college fund and the Christmas fund. At four years old, Aiden had a wish list for Santa Claus that ran toward a big-boy bike, a train set, Lego blocks and the perpetual request for a puppy. Although they were in a no-pet rental now, once they had a house with a little yard—still two years to go on that goal—she planned to make his puppy wishes come true.

The Christmas lists would only grow more elaborate and expensive as her son got older. However, raising him alone was a decision she'd never regretted. Despite the challenges and the occasional longing for adult conversation, she enjoyed every high and low moment with her son while squeezing the most out of every dollar she could earn.

Daniel cocked a hip and rested a hand on the hammer in his belt. "You've done great work for us. I can certainly use more time in the coming weeks if you've got it to spare."

She wanted to leap on the offer and purposely bit back the instant agreement. Her budget was like walking a tightrope and everything had to be balanced with Rachel, the friend and neighbor who kept an eye on Aiden while she worked. "Are you talking about the charity house?"

"Yes." He stepped up to the window, peering out at the crew. "The timeline is ridiculously tight there, but we need to get it done before the weather changes."

As the end of October closed in, the temperature would drop and the first reward would be the trees going from bright summer greens to the burnished tones of autumn golds and reds. It was her favorite season. The transition meant longer sleeves and shorter days packed with trips to the park for Aiden to play and collect fallen leaves. How much of that time did she want to miss for the sake of enhancing her bottom line?

"That sounds like you want me doing more than painting."

"You're one of our best with tile. That new ADA shower is big, not to mention the flooring. Plus upgrades in the kitchen, too, that could fall to you. I mean to take this one beyond practical. I want it to be something special," he finished, his jaw set in a determined line.

That required lots of hours added on to her usual painting and finishing work with those tasks. She knew they were going with the best and most efficient crew there, for the family as well as the general company schedule.

When he shifted his stance to face her, the sunlight through the window seemed to disappear in his thick black hair and sparkle in his deep blue eyes. Belatedly, she realized he was smiling at her, patiently waiting for some reply.

"I can manage all of that." She resumed her painting, deliberately shaking off the lingering effect of her curious hormones. Gorgeous and hot Daniel was her boss. While she had yet to count herself out of the dating game, being a single mom cast a big shadow over that aspect of her life.

"What's on tap for the rest of your weekend?" Daniel asked.

"Nothing too exciting." At least nothing he would find exciting. She and Aiden had a standing plan of action on Saturdays. After the obligatory trip to the park for slides and swings, there would be a big cheese pizza to go with the cartoon superhero marathon tonight. Once Aiden was in bed, she planned to tape off her tiny kitchen and give it a fresh coat of paint. "I'm giving my kitchen a little face-lift."

"Need any help?"

She carefully set the brush across the cup of paint. Avoiding his gaze, she floundered for a polite way to turn him down. He had to know she had a son. She didn't keep Aiden a secret from the crew, and Daniel had been on the site at least once or twice when she'd had Aiden with her to watch the big delivery trucks or cement mixers. On his fourth birthday, the crew had given him a tool belt complete with plastic tools so he could pitch in when she brought him to visit a site.

In her back pocket, her cell phone buzzed, belting out the old-school ringtone she used for unknown calls and text messages. Saved from the awkward moment, she set aside the paint cup and pulled out her phone, swiping the screen to view the text.

No words, only a picture of her son. He was strapped into a car seat, his shirt rumpled, his pale blond hair windblown, and his cheeks and eyes were red. His lashes were spiked with tears and his lower lip thrust forward in a pout.

What had happened? Why would her neighbor send this rather than call? Then she realized what she was looking at and her heart thudded in her chest. The fabric on the booster seat was all wrong and Rachel's van didn't have black leather upholstery.

Staggered, terrified by her worst fears, she dropped the phone as she doubled over, clutching her stomach as if she'd taken a punch.

Daniel caught the phone and steadied her with a hand at her elbow. "Shannon? What's wrong?"

"I—I'm not sure."

The ringtone sounded as another text came in and she grabbed the phone from Daniel.

If you want to see your son again, tell his father to cooperate.

Her stomach clenched and she clapped a hand over her mouth. Whoever was behind this had chosen the wrong leverage. She'd never had any influence over Aiden's father. Naturally, the sender's number was blocked, but she hit the icon to call back anyway. It rang and rang, and no one answered.

"I have to go," she said. With tears blurring her vision, she scrolled through her call history and dialed the sitter. No answer. She tried Rachel's house phone, stumbling out the front door of the nearly complete job site.

"Hang on," Daniel said.

"Can't." She had to get over there, had to find Aiden. Dreadful scenarios tore through her mind, each worse than the last as she bolted across the lawn for her car.

How had anyone connected Aiden to his father? It seemed all her precautions had done no good at all.

"Shannon!" Daniel's voice followed her, the sound faint as if reaching for her from the far end of a long, dark tunnel.

She ignored him, focused solely on getting to the sitter's house. Denial warred with logic, all of it blurred by a frantic desperation. Digging into her front pocket, she found her car keys.

She'd barely pressed the unlock button when her wrist was caught. Bigger, calloused, Daniel's hand took her key and held her in place.

"Let me go." She reached for the key, missed.

"You're in no condition to drive," he said in that unflappable way he had.

"Let me go!" She twisted against his grip, made zero progress.

His eyes were filled with concern. "What happened?"

"My son is—is…" She couldn't finish the sentence, not until she had proof this wasn't some sick joke. She had to see for herself that Aiden wasn't safely where she'd left him early this morning. "The sitter called," she fibbed.

"I'll drive."

"No." She couldn't, this was *her son*, her responsibility. "I'm okay. I just need a second." She gulped in air, forced it out. "The call startled me, that's all." She held out her open palm for the car key. "I'm okay. I need to get over there." Another breath. "I'll come right back." A cold wave of fear crashed over her. *Please don't let that promise turn into a lie.*

Through narrowed eyes, his mouth thin and tugged down on one side, her boss studied her with the same drawn-out assessment he gave to imperfect corners and uneven subfloors. Reluctantly, he handed her the car keys.

She pushed her lips in to a smile, knew she'd failed to sell it when he scowled. "I'll be right back." Opening the car door, she slid behind the wheel. As she pulled away from the curb, she used the hands-free button on her steering wheel to dial Rachel again.

With every unanswered ring, she cursed Aiden's father, cursed herself for falling for the glossy facade hiding his ugly nature. She reminded herself that without him, she wouldn't have Aiden, the love of her life. Of course, without her brutal ex she wouldn't be terrified for Aiden's safety right now, either. It was a circular, unwinnable chicken-and-egg argument that had no real bearing on the crisis at hand.

In her rush to get to the sitter's house and see first-hand what was going on, Shannon pushed the speed limits and ran yellow lights, heedless of the truck following her.

She'd left her husband nearly five years ago, relieved for once that his connections paved the way for what might have been the fastest divorce on record in New York. After much deliberation, she'd chosen Philadelphia to start over, creating a new life for herself just in time to become a mother.

How had anyone tied Aiden to his father? She'd changed her name and left her ex's name off Aiden's birth certificate, refusing to saddle her son with that burden.

She parked in front of the sitter's house and raced up the lawn, shouting for her friend and her son. "Rachel! Aiden!"

Dialing Rachel's cell phone again, she followed

the sounds around to the backyard. Her breath stuttered when she saw the gate swinging back and forth in the breeze, the latch broken. She pushed through, still shouting.

The yard was empty and far too quiet. The swings on the playset swayed listlessly, no boyish laughter spilled from the fort and the trucks in the sandbox were stalled out.

Aiden had raced to the playset when she'd dropped him off this morning while Rachel's twin boys, a year older than Aiden, had been carving ruts in the sandbox with their dump trucks.

As she turned for the kitchen door, her heart leaped into her throat. The door had been forced open, the doorjamb a splintered mess above and below the lock. Her phone rang in her hand as she debated whether or not to call for help.

"Hello?"

"If you call the police, I'll send the kid back to you in pieces," a man said.

She blinked and turned her face to the sun in an effort to erase the terrifying images the rough, mean voice created.

"Mommy!"

Aiden's voice carried over the line, bringing her a rush of relief along with the pain of knowing a stranger held her son hostage. "Let me talk to him," she pleaded.

"Sure thing. Just as soon as his father toes the line. I want my property and an apology to go with it."

The call ended and the cruelty in that unfamiliar voice quashed Shannon's hope. Aiden would not be inside the house.

A sob tore free from her throat on a tide of emotion. Her son was gone, out of sight and out of reach, but still alive. Would the same be true for Rachel and her boys? If her ugly past had brought harm to her friend and neighbor, too, she'd never forgive herself.

"Stop!"

She spun around, struggling to fit her boss into the miserable context of this godforsaken day. "Daniel?" He should be at the site, not here. "How did you…?" Her voice trailed off as she figured it out.

"I followed you," he replied, confirming her guess. "What are you doing here?"

Rachel's phone had gone silent, so she hit redial. "My son." She choked. "Should be here. H-he's not." Daniel wasn't a cop, but he knew plenty of them. She had to tread carefully. Aiden's life depended on it. "The sitter should be inside." With the phone in her hand, she fought tremors as she pointed to the busted door. "I need to check on them."

"Hold up." He stepped in front of her. "We need to call the police first."

"No!" She made a grab for his phone. "You can't call anyone or he'll hurt Aiden."

"He who? What's going on?"

"I don't know yet," she admitted. "Just hold off on the police for a minute and let me check on my sitter and her kids. I'm going inside." She used her elbow to nudge aside the broken door, calling Rachel's name again. Daniel followed, silent as a shadow. She found her friend's cell phone under the toe kick of the kitchen island, the screen cracked.

As the ringing died and the voice mail message came through her phone, Shannon caught the unmistakable sound of crying children from the other side of the basement door. The doorknob was broken off, preventing their escape.

"Rachel? Boys? Are you okay?"

The crying faded and she heard shushing noises. "Shannon, is that you?"

"Yes." Relieved, she felt her hammering pulse ease a bit, though her friend's voice was faint and full of pain. "Are you hurt? Should I call an ambulance?"

"No. No police!" Rachel coughed and sputtered, tried to talk again. "I'm fine. The boys are fine. They said no police."

They. So more than one person attacked her neighbor, kidnapped her son. "I know. It's okay," Shannon assured her. "She sounds weak," she murmured to Daniel. "How do we get her out?"

Daniel ran his hands over the door hinges. "On it. Give me a second." He jogged out of the house.

As she spoke through the door with the boys, they confirmed Rachel's claim that they weren't injured. She hoped the same held true for their mother.

Daniel returned, tool belt slung over his shoulder. He made quick work of popping out the hinges and Rachel and her boys emerged from the basement.

For a long moment, Rachel clung to Shannon, quaking from the ordeal. When she finally sat down at the kitchen table, her brown eyes were filled with worry and sorrow. Her gaze shifted between Shannon and Daniel. "You didn't call the police? He's not a cop?"

"No," Shannon replied. "This is my boss, Daniel Jennings. He followed me when I left the job site."

"Thank God." Rachel hugged her boys close. "Oh, that's horrible and I know it." She pressed her hands to her face, hugged her boys again. "They took Aiden. I'm sorry." Tears flooded her eyes, rolled down her cheeks. "They promised to come back if we called anyone. Not that I had a phone to use down there. How did you know?"

Shannon couldn't say the words, just pulled up the messages and showed Rachel. Daniel, too. No sense hiding the truth of this fiasco from him now. He scowled for a long moment at the phone, but he didn't say anything.

Meeting Shannon's gaze, Rachel only cried harder. Daniel handed her a roll of paper towels. "They had Aiden before I knew what was going on," she said, blotting her face dry. "I'm so sorry, Shannon. You know I love him like my own."

"I know." She sat down and hugged her friend, taking and offering comfort through an unthinkable crisis. "They didn't hurt your boys?"

"These two seem to be fine," Daniel said gently. He had the twins perched on stools at the kitchen island and had given them each a juice box. He handed Rachel a bottle of water. "Tell us how it went down."

"I heard a loud bang near the gate and suddenly two men stormed into the yard, out of nowhere." She tucked a strand of loose hair behind her ear and dabbed at her eyes.

"They smashed the gate like Hulk," one of the twins reported, while his brother nodded.

"I was over there—" she pointed "—at the sink, watching the boys play while I cleaned up breakfast. And…" She coughed again.

"Take your time." Shannon urged her to sip the water.

Rachel obliged. "One of them had my boys," she continued. "The other was hauling Aiden off the swing, toward the gate.

"There was no time to react. I grabbed my phone to call for help, but it was too late. The one with the twins kicked the door in and shoved his way inside with my boys." She went over and laid a hand on each head. "He pushed them through the basement door. I screamed and he sprayed something in my face. Knocked my phone out of my hand." Lost in the recollection, she stared at the cracked phone screen.

"How long ago?" Daniel prompted.

"Two hours, maybe?" She squinted at the oven clock. "No, a little more than that. We'd just had breakfast."

Shannon's vision blurred with tears. Two hours was a big head start. "They only called me a few minutes ago. They could be anywhere with Aiden by now."

"Did he say anything?" Daniel asked.

"Told me not to make a report or—or else."

Daniel's nostrils flared and Shannon had the feeling he was suppressing a string of choice words and opinions unfit for the ears of little boys.

"Did they say anything to you guys?" Daniel asked the twins.

"They were bossy," the first twin replied.

"And mean," his brother added. "They smelled like spaghetti."

"Seriously?" Daniel cocked his head.

The boys nodded in unison.

Rachel shrugged. "Maybe. Whatever he sprayed in my face made me groggy and choked me. I woke up on the landing, the boys crying over me and trying to wake me up."

"You always wake up when we cry," one twin declared.

"We can take you to a hospital," Daniel offered. "Get you checked out."

"I'm fine," Rachel said.

"The cough may be more related to the spray," he said. "You shouldn't take the chance."

"Not now, not today," she insisted. "What are you going to do?" she asked Shannon.

What could she do? "I'm not sure," Shannon confessed, staring at her phone. "I won't report it," she promised Rachel.

"You have to," Daniel countered. "The kidnappers are gone, coming back isn't smart."

She shook her head as Rachel gasped in fear. "I believe the threats. I won't put this family at risk." She pulled Rachel into another hug. "I don't know why this happened, but I don't want you in the middle of it."

"The men this morning put me in the middle of it. You're one of my best friends. You and Aiden are family. Whatever you need, we'll help."

Moved beyond words, Shannon could only hug her again.

Daniel pulled out his phone. "I'm calling one of the guys to take care of this door and the gate." He turned the phone to Rachel. "Is there someone else to stay with you when he's done?"

"My husband's traveling on business. He won't be home until next week."

Shannon caught the flare of concern in Daniel's dark blue eyes. "I'd feel better if you could go somewhere else for a few days at least. You shouldn't be here alone," she said.

When Rachel agreed, Shannon helped her and the boys pack while Daniel and one of the Jennings carpenters she didn't normally work with repaired the damage. She kept expecting another message from the kidnappers, some proof of life or a demand she could work with, but nothing came through.

She leaned against her car door, trying to smile as she waved to Rachel's boys as the family left their house to visit her mother a few hours away in New Jersey. "At least they're out of harm's way. What now?" she murmured, at a complete loss.

"You need to call the cops," Daniel said flatly.

"I can't. You heard Rachel."

"They took your son," he said, incredulous.

"I know!" She bit her lip against another outburst.

"What aren't you saying?"

"He called," she said. "When I got here. When I walked into the backyard, he called and said…" She couldn't get the words out. "He said he'd send Aiden back to me in pieces if I involved the police."

"Oh, Shannon." He rubbed her shoulder.

The immense sympathy in those two words overwhelmed her. She didn't know if she should lean into him or run away. "Thank you for helping her and fixing everything."

"I followed you to help *you*," he said, a lick of impatience in his voice. "You need to report this."

"If I do and they hurt my baby, it will be my fault. I can't live with that."

"What's really going on?"

"I don't know much more than you do." She didn't realize she was crying again, or that Daniel had her wrapped in his arms, until the fabric under her cheek was damp.

"Will you trust me?" he asked when she quieted.

It seems she already did. She eased back from his solid warmth and tried to regain some distance and some dignity, a lost cause at this point. "I won't speak with the police. Not yet, not after those threats."

"How do you feel about former police?"

She shook her head. "Daniel—"

"Your place is nearby, right?" He looked toward the corner, squinting at the street signs.

"Around the corner," she answered, caught off guard by the shift in topic. She supposed he knew her address from her personnel file.

"We'll drop off your car and then you're coming with me."

"You need to get back to the job site." She should go back as well, there wasn't anything she could do other than wait for the kidnappers to make a demand she could work with.

"Ed's got it under control."

She groaned, thinking of her immediate supervisor and the project manager on the house they were finishing up. A little older, Ed Scanlon was patient and easygoing most of the time. Over the past few years, she'd come to think of him as the older brother she'd never had. "I need to call him, let him know I won't be back." She pushed a hand through her hair. "What am I going to tell him?" He doted on Aiden. If she told him the truth, he'd be relentless about pressuring her to call the cops. Daniel posed plenty of opposition without Ed chiming in.

"I handled it," Daniel said. "I outrank him, remember?"

Ed was a friend as well and she didn't want to hurt him. "Handled it how?" She gaped at her boss. "You didn't tell him the truth."

"No, I didn't. And the guy who helped me with the repairs got a story about an attempted home invasion. Come on now."

"I'm not talking to the police."

"Trust me, I got that part loud and clear." He reached

around her and opened her car door. "First, your place. Lead the way."

She fought back tears as she drove, wishing the phone would ring. Threats or demands, she didn't care, as long as whoever held Aiden gave her another glimpse of her son, alive.

"I'll find you, baby," she vowed to the empty booster seat in the back. "You'll be home soon." She put all her thoughts toward how they would celebrate his homecoming and *almost* succeeded in blotting out the worst-case scenarios.

Daniel followed her to a tidy little rental in a duplex on another quiet street in the established, family neighborhood. Either she or the landlord took good care of it from what he could see out here.

His money was on her. Shannon's work ethic and positive attitude inspired and spurred on the others. No surprise. His father, as the head of Jennings Construction, made a habit of hiring quality people and doing everything possible to keep them happy on the job. Fewer employee turnovers meant better profits. Having seen her on various job sites, he knew how much the crews liked her and her son.

He'd known her address and phone number from the employment records, noticed she'd been in the area for almost five years and at this address for just about four. No mention of a spouse in her file, current or ex. He knew from the chatter around the job sites that she didn't date a lot, either.

Jennings was her only employer after her son had been born and her two local references came from a little restaurant where she'd been a waitress and the owner of a tile store where she'd been a showroom assistant. Shannon had juggled the two jobs through most of her pregnancy.

Daniel felt like a stalker for being able to pull all of that right out of his head. He'd never reviewed employee records for personal reasons before Shannon Nolan. After today, he never would again. If he wanted a date, he was better off using one of the apps the guys at the firehouse talked about.

Except something about her and her son had appealed to him from the first time he'd spotted her painting the intricate spindles of a porch rail on an exterior remodel project.

Late spring, he recalled, a fresh and clear afternoon. Her painting hand, those long fingers tipped with short unpainted nails, had been steady as she rocked the baby seat gently with her toe in time to the music Ed had pumping from the radio around front. The sunshine had highlighted the many shades of her fair hair. She'd worn it long then, had cut it some time ago, leaving a fringe of bangs that framed her wide brown eyes in a fine-boned face.

That scene had stayed with him all this time, daring him to stop wishing about it and take action. For years, he'd fabricated excuses that centered around her being an employee and off-limits. Now, on the day he'd been ready to ask her out, disaster struck.

"Take the hint," he muttered. "Some things just aren't meant to be."

He could write off the idea of asking her out, probably for forever. Lousy timing didn't get worse than this. She'd always associate him with her son's disappearance, no matter how things turned out, and he hoped like hell they'd turn out right. Good people should have the happy endings in life.

Quickly veering away from that line of thought, he watched her leave her car, relieved when she walked down the drive toward his truck. At least he wouldn't have to chase her down and haul her bodily into the vehicle. He couldn't fault her reasoning behind cooperating with the kidnapper and yet he couldn't step back and let her deal with it alone. Just wasn't wired that way.

She didn't say anything when she climbed into the truck, buckled up. He didn't know what to say, so he let the silence fill the cab, the situation percolating in his head while they drove out to the Escape Club.

The club owner, Grant Sullivan, had created a hot spot for local bands and music lovers at the pier on the Delaware River. While business boomed, so did the side work. As a retired cop, Grant persistently and quietly built up a reputation for using the club to help people in the community.

It had started with giving short-term jobs at the club to cops and other first responders, and little by little, the concept had grown into something bigger and yet more flexible.

When a case slipped through the cracks of normal law enforcement, often Grant and his connections proved effective and helpful. Daniel knew of several instances of Escape Club staff helping locals out of tough spots, large and small. He'd been peripherally involved on recent cases involving two of his friends from the fire department, Mitch and Carson. With Mitch's assistance, a murderous stalker had been stopped, and for Carson, a drug-dealing scam had been exposed and justice served.

He didn't expect Shannon to believe him about Grant's effectiveness, and he'd leave the sales pitch to

Grant. At this point, he could only pray Shannon would listen and give Grant a chance to try.

Shannon leaned forward as he parked in the delivery lot near the kitchen. "Escape Club?"

"You've heard of it?"

"Rachel and her husband have had date nights out here." She didn't look at him, her face turned toward the river rolling by. "They say the music is always great."

"They'd be right." He released his seat belt and shifted to face her. "The owner, Grant Sullivan, is a former cop. Hang on." He held up a hand to stop her protest when fear flooded her big brown eyes. *"Former,"* Daniel repeated. "He has connections and resources on and off the force. Believe me, I understand why you want to cooperate with the kidnapper."

"You have children?"

"No." He couldn't quite laugh it off. He wanted kids, had always assumed he'd be a husband and father. At thirty-two, he'd expected to be on that path by now. He had a foggy picture in the back of his head of noisy family dinners with his parents doting on grandkids and a strong, caring wife to help him navigate life. He just hadn't met her yet, the woman who could love him and stand by him despite his career as a firefighter. "That doesn't mean I can't see that this is hell for you."

She swiped a tear from her cheek and rubbed her hands on her torn and paint-stained work jeans. "What can Grant do?"

"It's always a surprise," Daniel replied, hopeful. "Come on." He eyed the traffic on the street, but didn't see cars circling the block or people paying specific attention to them. The club, usually bustling by noon on a Saturday, wouldn't open until four tonight in anticipation of a special concert. Daniel was on the schedule to arrive by seven to help at the bar through closing.

Opening the back door, the hard thump and kick of the drums poured out. More than likely, that was Grant enjoying a jam session before the band arrived for the final sound check. The man loved to sit in with the bands whenever possible.

Guiding Shannon down the hall and into the club, Daniel paused at the end of the bar. "That's Grant up on stage," he said to Shannon.

"All right." Doubt clouded her features as she watched him work the drums.

Daniel tried to see the club owner through her eyes. With his dark hair going gray at the temples, his stocky build and perfect rhythm, Grant looked more like a rock star defying the years than a savvy club owner with a gift for private investigations.

"He knows how to be discreet." Daniel forced himself to stop talking. She'd held up remarkably well considering strangers had snatched her son and threatened his life, but no one had adequate words to ease her distress.

Her lips pressed into a tight line, she wrapped her arms around her midsection and glanced around the space while they waited. Grant had transformed the run-down warehouse into a gleaming, popular night club. Daniel couldn't help wishing he'd been on hand for some of the build.

Grant finished the song and pushed his headphones off his ears, waved when he spotted them. "Be right there." He stepped away from the drums and tucked the sticks into his back pocket. He ducked out of sight for a moment, then reappeared from backstage, hurrying forward, his limp barely noticeable.

"Daniel." Grant reached out and the men clasped hands with a comfortable familiarity. "You're early." His astute brown eyes swept over Shannon. "I take it this isn't a social call."

"No, it's not," Daniel said. "This is Shannon Nolan. She's had some trouble today and we could use some advice."

Grant's thick salt-and-pepper eyebrows arched up and he reached out, shook her hand. "What kind of trouble?"

She started to answer and stopped herself with a quick shake of her head. "I should go."

"Not alone," Daniel said. He waited until she lifted her despondent brown eyes to his. "Not alone," he repeated. She did too much on her own and this wasn't a situation anyone could be expected to handle without help, regardless of the kidnapper's demands.

"Come on back and fill me in," Grant said in a friendly tone that softened what could easily have been an outright order.

He led the way down the hall, gesturing for Daniel and Shannon to enter the office first. "Have a seat," he said, closing the door.

Daniel appreciated the consideration as they sat down in the mismatched guest chairs in front of Grant's desk. Though the club was deserted right now, the prep crews would be coming in soon, along with the featured band and the warm-up acts. He didn't want anyone overhearing what Shannon had to say.

Grant's chair squeaked as he settled in, and he gave Shannon a cautious smile. "What happened?"

"My son was kidnapped from the sitter's house this morning." Tears welled in her eyes, but her voice was clear and steady as she relayed the story.

Daniel made mental notes, only chiming in when Grant asked a question about the damage, the timing. While she explained it all, Grant looked over the first text messages on Shannon's phone, reviewed the less-than-helpful incoming call log.

"Nasty work using kids as pawns," he grumbled. Grant's famous scowl was edging toward the ferocious end of the spectrum as he handed Shannon's phone back to her across the desk. "Who is the boy's father?"

She fidgeted in her chair, shoulders hunched and her palms pressed between her knees. "I don't have any influence over him. The only time he cooperated with me was when he granted me the divorce. I haven't even been back to New York."

"You never told him he had a son?" Grant asked.

"No."

At Shannon's whispered answer, Daniel felt his heart clench. Twice now, in text and by phone, the kidnapper had told her she'd only get Aiden back once the father cooperated. If she didn't have any influence over the man, it was no wonder she didn't show much hope.

"Could the boy's father be the kidnapper?" Grant asked, echoing a theory Daniel shared. "Maybe he found out and decided he wanted to be a dad after all."

"No." Shannon sat up straight. "He would have been furious to learn I was pregnant. I left him—left town—before he found out."

As she nibbled on her lower lip, Daniel sensed she left something dark and ugly unsaid.

"Why?" Grant pressed. "You were afraid of him?"

"Yes." She closed her eyes, her hands fisted on her knees hard enough to turn her knuckles white under the spattering of gray paint. "He turned into a different man after the wedding."

Daniel could see she wanted to leave it at that. Just as he could see Grant's cop instincts were humming. He had his teeth into this now and wouldn't let up until he had all the facts.

"Who is the boy's father?"

"It's irrelevant." She sniffled and another tear rolled down her cheek.

Grant's chair squeaked as he leaned back. "I don't think so."

"Can you help me find my son?"

Daniel wanted to give her another hug and let her cry it out, though it wouldn't help anything. He recognized the defeated look in her eyes, the utter helplessness dragging at her, having seen it in the faces of people certain they were going to die even as first responders did everything possible to save them.

"If you give me the whole picture, we have a much better chance of success." Grant drummed his fingers on the desktop, watching her. When she refused to volunteer any information, his penetrating gaze shifted to Daniel. "How did you meet Shannon?"

"She's a Jennings employee," he replied, taken aback.

"How'd you get yourself involved in this?"

Daniel didn't care for his tone and his temper started to simmer. "*This* isn't her fault." Grant flicked his fingers, urging him to answer. "I was talking with her on the job this morning when the kidnapper first made contact."

"So you trust her?"

"Yes."

"I'm right here," Shannon snapped.

"I know." Grant gave her a cool stare. "Until you give me what I need, I'm forced to tackle this from a different angle. How can we help you if you don't help us?"

"The kidnapper said no police," she replied.

Grant pointed at himself. "I own a nightclub." He aimed that same finger at Daniel. "Firefighter and contractor, right there. I don't see any cops here."

Again, her silence stretched, filling the room.

Grant opened his mouth and Daniel knew what was coming. "Not so fast," he said to both of them. "She needs us," he said to Grant, then shot a glare at Shannon. "No disrespect intended, Shannon. You've done a great job on your own from what I've seen, but this isn't a matter of independence or providing. You're up against hard men, criminals who've done this before, in my opinion."

"I'd agree, based on the sitter's account," Grant added.

"Shannon, you need Grant's connections to get your son back safely."

"They will send Aiden back to me in pieces." She curled into herself, rocking a little. "It doesn't matter who has connections." She hiccupped as tears slid down her face again. "I h-have no influence over Aiden's father. When the kidnappers realize it, Aiden is no use to them."

Grant pushed to his feet, sent the chair rolling back as he leaned over the desk. Daniel had never seen him take such an intimidating tack with a person asking for help. "Tell me who the father is."

Shannon's shoulders trembled and her eyes were locked on her work boots. "Bradley Stanwood."

"I'll be damned." He yanked his chair back into place. "Stanwood of New York." The chair protested with another loud creak as he dropped into it. "I knew you looked familiar."

"Pardon?" Daniel looked from Grant to Shannon and back again. Had she been a celebrity or married to one? That wasn't something he kept up with, though there were people on his crews that did. "You know her? How is that?"

"Her ex-husband has ties to organized crime up and down the East Coast." Grant rubbed at the lines creasing his forehead. "When I was still a cop, Stanwood and his less-polished associates were connected to more than a few crimes here in Philly. My guess is one of his enemies grabbed their son for leverage."

With better context, the name clicked into place for Daniel. He managed to smother an oath before it slipped out.

Shannon sniffled, rocking gently again. "You can't help me at all, can you?"

"On the contrary," Grant said, fingers drumming on the desktop again. "Now that I know what we're dealing with, I've got a few ideas brewing already."

Chapter 2

Shannon stared at Grant, wishing the floor would open up and swallow her whole. This was the first time since leaving New York that she'd faced someone who understood what a big mistake her marriage had been. Settling in Philly, she'd been able to start over with a new name and a clean slate, free of Bradley's unpleasant baggage. From the sound of it, this former cop knew her husband better than she had before she'd said her vows.

Yes, she'd found her backbone and negotiated a divorce before their second wedding anniversary, but that victory felt small and empty now.

"What sort of ideas?" Hope warred with caution. Her ex had a long reach, obviously, and serious connections as well. What a fool she'd been to think Philly was far enough removed from his circle of power in New York.

Grant studied her, the anger and intimidation replaced by kindness and compassion. She felt small and petty for being irritated by it. Her wounded pride did Aiden no good. She needed Grant's help, his plans, if they were to rescue her son quickly.

The former cop countered her question with another. "There hasn't been a true ransom demand?"

She shook her head as Daniel said, "No."

Sliding a look at her boss, she still couldn't figure out why Daniel hadn't bolted. "Shouldn't you get back to the site?"

This time, the "no" came from Grant and Daniel simultaneously.

Grant leaned forward in his chair. The sympathy in his warm, brown eyes made her want to rage and scream. Yes, she'd been an idiot to marry a madman, but she was different now, older and wiser after the harrowing experience. She didn't want anyone to see her as helpless, no matter that it was true. She checked the urge to pound on the nearest wall. Barely.

"I may run a nightclub now, but I still have connections within the police department." He barreled on before she could launch a protest. "I'm going to make some discreet inquiries about your ex-husband. I'll find out if he's been seen in the area, catch up with any gossip on the latest investigations, that sort of thing. I can couch it within the context of the business. Not everyone doing business near the river is legit."

She turned her phone over and over in her hands, willing it to leap to life with some news of Aiden. "And what do I do? Just sit at home and wait?"

"Actually, I'd rather you didn't sit at home," Grant said.

Shannon raised her head in time to catch the glance Grant exchanged with Daniel.

Daniel rolled his eyes. "Fine."

"What's fine?" She didn't appreciate decisions being made on her behalf, without so much as a discussion. Although the two men in this room were honorable, nothing like her ex-husband, the lack of input or control only stressed her out more. "This is my son's life we're talking about."

"Yours, too," Grant said baldly. "I'd like you to stick close to Daniel for the next few days. I know it's inconvenient, but I see it as a necessary precaution."

"I need to be at my place or at work." If she didn't stay busy somehow, she'd lose her mind in the bleak pit of worry. "Shouldn't I be where they know to find me? In case they bring Aiden back." It sounded like a starry-eyed fantasy as the words tumbled from her lips. She couldn't let her trouble disrupt Daniel's life. He had enough to juggle managing the nearly finished project and the charity house.

"Alone, you'll be a tempting target," Grant explained. "They could pick you up on a whim and we risk losing you both."

Daniel lurched up and out of the chair, pacing in front of the closed door, one hand shoving at his black hair.

"Better that than a burden," she protested, avoiding Daniel's restless gaze. "He has a life and two jobs already. He doesn't have time to babysit me."

"It's fine." Daniel leaned back against the closed door. "I'm using personal leave from the PFD so I can oversee the charity house. I was going to assign you to that next anyway. We'll save time and gas and all that if we're together."

A few hours ago, working on the charity project had been her biggest hope. Now, it felt flat and insignificant. "You've insisted on only the best crew over there. I can't imagine I qualify with my mind on Aiden." Her heart was broken. "I know keeping busy would help, but my concentration is gone."

"I can find something for you," Daniel promised.

Nothing short of holding her baby again would restore her. She'd seen enough documentaries to know kidnapped children were rarely returned. Children stolen to manipulate crazy ex-husbands…well, she didn't want to contemplate the long odds there.

Grant cleared his throat, gaining her attention. "It's imperative you have someone with you at all times. I can assign someone else, but Daniel is here and available," Grant said. "He's familiar with you and your son. He has reason to come and go from here as well, without raising suspicion."

"Won't your inquiries at the police department raise more suspicion?" she asked. By accident, she'd overheard her ex bragging to a friend about having an entire narcotic squad in his pocket. It had been a transforming revelation, one that hadn't gone well for her when he found out. "Couldn't it get back to Bradley or whoever has Aiden?"

Grant tipped his head to the side, wrapping one hand with the other. "It is possible Stanwood or his connections in Philly have cops on the payroll," he admitted. "That's just the nature of the beast when it comes to criminal syndicates. More often, lately, they think they have more pull than they really do. I can promise you I'll be careful. Your name won't come up until I'm sure it's necessary."

Somehow his candor did more to soothe her than any overconfident assurances. It was nice that he understood that her ex and his enterprises could mean serious danger for any uninvited party poking around.

She turned her phone over and over in her hands, wishing it would ring with another picture or a demand she could fulfill. "I don't have money," she murmured. What she had were secrets—secrets she couldn't share without putting the two men trying to help her on Bradley's radar.

"Remember, your son is leverage," Grant said. "The kidnappers know that and will treat him accordingly."

She considered the safety seat they'd used and silently acknowledged Grant's point. "Organized crime and reputable construction companies don't go together. It might be best for you and the company if I use my saved vacation days." She didn't want to undermine all the good work he and his father did.

"You can't be alone," Daniel stated.

Hearing the tone he used when he ran up against a hard decision on a job site, she knew it would be useless to argue. Still, she tried. "Maybe Grant should assign someone else. It doesn't have to be you hovering as my shadow."

He glared down his nose at her, his arms crossed over his chest, his short sleeves struggling to hang on as his biceps flexed. "You have a problem with me now?"

Yes. She liked him, respected him, and she knew how important he was to his company as well as the PFD. Besides, he couldn't possibly *want* the added responsibility Grant was giving him. Sure, anyone could be hit by a bus crossing a street on any given day of the week, but her past had caught up to her. Her odds of getting hurt—or worse—were much higher. Whoever stuck by her would also be in greater peril. "You have other things to do. If it gets out that I was once Mrs. Stanwood, it could become a serious problem."

"If it does, we'll deal with it," he said with a shrug.

It wouldn't be that easy, not with her ex in the picture. Grant had a good idea what Bradley was capable of, but very few others could comprehend the uncontrollable threat he posed.

"Satisfied?"

Not even close. She held up her hands in surrender. "Fine, I won't be alone." She swallowed another spate of tears. "My son is. Say what you will about leverage and safety, I want to hear every aspect of your plans to rescue him."

Grant swiveled the chair back and forth. "It will take some time to ask around, get some answers. Once the kidnappers state specific demands, we'll have a clearer path."

She understood the logic. Too bad she had no idea how she was going to hold up if they didn't find Aiden quickly. On his best days, Bradley had been arrogant and unsympathetic as he dealt with people who interfered with business. His enemies clearly held the same standards. She worried over what her son would see and hear and how he'd be treated.

"What do I say if they call?" she asked.

"Hit record if you can," Grant answered. "We can listen for any clue in the background noise. Do your best to cooperate without promising anything. I'll stay in touch through Daniel."

He had to know he was asking the impossible. She'd willingly give up anything, promise anything, to have Aiden back home safe.

"Shannon."

She met Grant's gaze when he repeated her name, gently pulling her attention from the brittle edge of shock and misery. "I'll try."

"You'll make it," he said with a confidence she didn't feel. "You were strong enough to leave Stanwood. That couldn't have been easy." His eyes flicked to Daniel and back to her. "You're strong enough to handle this the right way. We're here to help you."

He meant it, she could see the concern in his serious brown eyes, and feel the determination emanating from Daniel as he helped her to her feet. "I appreciate it." Her throat closed as more tears threatened.

They didn't know her ex like she did. Bradley could elevate ruthless to unprecedented heights. Looking back, escaping him had been nothing short of miraculous. Without the careful sleight of hand and unexpected sympathy shown by Bradley's personal friend and lawyer, she might not have made it to Philly. She should have thought of it sooner.

"There is someone I could call," she said. "The phone number I have is old, but it could be a lead right? If he knows what my ex is working on or where he is."

"That depends on who you're talking about."

"Gary Loffler," she said.

Grant rolled his eyes. "Stanwood's personal lawyer."

"You know him, too?" Daniel asked.

"I've heard the name here and there," Grant replied. "Why do you think he'd help?"

Shannon forced herself to say the words. "He was kind to me." When her marriage had turned into a nightmare, Gary had been the only friendly person in Bradley's household. "More than fair with me when he handled the divorce."

"Give me his number." He pushed a notepad across the desk for her. "I'll add him to the to-do list." Grant tapped the notepad. "Let's think this through. You'll stick together, but where? We need a safe place for Shannon to stay. I know you have a job to do and this situation complicates matters."

"It's fine," Daniel replied. "I'm already on leave and have plenty to spare. There's a house not quite done we could use for a day or two."

Shannon listened to them plan her next forty-eight hours and prayed she wouldn't be in this heart-wrenching agony for that long. Two days were unfathomable as each minute felt like an eternity all on its own. Daniel's hand moved lightly across her shoulder, soothing her as the conversation moved on around her. She wanted to spout apologies, though none of this was her fault.

"Should I come in tonight as planned?" Daniel asked.

"No." Grant reached into his desk drawer and handed over two tickets for the concert. "I'll find someone to cover the bar. You and Shannon can squeeze into that table of friends you had coming in."

Weary, Shannon scraped the tiny specks of pewter trim paint from a fingernail. "I couldn't possibly go out tonight."

"You don't have to stay long. With a little luck, I'll have an update by this evening." Grant pursed his lips, staring hard at the two of them. "Either way—" he caught Shannon's gaze "—I'm sure I'll have more questions. With the tech resources available, I'd rather do more face-to-face than over the phone. The concert is a better reason to come by."

Once more outvoted by sound logic. Frustrated, her emotions swirling, she agreed. What else could she do? She wanted her phone to ring, to hear her son's voice. She wanted to know what the kidnappers expected. Only then would they have a solid lead.

As Daniel stepped out into the hallway to make a few phone calls, Grant asked her questions about Bradley and New York, about what she knew of her ex-husband's habits.

She answered as best she could, considering she'd closed that chapter of her life so many years ago. All the while, questions more essential to her heart, her future, pounded inside her in a vicious cycle.

Where was Aiden? Was he frightened or hungry? At four years old, he probably couldn't reason out that she'd be searching for him. The despairing thought had her heart withering in her chest.

"Come on, Shannon."

She followed the sound of the deep voice to Daniel's face. She'd zoned out again and missed his return to the office. He held out a hand, strong and calloused from hard, honest work. Bradley's hands had always been soft and well-manicured.

"Come on, now," he said gently.

What else could she do except go with him? Sobbing and wringing her hands wouldn't save her son. She thought back to her pregnancy and the days and nights coping with alternating waves of emotion. There had been soaring highs of hope and anticipation of seeing her baby followed by bouts of anxiety over motherhood and wondering how she'd provide. To fill the time, she'd researched, taken classes and socked away every spare penny. She'd prepared and planned to the best of her ability.

She would do the same for Aiden now. Waiting didn't have to be stagnant. She could shift her focus to anticipating his safe homecoming. In the meantime, she would research her ex and prepare for a rocky road ahead.

Resigned, she put her hand in Daniel's and followed him out of the club.

Daniel kept half an eye on Shannon as he drove back to her place. She hadn't said a word since they'd left the club. Although the silence unnerved him, he didn't have good cause to break it. She had every right to curl up in a corner until they found a helpful lead on Aiden. He doubted that would happen, but she had every right. Single parenting was tough for anyone. Single parenting the son of Bradley Stanwood? Well, that took more courage.

He'd walked into the club hopeful and walked out more unsettled. He recalled a few national headlines about Stanwood's less-than-legit business practices. The guy slipped through the system every time. Although Daniel didn't have all the facts—didn't feel he had a right to them—she'd been married to a nasty criminal. That kind of mistake just didn't fit with the sensible, smart and lighthearted woman he knew as an employee.

No, he suspected she didn't have any influence at all over her ex-husband. Unless the kidnappers asked her for something else, this would not end well.

He shoved aside his doubts and reminded himself he'd seen more than one miracle in his life. As a firefighter, he'd watched people survive who shouldn't have made it. Faith and belief were core components in survival, as effective as ladders and hoses and medical treatment. His purpose here was to keep Shannon safe while Grant worked on finding her son.

He parked in the alleyway behind her car. Still keeping an eye out for anyone too interested in them, he followed her inside. Her design choices set a clear mood, homey, tidy and comfortable. The furniture was secondhand, in good repair and clean. She'd probably refinished and reupholstered everything herself. Gleaming hardwood floors anchored the modest living room, ran back through the dining space to the kitchen and into an alcove with a stacking washer and dryer.

Without a word, she went up the stairs that bisected the first floor.

Looking closer, he got the sense there were clear rules here about cleaning up, making beds and eating whatever veggies were on the plate. None of that surprised him. Shannon had a reputation among the crew for being prompt, clean and friendly. She pulled her weight—more than—with the crew and she held firm about how much teasing she'd tolerate.

The evidence of a young boy in residence showed up in the booster seat at the table, the basket of children's books under the stained glass floor lamp by the couch and a pint-size table in the corner of the living room bathed in light from the front window. Daniel smiled at the line of trucks—dump, cement, freight—waiting for their boy to come home and put them to work. He couldn't help wondering if the kid had a fire truck somewhere in his fleet.

"Should I take some of Aiden's things, too?" she asked.

He smothered his surprise, pleased her voice sounded stronger. Turning toward the stairway, he gave her a smile. "Only if it helps you. When the kidnappers release him, I'm sure you'll both be able to come home."

"Right."

The single word, loaded with doubt, tore him up. As he debated the wisdom of giving her more reassurances when he didn't have any guarantees, she headed back upstairs. He gave her a few minutes, checking the windows and door locks, wondering how to be respectful and polite in an untenable situation. Ten minutes later, concerned at her absence and more silence, he went up after her.

The bedrooms were on either side of the stairs, with a good-sized bathroom wedged in between. "Shannon?"

He found her in the smaller bedroom at the back of the house. Sitting in a rocking chair, she had her hands wrapped around a floppy blue rabbit and her gaze locked on her son's small bed. "Shannon, honey, we need to go."

"Why?" The strength she'd displayed minutes ago was gone. "We should stay, be here so they can bring him home."

He recognized the shock and denial that often set in amid crisis and dire circumstance. Kneeling in front of her, he covered her hands with his. "Is this his favorite?"

"From day one," she whispered, tears glistening in her eyes. "He doesn't sleep—can't sleep—without it." She held it to her face, breathed deep, lowered it to her lap. When her weepy eyes met his, his heart clenched. "He gets so grumpy when he doesn't sleep."

"He'll be all right." Daniel didn't want to give her false hope, and yet there was nothing else to offer. "Take it with you. It will make you both feel better when you're reunited."

"You sound so confident." She tried to smile, but her lips wobbled. "I appreciate it."

It took some prompting to get her moving and keep her on task as she gathered clothes and toiletries to spend a few days away from home. She would pause, her hands full and her expression empty. The stark terror in her brown eyes made him wish for the power to restore everything with a snap of his fingers.

Regardless of Grant's trust in Daniel to stick with her and keep her safe, he wasn't a bodyguard or an investigator. Hell, at this point he wasn't sure he could even keep Shannon in line with the plan or explain her presence on the job site tomorrow. She was devastated, unfit for work, and he didn't have a clue how to pull her out of the worry that kept dragging her down.

Going on instinct, he decided to start by making sure she wasn't alone and building on that foundation. He kept up a monologue of nonsense, sharing his ideas for the charity house while he packed her suitcase and stowed the things she handed him from the bathroom into a smaller tote.

"What about tonight?" he asked, noticing she hadn't selected anything special for their next visit to the club. "The concert," he reminded her. "Grant could have news," he added when he thought she might launch another protest.

With a heavy sigh, she returned to the closet, shoved hangers back and forth until she eventually pulled out a black dress. She repeated the mute search for heels and dropped them on the bed. Sitting on the velvet-covered stool in front of an antique vanity table, she gathered makeup and dropped it into the tote.

At last they were done and he carried her things downstairs.

"Where are you taking me?" she asked, trailing him to his truck.

He tucked her suitcase and tote in the cab behind the seats. "There's a flip I haven't quite finished over in Francisville. We'll stay there tonight. Once we get you settled, we'll swing by my place before the concert."

Her lips thinned, confirmed she wasn't happy with him shadowing her.

"Are you going back to the site today?" she asked as he backed out of the alleyway.

"No. Ed's got it under control." He weaved his way

through the neighborhood streets crowded with parked cars on both sides.

She groaned. "What did you tell him about me running off?"

"I only said there was a mix-up at the sitter about which kid got hurt on the swings and things are under control. He has kids, he gets it."

"I hate lying to him," she said.

"On the upside, the place is done." The news seemed to deflate her more. "It gives me a solid reason to take them out and celebrate at the concert."

"I'm not sure I can do that." She tugged at the seat belt, as if she felt choked. "I'm not sure I've done the right thing at all, going to Grant, putting you in this awkward position."

"I'm fine." How many more times would she need him to say it? "It was my idea to go to Grant, remember?"

"When he starts asking questions..." Her voice trailed off.

"You didn't disobey. Kidnappers say no cops all the time," he pointed out. "I think it's a standard step one."

"Maybe in the movies," she said. Her cell phone on her denim-clad thigh, she tapped her fingertips across the black screen as if she could summon contact from the kidnappers at will.

"Grant would support you if you wanted to file a report and get a formal search going."

"I want that very much. A formal search, I mean." She swiped away the errant tear rolling down her cheek. "If the kidnappers are like my ex, I doubt it would get us anywhere." She cursed under her breath. "I want my son home safe, sleeping in his own bed. I want to go back to yesterday and stay there, freeze time. Or fast forward to tomorrow or the day after, when he's home."

"Just keep believing you'll see him again."

She sniffled. "I want to. I want that so much, I'll co-operate with the first demand not to formally involve police."

"All right." Although he couldn't advise her one way or another, he could be grateful she was talking again and he'd be her sounding board.

"You can't think cooperating is a mistake after encouraging me to pack up and leave my home?"

"Didn't say that," he replied.

"Didn't you?"

Daniel glanced over, caught the flash of a fight coming into her brown eyes. "No." He wouldn't let her goad him into a futile argument. "You're hurting, confused and worried for your son. It's natural to second-guess every choice while waiting for a response or reaction from the people holding him."

"You're not second-guessing anything."

He shot her another look. She had no idea what was going on in his head and he intended to make sure that didn't change. He couldn't imagine her having a positive reaction if he told her he'd been trying to ask her out. "Taking orders is part of my job."

"In my experience, you give the orders," she said.

"Huh?" He scowled. "Oh, sure. I hand out task lists at the construction sites."

"More than that," she said. "You manage timelines, supply and personnel, too."

"Are you calling me bossy?"

Her lips twitched into something less sorrowful. "If the boot fits."

He cleared his throat. "About orders. I meant I'm the one taking orders at the firehouse."

"You're a lieutenant."

She must have heard that through chatter on the job. "Yes." He gripped the steering wheel tighter. "A lieutenant is one link in a long chain of command." Thankfully, they'd reached the house and he could change the subject gracefully. "The house is right here."

He parked in the spot reserved for the house he intended to turn into a big profit once they were done using it as a hideout.

One of the calls he'd made from the Escape Club was to the staging service they used for open houses. He didn't ask for the full treatment with all the mood and style bonus points, but he didn't want them sleeping on the floor. Meals would still be a string of takeout menus and prepackaged options. That couldn't be helped unless he stocked the kitchen with food and utensils. That kind of action felt too permanent. In his opinion, right now Shannon needed to believe this would all be over within a day or two.

"We can't stay here." Her gaze roved up and down the street as they walked to the door. "We just finished this house last week."

It wasn't as if he could take her to his place. He'd just moved into another renovation site and the place was a dusty construction zone. "The stagers will be here any minute so we'll have furniture," he said.

"That's not the point. You need to get it on the market."

He opened the door, nudged her inside. "It will go on the market soon enough." A few days, or even a week, wouldn't make a real dent in his bottom line. This was one property where the investment risk was all on his shoulders, though she didn't need to know that. He didn't mind putting off the listing for her sake. Her safety was more important to him than the profit.

He told himself he'd do the same for any employee and nearly laughed out loud. He considered the core of his crew friends, though Shannon was different. He wanted something more from her, and had for a long time.

Smothering his attraction for her was going to be tough enough in a neutral environment.

Shannon turned a slow circle, taking in the details. Ed had moved her to another job and she hadn't seen this house completely finished until today. It was sleek and modern and some happy buyer would snap it up in a hurry.

"This is a bad idea." Her voice bounced around the empty space. Real estate agents often claimed the hollow effect put off potential buyers, but to her ear it signaled a wealth of potential.

"How so?"

She shrugged, searching for the words to explain. Being in her house without Aiden, wondering if she'd ever see him playing with his trucks again had been miserable. Being away from the home she'd made didn't bring her any relief. "What if he gets away and tried to come home?"

Daniel opened his mouth and snapped it shut, his vivid blue gaze sliding away from her.

She knew what he was trying not to say. "That's a mother's fantasy talking, I know it. He's only four and they had hours to get him out of the city before we knew he'd been taken. We have no leads." She shoved at her hair. "I know."

"No leads *yet*," Daniel said. "You have to believe you'll see him again. That's your primary task right now."

She did believe. She *did*, but doubt was a dark, persistent undercurrent dogging her every thought. Doubt and dread. "I believe." She curled and flexed her fingers, made herself say the words again. "It's this helpless feeling I don't know how to cope with."

"Kidnappers prey on that, use it against loved ones to get their way. Your son is still in the city and you'll get him back."

"You don't know that," she said.

"You don't know I'm wrong."

"Fair enough." She wandered through the kitchen, ran her fingers across the smooth quartz countertops. "We can't stay here. If you're paying to stage it, you need to list it."

His dark eyebrows dipped low as he scowled at her. "Have you been talking to my father?"

"Not since last month," she replied, moving around the island and down the hallway. "I didn't agree when Ed installed the bead board. It works."

"That was my call," Daniel said. "No one liked it on paper. Now back up a second. Exactly when and why were you talking with my dad?"

She faced him. His bewilderment gave her a moment's distraction from the pain squeezing her heart like a vise. "You do remember I work for him?"

Only for a bit longer, though. If Bradley was behind the kidnapping, she'd have to move on as soon as she got Aiden back. "He signs my paycheck," she reminded him. "He comes around and checks in with each of us at least once during a project."

"No, he leaves that to his managers," Daniel insisted. "Especially on jobs like this one, jobs I choose."

She tilted her head, startled by his outburst. "I really thought you two got along."

"We do," he said through clenched teeth. "We didn't see eye to eye on the timing of the charity house, that's all."

He was genuinely upset. It seemed she was wrecking his day right and left. "I got the impression he wasn't happy you fronted so much of the financial responsibility there. I'm sure he'll be pleased with the positive publicity for Jennings."

"Yeah, he will." He shoved his hands into his pockets. "And I didn't realize he was snooping around the projects on my slate."

"Not snooping, taking an interest."

Daniel snorted in obvious disagreement.

She let the tender subject go. Walking through the rest of the house, envisioning how she and Aiden might fit in. The mental exercise always kept her in the right frame of mind, happy and eager to do her best for the eventual homeowner.

"Getting hired full time with Jennings was the best thing that happened to me after Aiden was born," she said.

"Did Dad hire you?"

"Not directly."

Her mind drifted back to those first months in Philly, juggling the hours at the tile supply store with her waitressing job. Banking her tips, her back and feet aching more each week as her pregnancy progressed, she'd lost more than one night's sleep wondering what she'd do after she delivered.

"Ed would come by the diner where I worked with

the lunch order at least once a week and we'd talk while he waited. I had some ideas for updating my place, and he gave me some advice as I cleared each project with the landlord. About a week before I delivered, he asked if I was interested in picking up some extra cash doing touch-up work after the baby came. One thing led to another."

She rolled her shoulders. As soon as she had Aiden back again, her past would shove them into another new start. Would she be as lucky to find good work when she found her next place? She had her emergency fund and a decent savings built up. She supposed how long the money lasted would depend on where she ended up. She made a mental note to start researching the most affordable cities nearby.

"That was a Victorian remodel," he said. "You had the patience of a saint, painting that detail work."

She smiled. "Aiden was about a month old. I was going a little stir crazy alone in the house. Ed saved my sanity. Aiden napped in his car seat through most of that job." It was bittersweet, thinking of those days, full of such pure relief and endless joy that she was a mother, raising her son her way. "The fresh air put him to sleep every time."

"Ed was smart to bring you on. You did great work on that job. And every job since."

"Thanks." She wasn't sure how she felt about him taking such notice of her particular efforts. She'd noticed him, of course, and for several reasons that were far less professional. "I'd ask for a reference for when I leave, but I couldn't use it."

"Leave? What are you talking about?" His gaze went razor-sharp as he stared her down. "You've made a good life for yourself here."

"It's common sense. Once I have Aiden back, I'll have to relocate. I can't count on my ex or his enemies leaving me alone after this. I won't let him have anything to do with Aiden."

"You're planning to run away?"

"Relocate," she repeated stubbornly. She refused to call it running, wouldn't give Bradley that much control, even in her mind. "Isn't today proof that it's not safe for people to know who I married, who fathered my son?"

"Running." He scowled again. "That's no life for you or Aiden."

She didn't care for the judgment in his tone or the subtle disapproval in those deep blue eyes. In self-defense, she ignored him and moved on down the hallway and peeked into each of the three bedrooms, two baths.

As if she *wanted* to leave Philly. She'd done well here, rebuilding herself from the inside out and providing for her son. There was no reason for her to pop up on the radar of someone looking for her ex, yet somehow his enemies had stolen her son simply for the sake of leverage.

"Shannon, I'm sorry," he said, blocking the doorway of the hall bathroom. "I didn't mean to offend you. It's just wrong for this to drive you away from a good, stable situation."

"I agree."

"Then stop planning to leave. Focus on how you'll stay."

His intensity had her leaning back, looking for a way around him. Although he didn't understand what he was suggesting, she was too weary, too grief-stricken to try and explain further. Her plans to leave Philly weren't a result of defeat or self-pity, it was simply her reality. Only someone who'd been close to Bradley could comprehend the fear he invoked in those who disappointed him or went against his wishes.

"It was a miracle he granted me a divorce in the first place," she said. "If he decides he wants to know Aiden, everything I've worked for falls apart."

Daniel started to say something and stopped when they heard voices in the front room. "That would be the stagers. I'll get them started. You keep thinking positively."

Shannon was positive she would have to make a move, have to take some action or she'd never take another easy breath. She couldn't raise her son while looking over her shoulder, waiting for his father to strike.

With her phone set to full volume, she tucked it in her back pocket and said a prayer the kidnappers would call. It had been almost six hours without any contact. No amount of spinning could turn that into a positive.

Unable to stand around idle, she made herself useful hauling in counter stools, chairs and abstract art for the mantel. Dreamer that she was, she and Aiden had occasionally been through the houses Daniel flipped, so she had a feel for the easy, transitional style he preferred.

She stepped back, eyed the mantel and then stepped forward to make another minor adjustment.

"Can't sit still, can you?"

"Could you, in my shoes?"

"Absolutely not," he admitted. "You have a good eye."

"Hmm. It's not a stretch to know what you're after," she said without thinking.

"It's not?"

He didn't miss a detail, something that surely worked for him in both his careers.

"After a few years with Jennings, I've picked up a

thing or two." At his cocked eyebrow, she gave him the fastest reason she could come up with. "Come on. Staging a house is basic logic. The goal is to make it feel like a home and present the space as stylish and roomy without driving away potential buyers."

"Let me guess, you worked in staging somewhere along the line."

His tone, light and friendly, made her smile. "No, but I've seen several examples. On television," she added before he pegged her as a real estate stalker. To get out of the way while the stagers tweaked the furniture placement in the front room, she retreated to the kitchen and he followed.

She didn't feel comfortable admitting how she appreciated his understated style. He went beyond the boring beige palette when he flipped houses and he delivered quality on his remodeling projects. She admired the dedication and organization he and his father used that kept Jennings crews hopping and sites well managed. Daniel in particular had cultivated a winning manager in Ed, who kept things moving while Daniel was on shift at the firehouse.

Maybe she should follow his example and be bolder when she relocated. With four years of experience, she could accelerate the timeline of owning a home and a business. "How long did it take to get your general contractor's license?"

His gaze narrowed. "You don't need a contractor's license to flip houses if you partner with someone reasonable and reliable. Better not to shell out all the capital anyway, especially if you're new to the business or the area."

No, he didn't miss a detail. She bit her lip, keeping more questions to herself for the moment.

"We're nearly done here," Daniel said. "Then you can unpack. Take the master."

The shrill ringtone from her cell phone prevented a reply. She pulled it from her pocket, showed Daniel the Blocked message on the caller ID. He urged her to pick up, to use the app that would record the call.

"Hello?"

"Your son is safe." It was the same mean man who'd contacted her earlier.

"I want to see him," she said. "Another video."

"Not yet."

Daniel moved to usher out the stagers and closed the front door behind them. When he walked back into the kitchen, she put the phone on speaker.

"What do you want?"

"Everything," the caller said. "All you have, in fact."

Terror turned her knees to jelly. Bradley had given her those very words on their third date. At the time she'd found it romantic, since he'd promised her she'd have all of him. Why hadn't she seen through him? How could she have ever mistaken his greedy and possessive nature as love? "My son is my everything," she said, her throat dry and tight. "And you have him."

"Good."

She stifled a whimper at the cruel sound in that single syllable. Demands backed up in her throat, along with useless threats and promises, but she held her tongue, waiting for the caller to say something. "Can I talk to him?" Maternal worry eroded her patience.

"No. What you will do is follow my instructions to the letter."

"Yes." She rifled through her purse for pen and paper.

"First, you will maintain your routine as if nothing is

wrong." Each word was spoken carefully, as if he was reading from a script.

She'd put a numeral one on the page, now her pen stilled. "What?"

"You heard me," he snarled. "Maintain your routine to the letter. Make any deviation, make any report and your son will come back to you one piece at a time."

She couldn't smother the primal cry of despair.

"Shut up!" he shouted.

She jumped, the outburst reminding her of the sting of Bradley's palm on her cheek the first time he'd slapped her. This wasn't Bradley's voice but it was definitely his vocabulary. She clapped a hand over her mouth, praying for courage.

"I'll do anything for you," she said, pleading as she'd done in her marriage. "Just let my son go."

Daniel waved a hand in front of his throat, signaling her to end those offers.

"Maintain your routine and I will call back with further instructions." The caller sounded more natural now, with less stiffness and space surrounding each word. "Do you understand me? Yes or no?"

"Yes." She wanted to ask for proof of life, knew she wouldn't get it.

The call ended and she clutched the phone, giving in to the fresh wave of tears as she folded in on herself.

Daniel gathered her into his arms, his heart beating steady under her ear. He spoke to her, but lost in her grief, swamped by fear, she couldn't make out the words.

Her phone chimed with an incoming text with one word: routine. A second message arrived with a link to a website. She clicked on it immediately. It was a video of Aiden sitting on a twin bed in a small room.

Only fifteen seconds long, she watched her son wave at the camera and say, "Hi, Mommy," when prompted by someone off screen.

Shannon blinked away the tears so she could see clearly. She saved the video to her phone, just in case the sender removed it from the site. Then she replayed the video over and over, soaking in every nuance on her son's sweet face.

"He's confused. His eyebrows furrow right there when he's confused." She tapped the screen and paused the video. "Does he look scared to you?" She angled the phone for Daniel. "What do you think they told him?"

"No idea," he said. "You can ask him once he's back home. Give me a minute to update Grant."

"No," she protested. "They said normal routine." Panic sank deep in her belly, clawed at her. "I've never been to the Escape Club. I never helped you stage a house." She leaped to her feet, grabbed her purse. "I have to go."

"Slow down." He nudged her back to her seat, held her there with the lightest touch of his hands on her shoulders. "I heard the order. We'll get back to the routine. Grant needs this so he can have someone with the right skills analyze the link and the video."

He was right. "Okay." She forwarded the video to the email address he gave her.

"Bradley's behind this," she murmured as he exchanged messages with Grant. "The demand to make him cooperate with himself doesn't make sense, I know that. But he's behind it. The caller was using his words."

"A script? It sounded stiff, I'll give you that," Daniel agreed. "If he wants his kid, wouldn't he—"

"Don't say that. He can't want Aiden." She didn't have the resources to fight that kind of custody battle. "He can't have my son." Her breath came fast and she couldn't slow it down. Her arms tingled. She was too young for a heart attack, she thought as the room started to spin.

"Whoa, slow down. You're hyperventilating."

She reached for him, clinging and desperate. "Help," she wheezed.

"It happens," he crooned. "Breathe like this." He pursed his lips and she did the same. "There you go, just take it easy. You'll be all right. Easy, easy now. Slow it down. You're doing great."

His solid, gentle voice was wonderful, but she still felt horrible. Closing her eyes made the dizziness worse.

Daniel shifted his stance. "Let me help?"

She bobbed her chin, locked her eyes with his. He had the most amazing eyes. She focused on that deep, deep blue as he moved her hand over her mouth, held it there. He pressed a finger to one nostril.

"Keep breathing. You're doing great."

Slowly, her lungs recovered and she felt better as the strange method brought her breath under control. He carefully released the pressure on her nose while keeping her hand over her mouth.

"Better?"

"Mmm-hmm," she managed around their layered hands. The dizziness passed and her arms were back to normal.

"You're sure?"

She eased back, more than a little embarrassed that she'd lost it. Again. "How many times do you think you'll have to rescue me from myself today?" His smile, so open and easy, soothed her immeasurably. "Thank you."

Daniel gave her shoulders a squeeze. "It will be okay."

"I don't want to stay here. Not after that call."

"We're going. Back to your place," he added, preempting her next question. His phone sounded off and he showed her the reply from Grant. "See? He already has someone tearing into the video."

"All right. Thanks." She stood up, needing his assistance for only a moment before she felt steady. She checked the time. "This is about the time I'd be home with Aiden on a Saturday afternoon."

He pulled out his keys. "Then that's where we'll be." His phone rang with an incoming call this time. "Grant," he said, picking up.

"I'll turn out the lights." Shannon worked her way from the master suite, through the bedrooms and back to the hall bathroom where she stopped to splash cool water on her face.

Her routine and normal behavior didn't include crying jags or hyperventilating. She had to get herself together or she wouldn't stand a chance against whatever Bradley had planned. She didn't have any idea how she'd manage to pretend everything was fine while her son was being held hostage who-knew-where. She only knew she had to be convincing. She had no doubt Aiden's life depended on her performance in the hours—probably days—ahead.

Nothing was off-limits and no one was safe when Bradley set his mind on owning or controlling something. Seven years ago, when he'd spotted her in the bar during a conference in Miami, that something had been her. She'd been swept off her feet, falling for the charming façade.

"You were naive," she told her puffy-faced reflection.

"Not anymore." She raised her shirt to dry her face and gave herself another long look. "He fooled you, held all the cards." And she'd escaped. "Not anymore. You're stronger than he knows."

She ran her hands over her hair, tugging the wispy bangs into place over her forehead. The only hope for her eyes was dark sunglasses. All traces of the mascara she'd swept on this morning were long gone. Didn't matter.

"Believe." Daniel said that was her primary task right now. "Aiden is coming home. Believe it."

Chapter 3

Hearing her in the hall bath, Daniel backpedaled to the kitchen. He didn't mean to catch her coaching herself, yet he'd worried when she hadn't come back right away. The overhead light in the hall winked out and she paused in the kitchen doorway.

"Feeling better?" he asked.

"Getting there."

He'd relayed everything she'd said to Grant, caught between trusting her assessment of her ex's involvement and common sense. There hadn't been enough time to develop a real lead, though the video could prove helpful. Though learning construction at his dad's hip had taught him patience, he knew the waiting would wear down her resolve. He'd just find a way to help her through it.

"Do you date at all?" he asked.

Her pale eyebrows furrowed over her nose same way her son's had. "Beg pardon?"

"I'm thinking about the concert." He felt like a jerk for bringing it up, for pushing her more after such a traumatic day. "We need to go, but if dating isn't normal for you, I'm not sure how to proceed. Grant's leaving the decision to us."

"Oh."

That wasn't exactly the clarification he needed. "Do you ever go out with girlfriends? It's Saturday night." He watched her closely while his mind sifted through the tasks ahead. Training with the PFD had conditioned him to dive in, to problem-solve and help. In that role, he rarely felt helpless, thanks to training and teamwork. Assisting on a kidnapping in any capacity was way more than he'd ever expected to do.

"How can they ask me to be normal?" she demanded in a hoarse whisper, staring at her phone. "What could possibly be normal about my life while they have Aiden?"

She was on the verge of cracking again. He could see it in the hard set of her shoulders. A stiff breeze would shatter her. He took away her phone, caught her hands when she reached for it in a blind panic. "Shh. I'll help you through it, Shannon."

Her hands fluttered under his like trapped butterflies. "I have to be alone. They said normal." She sucked in a breath, held it while she lifted her gaze to the ceiling, blew it out slowly. "I am not going to lose it again."

"It's okay if you do." He let her go, missing the contact more than he should.

"No." She took another deep breath in and out. "No, I don't really date." Her eyes slid to a point over his shoulder. "Saturday night is usually Aiden, me, pizza and a movie." She got through without another tear.

"Nicely done." He admired her grit and resolve. "You and Rachel never go out?"

"Well, sure. A few times a year."

"They don't know your routine," he said, theorizing

on the fly. "It's another hoop for you to jump through, buying them time."

"That fits Bradley's methods," she allowed.

"It's something to consider." He released her hands and picked up his keys. If he was lucky, it would give her mind something to do besides worry. "Now let's get moving. We'll go back to your place and I'll stay over. Tonight we'll go out, as if we'd made plans like normal people."

"Like a date?" She flicked her hands up and down. "Look at me. I can't do that."

He swallowed the immediate protest. From his vantage point, she looked beautiful and he was sure she could do anything she set her mind to. Under the sadness and the stress, the qualities that had always drawn him to her were still there. She personified commitment and tenacity, managed to keep her balance between a demanding job and her young son. The packaging of her pretty face and lovely curves was simply icing on the cake.

"I'm trying to help, Shannon."

"I know." More tears shimmered in those wide brown eyes. "A date is hardly part of the routine for me. Dating *me* isn't in your routine, either."

He made a mental note to figure out what she meant by that. Later. This wasn't about him. "We need to buy time for Grant," he said. "And I don't see a better option than the club. It's the safest place to talk with him and we'll be surrounded by friends. It's bad luck for them that they attacked right when you started dating someone new."

With a roll of her eyes, she shook her head. "No. My ex is behind this…Just, no." She used her shirtsleeves to blot her eyes. "Take me home and I'll find a way to deal with him on my own."

"No, right back," he said, bracing for an argument. He knew all about her independent streak and her pride on the job. He'd seen her house, noticed all the evidence of the same traits. "This isn't a situation you can 'deal with.' Routine or not, you're not going through this alone."

"Daniel."

Hearing her say his name with an exasperated sigh only spurred him on. "Remember what Grant said. Alone, you're a sitting duck and what good will that do Aiden?"

He'd never been happier to have a woman shoot daggers at him. "That's low."

"You'll find I get creative when lives are on the line."

Her lips parted and snapped shut. Nudging him aside, she walked over and turned out the kitchen light. He interpreted the move as a minor victory, though he was sure there were plenty of battles ahead of them.

"We'll swing by my place," he said, meandering through the neighborhood side streets. "I pack fast, don't worry. We'll be settled at your place right away. Later, we'll meet Ed and the guys at the Escape Club for the concert. We'll stay for one set, get Grant's take on any news and go home."

"Home to my place." She drummed her fingertips on her cell phone.

"That's right."

"You may want to pack a bed, too. Aiden's will be too small for you."

He gave her a long glance while they waited for a traffic light to change. "The couch is all I need."

She didn't reply and he couldn't get a read on her with her face turned toward the window. The sound of his phone caught her attention. The hands-free setting showed Ed's name on the truck's radio display. "I'll call him back."

"You should pick it up. It's probably about the charity house."

He did as she asked, hoping for the best. He'd bitten off a big goal aiming to finish the project before he went back to his normal shifts. Suppliers had the materials standing by, and Daniel had put his best people on the job, including Shannon. Despite his father's doubts, he was confident they could pull it off.

"What's up?"

"I went by Officer Caldwell's house," Ed said, referring to the pro bono project. "Found a water leak under the bathtub."

"We suspected we'd have to re-pipe."

"Yeah, but this has been long and slow. Subfloor is rotted nearly through."

Shannon winced in sympathy.

Daniel sighed. Nothing kept a man as humble as working construction. "Did you send the material order to the office?" Jennings kept a warehouse of the basic materials on hand for smaller jobs and situations like this one. Based on his recollection of last month's inventory sheet, pulling from the stock wouldn't pinch any of his Dad's projects.

"I've got it worked up and ready to send over. Just giving you a heads-up."

Daniel forced himself to smile, hoping it translated into easy confidence over the phone. "I appreciate that, man."

"You're meeting us at the concert tonight?"

"Wouldn't miss it," Daniel promised, raising his eyebrows at Shannon.

She gave him a thumbs-up with plenty of sarcasm.

"Great. My wife's been talking about this one since you gave us the tickets."

"And the first round's on me even if I'm not tending bar," Daniel said, the smile on his face feeling natural now.

"You've met Ed's wife, right?" he asked after Ed hung up.

"She's great," Shannon replied. "Lying to her won't be easy."

"In your shoes, they would do the same thing," he said. "When it's over, I bet they'll be the first to hold a celebratory barbecue."

"They do that nearly every nice weekend since we put in that backyard kitchen."

"Still." Checking the clock on the radio display, he gave thanks for the weekend. As it was Saturday, he figured he had about fifteen minutes before his dad called about the unexpected order for materials rather than the stingy five minutes max if it were a weekday. Plenty of time to pack. "Here we are."

"You live here?"

"Don't you like it?"

"It looks great." She hopped out of the truck and perused the other houses on the block. "Not quite what I pictured for you."

He laughed it off, though he wondered what she did see when she looked at him. "Someday you'll have to explain that." Pulling out his key for the side door, he led her around. "Short-term thing," he explained. He caught her eyeing the temporary stairs and the cracked siding doing little to protect the crawl space. "And it's torn all to hell right now."

"I've seen worse," she said.

"You and me both." He opened the door to the honest scent of sawdust and sweat. "I'm sure we'll see worse again."

The first floor was torn down to the studs and looked more like it was ready for a wrecking ball than drywall. "Mind your head if you move from this spot," he advised. "I won't be long." He hesitated, debating the wisdom of leaving her alone.

She arched one honey-gold eyebrow. "Problem?"

"Promise to be here when I get back?" He wouldn't put it past her to call a cab or ride share and leave him behind. It didn't matter that he knew she'd go straight to her house. The idea of her out in the city alone while someone was bent on causing her trouble slid like ice between his shoulder blades.

She made an X over her heart. "Promise."

Trusting her, hoping he wouldn't get played for a fool, he took the stairs two at a time to the bedroom he was using upstairs. Living out of a duffel made it easier to pack. He grabbed up his clothes, double-checked that he had a dress shirt and clean jeans for tonight and jogged back downstairs.

Shannon was replaying the video. He could tell by the blend of longing and sorrow on her face. "Something new?" he asked.

She jerked her head up and pocketed her phone, looking guilty. "No."

It broke his heart watching her suffer. More than anything he wanted to hold her and promise they'd rescue her son. He just couldn't do it. If things went south, she'd never trust him and he'd never forgive himself.

"I remember Ed telling me you go out with the guys occasionally after work."

"That's not dating," she insisted. "Aiden sleeps over at Rachel's place once in a while."

"Close enough for me," he said.

"That hardly explains how we went from boss and employee to you moving in within a day."

"I don't plan to explain anything to the bastard who took your son." Daniel stopped short of venting his full opinion about her ex—though his involvement didn't make any sense—or the team that snatched Aiden from the sitter's house. "We need a plausible story for the guys tonight."

"Not if we skip it," she said, her chin cocked stubbornly.

She wasn't inviting a kiss, though his brain went there automatically. With deliberate motions, he ushered her out of the house and back to the truck. This wasn't going to be simple for him, watching over a woman he'd hoped to date. It never would have been easy, considering she worked for his company, but until this morning he'd felt like he had a pretty good shot.

Not now.

"No one needs to know we're staying in the same place," he said, when they reached her driveway.

With a sniffle, she put her phone away, having watched the video again on the drive over.

From his perspective, she was torturing herself watching that video nonstop. What did he know? He wasn't a parent. No amount of compassion or sympathy gave him a full understanding of what she was going through. Smothering his attraction to her was an annoyance compared to her struggle. Nothing he did or said would ease the wounded look hollowing out her brown eyes.

They didn't talk much as he unloaded the truck and carried their bags inside. He put her suitcase and tote just inside her bedroom and stashed his bags in the closet downstairs. Maybe if he stayed out of her way, kept himself as out of sight as possible, she'd relax.

"I'm going to take a nap," she said. "Just do...whatever you want."

He started to reply and she held up a hand, cut him off. "I know we have to go to the concert. I'll set an alarm and be ready on time."

Checking on her once, he found her curled up on the bed, Aiden's blue rabbit tucked under her chin, phone charging on the nightstand. Her eyes closed and her breath deep and even, he figured sleep was her best defense against the senseless situation.

Restless, he meandered through the house downstairs. He found three paint chips taped to the wall in the kitchen and eyed them critically. He was debating between two good choices when his cell phone rang. He picked it up without looking at the display. "Daniel Jennings."

"You can't just take whatever you want and write it off, Danny." Matthew Daniel Jennings was calling to take a strip out of Daniel's hide.

"Hi, Dad." Daniel stifled the sigh just in time, pinching the bridge of his nose as he stepped out on the small back porch. Conversations between them had a tendency to get loud and he didn't want to wake Shannon. "I checked the inventory," he began.

"Well, you didn't check the new work orders for next week," his dad snapped. "I can't spare the subfloor. You'll have to order it."

Waiting on delivery meant his crew would be standing around Monday morning with nothing to do. A costly decision on a charity project he needed to finish within the next two weeks. Usually he and his father were both a little bit right when they butted heads on things like this. He forced cheer into his voice, hiding his weariness with the constant pushback. "How about my crew meets yours and helps with your subfloor. Then they can take any leftovers, swing by the—"

"No. Too many hands only jam things up."

"Right." Daniel practically growled the word. Cooperation, support weren't part of the elder Jennings's vocabulary when it came to his sons.

"You bit off more than you can chew on this one. Thinking with your heart, not your head."

"Stop," Daniel barked. He'd memorized the lecture, having heard it all his adult life. "The Caldwell project is mine. My mistake assuming we could pull from the available supply."

"I didn't say that."

"You just did," Daniel pointed out.

"You didn't even ask!" Matthew shouted.

What the hell was the supply order if not a request? Daniel wanted to shout back, thought of his mother's reaction if she heard they'd gone another few rounds. Anticipating her disappointment drained the fight out of him.

"Sorry, Dad. I'll let the crew know the change in plans."

"Good."

"We wrapped up the job in Garden Court."

"I heard."

Although his dad sounded less than pleased, Daniel refused to bite. "And I got the place in Francisville staged."

His dad made a noise that could be interpreted a number of ways. Daniel took it as a positive, if only to annoy the elder Jennings. "I'm happy, too. It should sell fast."

"We'll need the profit with you handing out subfloor like candy."

Daniel laughed, though there wasn't any joy in it. "Well, it's been a long day, Dad. Give my love to Mom."

Matthew cleared his throat. "You're not coming by for dinner tomorrow?"

Even if he wasn't helping Shannon, he wasn't about to put himself in his dad's crosshairs again so soon. "Maybe next week." He yanked open the screen door and found Shannon in the kitchen, staring about, lost, dark circles under her eyes.

"If this is some kind of punishment," his dad started ramping up again.

"It's not. Bye." He ended the call on his dad's sputtering protests and pulled the door shut, threw the deadbolt.

"You okay?" she asked.

"I should be asking you that question. I'm fine. A little father-son bonding is all."

Her lip quivered, though she stopped it with a nip of her teeth.

He wanted to knock down a wall, letting his dad get under his skin. "That was insensitive. I'm sorry."

"Don't. You can't walk on eggshells around me."

"You're hurting."

"True." Standing at the open pantry, she gave him a long look over her shoulder. "You, too."

He shoved his hands into his pockets. "Did my conversation wake you?"

"No." She laid a hand over her stomach. "Hunger did. Now that I'm up, nothing sounds good."

He crossed the kitchen in two quick strides and nudged her into a chair at the table she'd placed under the sunny back window. "Let me handle it."

She didn't argue as he rummaged through her kitchen, coming up with a can of tomato soup, bread, cheese and butter. He set the soup simmering and had the sandwiches browning in the skillet while she stared out at the backyard. He was relieved that though her phone was nearby, she'd stopped replaying the video.

"Can't go wrong with comfort food," he said, serving them both at the table.

"So named for a reason," she said. "Thanks."

There wasn't any sparkling conversation while they ate, but she did eat, which mattered more to him. When she stood up to clear the table, he took over, handling the dishes while she went upstairs to dress for the concert.

She came downstairs in the black dress and heels she'd stuffed into her suitcase earlier. The hem of the skirt stopped just above her knees and the fabric seemed to hug her from her shoulders to her trim waist before flaring out over her hips. Far better on her than it had been on the hanger. On a normal date, he'd offer a compliment. Tonight? He had no idea if she'd even hear him, much less find the words sincere.

"You clean up nice," she said.

Clean jeans, dark blue dress shirt and loafers paled in comparison to her. "I'll do better next time," he said without thinking.

Her lips curved in a ghost of smile and he felt as if he'd slayed a dragon for her.

He timed it so they were the last to arrive at the club and the others would be distracted by the entertainment. It was all he could think of to make a challenging outing easier for her. The band up on stage had the crowd jumping to the throbbing beat as they navigated around the dance floor to find their group. Ed and his wife Toni were holding the hi-top table while Lou and Craig—both single—stood by, watching the women dancing in the crowd.

He didn't think an Oscar-winning actress could pull off the performance Shannon gave as she greeted everyone with her typical, friendly enthusiasm. Through some female miracle, she'd erased all signs of stress and tears from her face. Her smile wasn't as bright, but that was the only clue he could see to the burden she was hiding from the others.

"How is Aiden?" Toni asked, clearly concerned. "Ed told me there was an emergency."

"A mix-up over the phone," Shannon replied. "I thought Aiden was hurt…" She paused, cleared her throat. "It was one of Rachel's twins. He's fine now. Didn't mean to worry everyone," she finished sheepishly.

"Your mind just leaps to the worst-case scenario, doesn't it?"

"All the time," Shannon said.

Daniel bumped her knee with his under the table, lending her subtle support.

"Ed says I'm a drama queen." Toni beamed at her husband. "But those 'come right now' calls just grab your heart and don't let go until you can see for yourself that your baby is okay."

Though Shannon's smile wobbled, her voice was steady. "They really should put a warning label on kids, or at least cover it in the motherhood books."

Toni and Ed chuckled in agreement.

Oscar-winning performance indeed. He ordered a pitcher of beer for the table when the waitress came by and turned the conversation to business for a few minutes, filling in Ed on the subfloor supply issue.

Ed shook his head and asked Shannon to dance.

She hopped up cheerfully, making it look like she was having a grand time.

Daniel wanted to dance with her himself and decided he'd wait for a better day. She probably wanted a break from him, from his constant presence reminding her of the trouble. Until this morning, he didn't know anything about her ex or his businesses. Tonight, he despised the man on principle for slamming into her day like a runaway truck.

The band took a break and Grant wandered over to say hello as he made his rounds.

"Mind if I steal you away for a professional assessment?" Grant asked. He smiled easily at the others as he explained. "We had a fight out back last night. Perils of running a nightclub. Your date can join us," he added.

Daniel ignored the odd look from Ed as they followed Grant back to his office. "Nicely done," he said when they were safely behind the closed door.

"Do you have any leads on Aiden?" Shannon laced her fingers together in her lap, her forehead lined with worry.

Daniel wished he could soothe her, knew it was an impossible task until she was reunited with her son.

"We don't have a lead on Aiden's location yet. People

are working on the video. I'm told we shouldn't expect much since they kept it short."

"You think the video was short on purpose?" Daniel asked.

"It's a definite theory. Shannon gets proof of life, anyone helping her gets little to nothing to go on. We haven't ruled out much of anything." Grant massaged his hand. "Yet."

"Why not?" Shannon's entire body was stiff and he saw her fighting for control over the tears welling in her eyes. "I know Bradley's behind this. Those were his words, if not his voice. Daniel told you that, right?"

"He did," Grant assured her. "My detective friend in organized crime is quietly shaking every tree to get a location on Stanwood or catch wind of a kidnapping order."

"He's not in New York," she insisted. "He may not be staying here in Philly, but he must be close. He wouldn't have sent that kind of script through an email or text message."

"Good point," Grant said. "Still, it's possible he's handling this remotely. I've listened to the call you recorded and watched the video. No one is discounting any possible scheme at this point, Shannon." He turned to Daniel. "You're all settled in at her place?"

"We're good there." Daniel shrugged, not wanting to dwell on that subject. "What's the next move?" He wanted to hear any and all ideas for resolving this swiftly.

"Patience is the move. Follow your routine as closely as possible. We want the kidnappers to believe you're cooperating while we work behind the scenes."

Shannon sucked in a breath, blinked rapidly.

"You've got a team at your back, I promise." Grant

leaned against his desk. "Because we're a team, I want your take on some other news. I learned Gary Loffler has made two visits to Philly in the past three months. Did he contact you at all?"

"No." Her eyebrows snapped together. "Gary escorted me out of the house the day I left. I haven't spoken to him since the divorce was final. I still think he'd help us pin down Bradley if I called him. Told him…"

They all knew how that sentence ended.

"So he doesn't know you had a son?" Grant asked.

"I never told him," Shannon whispered. "Even if he knew, Gary wouldn't do this."

"Not even for his best friend, his best client?"

"Gary was the only thing left of Bradley's conscience. Assuming he had one to start with."

"Well, it's one more avenue. Apparently, the organized crime and intelligence unit has been hearing rumors about a major deal brewing. Until your son was taken, no one had a clue about what, why or when anything would happen.

"You have to see that to an outsider, taking Aiden implies you have something or know something that can impact the deal Stanwood is trying to make."

"I'm aware how it looks," Shannon said. "Trust me, I'd happily give up any information on Bradley or his businesses to have Aiden back right this minute."

"The kidnappers believe you're cooperating," Daniel reminded her. "The police will catch a break soon."

"The demand for a routine makes me wonder if the kidnapper—"

"Bradley," Shannon interjected. "I know it doesn't add up, but he *is* involved."

Grant tipped his head. "Bradley," he echoed. "I wonder if he's hoping that forcing you to maintain a routine gives him a window to search your place."

"He had plenty of time today while we were traipsing all over town," Daniel pointed out. "She was at work when they took Aiden and they waited a couple hours to make contact."

"And yet." Grant spread his hands. "Patience is what we have to work with right now."

Shannon's mouth thinned with worry. The temper and need to act burning in her eyes were at war with Grant's persistent logic. "I'd hoped for more from this meeting," she admitted.

"I know."

"Do you have children?" Shannon asked.

"Not been blessed in that way yet," Grant replied. "Doesn't mean I'm not one hundred percent committed to getting your son back home to you."

"I apologize." She stood up to pace the small office, cracking her knuckles and worrying that wide lower lip. "The timing," she muttered. "A deal? Did your detective in organized crime have any idea who Gary met with during his recent trips to Philly?"

"He visited the Marburg Law offices. Our contacts there are making inquiries."

Daniel could practically see the gears turning in Shannon's mind. "What are you thinking?"

She shook her head. "Between Gary's visits, the kidnapping and the rumors you've heard, the timing bothers me. When I left New York, Gary gave me his personal number. He told me to call if I had any trouble and I know he meant it as a friend, not a ploy for Bradley to keep tabs on me." She pushed a hand through her short, sunny hair. "Bradley was happy to send me packing. I'd let him down. Without Gary..." Her voice trailed off. "Anyway, Gary was the only point of compassion when my marriage fell apart. He was an unexpected source of kindness."

"You were friends?" Daniel slid a glance at Grant, caught the speculation in his gaze.

"After a fashion," she murmured, clearly lost in the past. "I think we were both surprised to find a likeminded person within Bradley's merciless sphere. When the honeymoon was over and I was searching for a way to stay afloat in my marriage, Gary and I had several conversations about pursuits Bradley might allow."

Daniel wondered what a younger Shannon had wanted when she'd found herself caught in an untenable marriage.

"Such as?" Grant prompted.

"Local chapters of national charities." She rattled off three familiar program names. "Real estate." The bitter laugh that followed prickled along his skin. Her lips tilted into a half smile full of irony. "Can you imagine the kickbacks Bradley might have pocketed if I'd done that?"

Her ex had been a piece of work, and the way he'd manipulated her had taken a toll. Daniel wanted to meet him, if only to plant a fist into the jerk's face. He marveled that she'd gotten out and made such a good life for herself and her son.

The idea of her moving on, starting over again, lit his temper. Who was her ex that he thought he could get away with this kind of stunt? And what kind of monster would put a mother through this torture and turmoil? "Wherever they're holding Aiden, we'll find him. Right, Grant?"

"Yes. There are ears and eyes everywhere, combing the city for clues." Grant's fingers tapped in a rapid-fire staccato on the desktop. "Which means you two should get back to your night out. Keep up appearances."

"Normal," Shannon said, plastering a patently false and somewhat scary smile on her face.

"Believe." Daniel took her hand as they left the office.

"What if he does a paternity test?" she asked, pulling Daniel back at the verge of the club. "I've been thinking about it all day."

The question startled him. On the other side of the wall, the crowd sang along with the band onstage. Daniel had to lean close to be heard without shouting. The tangy lemon scent of her shampoo tantalized his nose. With another woman—with Shannon amid other circumstances—he would have used the opportunity to steal a kiss.

"Why would he do that?"

"I don't know," she admitted. "I'm just trying to figure out who's after what here. Bradley or someone who knows him well wrote that script."

"Loffler, maybe?"

She tipped her head side to side, chewing on her lip.

"Would he find something unexpected?" Daniel asked.

"Learning he's a father would shock him." Her nose wrinkled. "If he ordered the kidnapping to manipulate someone else, who knows what he'd do to Aiden if he realizes he's holding his own son."

"You said he had no interest in fatherhood."

"He always has an interest in what can be used as leverage and useful tools," she said, peering over his shoulder into the club. "He never had an interest in accommodating me."

"Relax," he said, knowing it was an impossible request. "If he was here, Grant's men would be all over him by now."

"Okay."

He gave her hand a squeeze to reclaim her attention. "Is there something you're not sharing?"

She shook her head. "No. I'm trying to rush things along and I'm only making myself crazy. You, too, probably. My mind is running like a hamster on a wheel. Bradley or whoever is behind this will make some kind of demand eventually."

As they finished out the evening with friends, Daniel's mind raced as well. He kept mulling over her concerns about the timing and purpose behind Loffler's visits to Philly. Could the lawyer have been checking on her, determining potential targets for his boss? Daniel couldn't blame Shannon for wanting to leave what was a traumatic time in her life in the past, but he too sensed there was something bigger at play.

Something about the kidnapping, the odd demands to keep a routine, reminded him of a fire breathing just under the edge of a door. Craving oxygen, without a vent, the fire would eventually attack, tossing everyone and everything aside.

Why steal a kid he never wanted or pester a woman he'd been happy to boot out of his life?

"You don't have to stay over," she said as he pulled to a stop behind her car in the narrow driveway. "It's not routine."

"It is until your son is home," he replied. "Grant expects me to stay close and keep you safe. You've never had to answer to him," he added, hoping to lighten the mood. "He might be a little older, but there's no doubt he could still take me down if he wanted to."

"What's his story?" she asked as they walked to her front door.

"Shot in the line of duty, partner died, and he had to retire for medical reasons. Bought the club and loves it. He just can't seem to stop helping people."

They walked inside and she closed the door, leaned back against it. "He has a way about him," she said.

"Good or bad?"

"Solid." She shrugged out of her coat and dropped her keys into her purse and her purse on the end of the kitchen counter. "Reassuring. A lot like you, actually. Must be a first responder thing."

"Huh." Feeling a little lost by the direction of the conversation, he rocked back on his heels. "Everything looks normal in here." Part of him hoped for a decisive move from Aiden's kidnappers while another part of him was relieved not to add any more drama to the rough day. "Do you mind if I clean up?"

"Go ahead. I'll get out linens for the couch."

"Great, thanks."

"And Daniel?"

He glanced back, one foot on the first stair. Something inside him unraveled, yearning for the impossible when he saw the gratitude shining in her brown eyes. With reluctant determination, he hid the way everything about her gave his system a jolt of desire. If she knew that she'd starred in his fantasies for nearly a year, she'd lock him outside.

"Thank you," she said, breaking the silence. "I didn't want your help." Color rose in her cheeks. "I didn't want anyone's help. Thank you for being persistent despite my best efforts to push you away."

Flustered and embarrassed, he held his ground with a smile. "Must be a first responder thing."

He escaped the heavy moment, taking the stairs up to the bathroom and locking himself in. A cold shower was just what he needed.

Chapter 4

Shannon's mind and heart had been working overtime all through the night. She hadn't slept more than a few minutes at a time, dozing between prayers that either her ex or the men who'd kidnapped her son would reach out again.

Only more of the nothing, more horrible silence filled her mind. Dreadful images greeted her every time she jerked awake. *Nothing.* There hadn't been a threatening text about her going out on a Saturday night, no new link to a new video that could confirm her son was still alive and well.

Was he even still in town? Her stomach clenched. She'd seen Bradley's resources in action, knew that almost twenty-four hours after stealing her son, he could have him stashed anywhere.

She understood the logic Grant and Daniel kept emphasizing, that Aiden was leverage. His captors were more motivated to take care with him so she would cooperate. But they knew Bradley Stanwood by reputation, not the way she did. Logic was the first thing her ex dispensed with when it suited him.

Awake, her hands hugging her son's toy to her chest, her mind wrestled with what had pushed Bradley to have Aiden kidnapped. No logic there. Who else could know Bradley well enough to write the scripts the caller read from? And why bother with that kind of stunt? Until it made sense, she didn't think the police would put much theory into her ex's involvement.

"Believe." She said the word aloud, hearing Daniel's voice in her head as she did.

Wanting to bury herself under the covers and cry and wallow in her grief, she rolled out of bed, headed for the shower. Although she'd never thank her ex, maybe he was doing her a favor demanding normal, routine behavior. Wallowing wouldn't bring her son home. Crying wouldn't help her find any insight into why this was happening now.

Sunday was a mandatory day off at Jennings Construction at Matthew Jennings's insistence, and today she couldn't be more grateful. She could use the time to research recent headlines in New York, maybe call Gary Loffler despite Grant's advice against it. Dressed in soft leggings and a loose T-shirt, she finger-combed her short damp hair and headed downstairs to the kitchen for coffee and breakfast.

Daniel slept soundly on the couch, one knee pulled up, a bare foot peeking out from under the blanket. He had a forearm over his eyes, as if blocking the light, but the room was still dark. She made herself move on before the mother in her took over and she covered up his foot.

Daniel was her boss. He wasn't in search of or in need of her nurturing tendencies and he was crashing on her couch because he was doing her a favor. Maybe she'd be better off thinking of it as Daniel giving Grant an assist.

Her son slept with equal abandon, she thought, peeking back out at Daniel while she waited impatiently for the coffee to brew. Aiden flung his arms and legs as he pleased in sleep and somehow the silly blue rabbit always stayed within his reach. She wondered if he'd slept at all without it last night.

Inside her chest, her heart seemed to beat erratically. First slow and sluggish, then leaping too quickly as she worried over her son. There had to be something more she could do than just cooperate. If she played this game solely by the rules her ex had set, she'd never win.

Temper seared through her sleep-deprived mind more effectively than the coffee. How had her ex found her? Why target her son?

Bradley Stanwood didn't do things without a plan and a self-serving purpose. With the benefit of hindsight, she could see how her ex had covered up his twisted nature during their brief dating life. Within a month of her wedding day, she'd learned how vicious and calculating he could be. The first slap had been a shock, the handprint fading quickly. The deep bruise he'd left on her next had turned into a harsh lesson on proper concealer techniques.

Her thoughts veered away from the remembered pains and right back to the starting point: he wouldn't have taken Aiden, wouldn't have bothered with a child, without an end game in mind.

Coffee in hand, she stared at the paint swatches on the wall. Her landlord had approved all three, and considering her day job, given her permission to do the painting. He'd even agreed to let her deduct the cost of supplies out of her rent. With receipts, of course. If she owned the place, she'd go with a bolder color than the bland neutrals, but she could add pops of character and color with accessories. Maybe she'd paint while she waited on the kidnappers to reach out again.

She opened her laptop and started searching through the local news in Philly and the immediate areas. If she found anything she could give to Grant or his detective friend, it would be Bradley's fault. She'd been ordered to behave as if nothing was amiss. Being the mother of a young boy, Sunday morning was often the best time for her to catch up on recent events while Aiden slept in.

She clicked a few headlines on the real estate market, skimmed them quickly, along with obituaries and crime reports. Bradley was in for a surprise. She wasn't the downtrodden mouse he'd happily discarded. Motherhood had shifted her normal, honing determination into a toughness and desire to do more than merely survive or get by. She'd planted herself in Philly to create a thriving life for her and her son.

Just because her heart was currently caught in an unrelenting vise, and would be until Aiden was back home, didn't mean she had to stop thinking. The cops had their avenues, she had hers. No, she hadn't known the true Bradley when she'd become Mrs. Stanwood, but she'd always been a quick study. Kidnapping Aiden, dragging her back into his control, could only mean there was an overlap, an intersection between then and now.

She glanced over the edge of the laptop as Daniel sat up. He scrubbed at the stubble shading his sharp jaw and twisted around. Seeing her, he raised a hand in a sleepy wave. "Coffee?"

"Ready to go whenever you are."

He gave a nod, yawned and stood up to stretch. After folding the blanket, he stacked it neatly on top of the pillow before heading upstairs. She heard the shower and waited a few minutes before leaving her research to make his coffee.

He walked into the kitchen wearing faded jeans and a short-sleeved white T-shirt that emphasized both his physique and his dusky skin, tanned from hours of work in the sun. The man was a work of art, she thought, watching him eagerly gulp down the stout coffee.

"Thanks." He took another sip, a slow savoring this time, his eyes closed. "Great stuff." He opened his eyes and that intense blue gaze pinned her. "Did you get any sleep?"

"Am I looking that bad?" she asked, knowing the answer. "No, don't apologize," she added when he blanched. "I'm not fishing for compliments. I saw my reflection." The dark circles under her eyes and the lines bracketing her mouth would likely be there, and get worse, until Aiden came home. "I dozed a little. Was the couch okay for you?"

"Your couch is really comfortable." He busied himself making another cup of coffee.

She chuckled. "You're not a very good liar."

"Thanks." He studied her while the coffee brewed. "The couch is better than what I've had lately. What's going on?" He tapped his temple and then circled his finger in the direction of her face. "You've got a different vibe going on today. Did something happen?"

She figured that showed on her face as clearly as the dark circles. She'd never been good at lying either, which was why getting away from Bradley without revealing her pregnancy had been nothing short of miraculous.

"Nothing happened. After tossing and turning all night, I've found a good head space for the moment.

Determined. I won't roll over or cave in," she said. "I've decided there are steps I can take to find Aiden and bring him back home."

Daniel's gaze slid over her shoulder to the computer. "What kind of steps?"

"Research, right now. I'm not being an idiot." She decided being offended by his sigh of relief was counterproductive to Aiden's rescue. "The key to all of this is in the timing," she said. "I'm looking for anything that could connect the chatter Grant mentioned, Loffler's visits to Philly and the script the caller read from."

Daniel drank deep, motioned with his hand that she should keep talking.

"I have yet to find the common denominator, but I know Bradley. I will find it."

"How can I help?"

"You're doing more than enough already." Shame prickled along her skin. She didn't want anyone else poking through her past, seeing her at her worst in those terrible days of her marriage.

"Bull."

"Pardon?" Caught off guard, she stared at him for several seconds, struggling against the pain worming through her chest. If he was going to be rude, she'd manage this alone and he could explain the change of plans to Grant.

On the verge of saying just that and sending him on his way, she snapped her mouth closed, gathered her composure. It wasn't fair to vent her frustration on him when Bradley was the real problem. "I'm not sure what you think you can do."

He leaned back against the counter. "Talk to me and you might be pleasantly surprised."

"There's nothing to talk about." *Yet.* Her aloof tone

echoing in her ears annoyed her. "I'm hungry. What would you like for breakfast?"

"You're not cooking for me like I'm some long-lost relative, stopping in on vacation."

She didn't think of him that way at all. In her perfect, private fantasy world, Aiden would be sleeping off a slumber party at the sitter's house and breakfast would be sweet and hearty, refueling the two of them after a night of wild and passionate sex.

"Is it all right with you if I remember you're my boss and you're here doing me a huge favor?" She tried to scoot around him and quickly gave up. He dwarfed her small kitchen and where he lounged at the moment, he blocked her path to the refrigerator, his gaze drifting somewhere over her head.

"Daniel?"

His gaze returned to her. "I'm thinking."

She rolled her eyes, tried to get around those long legs without making it an issue. He caught her arm. Despite the light touch, with Bradley's sudden return to her life, she flinched and recoiled.

He let her go instantly. "What was that?"

"Nothing," she lied, making a study of her bare feet.

"I wouldn't hurt you."

"I know that." Well, she assumed it anyway, based on her interactions with him at job sites. He never showed any signs of taking out his temper in physical ways. "It's my problem, no reflection on you."

His coffee mug landed on the counter with a precise clink. He managed to do what she couldn't, stepping out of the kitchen without touching her. Taking a seat at the table, he propped his ankle on his knee. "I think this is our problem," he corrected her. "I need you to trust me."

"And I do." She opened the refrigerator, realized

she'd never stopped for groceries yesterday, her normal shopping day. Irritated, she closed the door, searched for a distraction. "More coffee?"

Unflappable, he ignored the question. "He hurt you."

She wanted to rail against the statement. Her hands shook as she poured water into the coffee maker for another cup. "It's that obvious?"

"No, but I've had some training on the issue."

Issue. In her head, she cursed her ex and the invisible scars he'd left on her heart and soul. She didn't want to be an issue. Not to Daniel. Not after working so hard to be strong and set a good example for her son.

"You can talk to me," he said gently.

Bad idea. "It's over." She stirred a spoonful of sugar into her coffee this time. If she told him what had happened, he'd forever see her as a victim. "I'm just over-tired."

"And miserable because Aiden isn't here," he said. "Two heads are better than one. Give me something to track down, use me as a sounding board. You have help, Shannon."

She could handle this on her own. *She* knew Bradley and his businesses, second only to his lawyers. Still, the argument that leaped to the tip of her tongue promptly dissolved under the soft warmth that stirred inside her when he said her name.

Defiant, she yanked open the refrigerator again and pulled out the carton of eggs. Four left. "How do you feel about sharing an omelet?" She could scrounge up enough leftovers and chopped veggies to make it worth-while.

"I feel weird having you cook. Brunch is a better solution." His blue eyes radiated kindness as he asked, "What do you usually do on Sundays?"

Emotion clogged her throat. Sundays were often the best days of her week and she refused to cry over what the kidnappers had stolen from her today. When her son came home, she'd find a way to make up for the lost time. It had only been a day. Bradly expected her to cave to the overwhelming fear and worry. She had to keep believing in a better outcome.

"We read the comics in the paper," she said. "I make pancakes or waffles, and then we alternate open-house tours with time in the neighborhood parks." She wouldn't hear Aiden's giggles or the crinkle of newspaper. She wouldn't feel his hand in hers as they walked through sparkling homes or laugh along with his delighted squeals as he pumped his legs to soar high, higher on the swings.

Daniel's eyebrows arched. "You do open houses on Sundays?"

"Almost every week," she said. "Why?"

"Me, too." He smiled. "I know a great brunch place, no tie required. We can take the paper or the laptop and make a plan of attack for the afternoon." He aimed a thumb at his chest. "And you can bounce around theories while we're out. Sounding board."

Did the man have to have all the answers to go with the sexy smile that had her belly quivering with impossible anticipation? Daniel wasn't for her. Couldn't be. He deserved a woman who would stand by him and she planned to run as soon as they found her son.

She went upstairs for shoes, automatically moving to Aiden's room to share the plans, stopping awkwardly by his door. Her vision blurred as the helplessness and grief came crashing down on her again, this time with an added dose of guilt. What kind of mother allowed attraction to distract her so much that she forgot her son was being held by strangers?

She didn't realize she was sobbing until Daniel had her wrapped up, crooning soothing nonsense at her ear. "Shh. He's okay. He's coming home. It's all going to be fine."

"You can't know that." She hiccuped, her cheek rubbing against his chest. "What if they—if he—"

His fingers rubbed at the tension gripping her neck, pushed up into her hair. "No what-ifs today. We'll go out and have as good a Sunday as possible."

Her hands clutched the fabric of his shirt as she leaned into the solid security he offered.

"Over brunch, I want to hear all about whatever put that glint in your eye earlier. I promise not to pick at any old wounds, but admit it, you need someone to help you assess theories. May as well be the person you're stuck with."

Reluctantly, she agreed. It was a blow to her pride that he was right. About all of it.

She changed into jeans almost as worn as his, ballet flats and a long-sleeve top. Grabbing the zip-up hoodie emblazoned with the hockey team logo to fend off the cool autumn weather, she sat down at the vanity. Her eyes were so puffy makeup would only be an exercise in futility. Smoothing sheer gloss over her lips, she'd have to rely on dark sunglasses while they were out.

The bright, sunny day was the polar opposite of her mood as he drove out to the restaurant he claimed had the best brunch in town. She made a concerted effort to suppress her misery and focus on the sunshine and almost succeeded.

With her laptop and real estate section in her purse, they were soon seated at a table to fuel up for the day on eggs, bacon, sausage, fruit, pancakes and diced potatoes, all served family style.

"You doubted me," he said, pouring syrup over his plate-size pancake.

"I did," she admitted. "My apologies." The little diner didn't look like much from the outside, though it was neat as a pin inside and sweet and savory aromas filled the air. "The food is incredible."

He raised his coffee cup in agreement. "Cops can have the doughnut shops. For real food, trust a firefighter."

"Duly noted." She appreciated his easygoing nature and the way he steered the conversation away from her troubles. "When Aiden comes home, I'm bringing him here."

"Good idea and great attitude." Daniel refilled her coffee from the carafe on the table. "Can I come along?"

"Sure."

"I bet his face would light up at a pancake this size."

She chuckled. "Pancakes are his favorite." She let herself imagine the homespun happiness of that scene for a moment before shoving it firmly into the mental box of fantasies unlikely to come true. The same box where she'd stashed her silly dreams of white knights and unicorns.

Daniel snagged another slice of bacon from the plate between them. "Can I ask you a dumb question?"

Better than an astute question, she thought. "Shoot."

"Your son loves trucks."

"Yes." She waited a beat. "That isn't a question."

"Why doesn't he have a fire truck in his collection?"

She sat back, smiling. "You're offended."

He poked at his eggs. When he raised those stunning

eyes to hers, she saw the self-deprecating humor dancing in the blue depths. "I am a little, yes."

"Well, you shouldn't be," she replied. "There's a very good reason."

"Oh, I am all ears." He sat back in the booth, folded his arms over his chest.

"He has dump trucks in many variations, a cement mixer and a big flatbed that hauls some of the other trucks occasionally."

"I'm aware of what he has, Shannon."

She wasn't the least bit intimidated by his mock scowl and the sensation of teasing him was a blend of surprise and delight. "All of the trucks in his collection came after he visited job sites with me. Jennings job sites."

"That is a good reason. And it makes me feel better about no fire trucks."

"Even his pickup truck is the same color as the official Jennings Construction trucks. Hadn't you noticed?"

"Guess I missed that."

"You wouldn't believe what I've taught myself about engines, tires and various types of trucks in the past six months. Some moms learn dinosaurs. It seems I have a budding mechanic on my hands." She sighed, bumping back to reality. "And, if he's missing his trucks half as much as I think he is, he'll be a plague to his captors."

Unless they had him locked up somewhere alone. The thought sent her heart arrowing toward the edge of that terrible abyss.

Daniel distracted her, drew her back from that sharp edge, by quizzing her knowledge of trucks. When he declared her an expert, they shifted gears and decided which open houses to visit while they finished up brunch.

"I'll take care of the check if you'll send Grant a text." He handed her his cell phone and slid out of the booth. "Let him know our plans for the day."

"Done." She took a final hit of coffee and was ready to go when he came back from the register at the front of the diner.

In the truck, he handed his phone back to her. "Can you let Grant know I haven't seen anyone deliberately following us?"

She did as he asked and put the phone back into the console between them. "Now what?"

"Now we enjoy the first open house of the day." He turned a corner. "It's at the end of this block."

He hadn't plugged the address into a navigation app or tool. "As a firefighter you must learn the city pretty quickly," she said.

"Most of us do. Over the years, our calls have given me a fast sense of neighborhoods, too, when I'm looking for the next flip."

He parked on the street as close as he could to the house and came around to open her door. "Looks like they're getting good traffic," she said.

They walked into the house, chatted with the realtor, and she started making mental notes on the design choices. Her nerve was tested walking through with Daniel rather than Aiden, especially when she saw one of the bedrooms done with bright colors and bunk beds in a heavy, rustic wood frame. It was exactly what Aiden would be asking for in a year or two.

Someday, she promised herself. Someday she'd have a house with a big yard in a place Bradley could never touch. She added a security system to the ever-growing wish list in her head.

Back at the truck, she reached behind the seat for

her laptop. "Can you wait here just a second? I want to make a few notes on this one." If she had to behave normally while her son was being held hostage, she'd make the most of it. That way when he came home, she'd be ready.

"What kind of notes?" he asked.

"Mainly notes about materials and style choices. What I liked, what I'd do differently on a shoestring or with an unlimited budget. Usually, I factor in what Aiden likes." She hit Save on the file, took a steadying breath and closed the laptop. "Usually, I make my notes while he gets the wiggles out running around the nearest park."

Daniel didn't drive away. He just sat there gazing through the windshield at the houses marching down the street in a neat row. "Does your boy like swings as much as trucks?"

She smiled, thinking of the wild shrieks he made when he wasn't sure if he was too high or not high enough. "Yes."

"Ever jump off midair?"

"Not yet." She closed her eyes and wrinkled her nose, knowing the stunt was inevitable. "He's getting close."

"Rite of passage." Daniel's mouth tipped up at one corner. "Don't worry. He'll nail it."

"You're pretty sure about that for never having met him."

"I've met you." He rested an arm on the steering wheel, his blue eyes calm and serious as he studied her. "I'd bet bravery and courage comes through his mother's side."

It was the perfect thing to say and she found great comfort in his words. She knew him as a conscientious boss and had heard more than a few stories about his heroics as a firefighter. She'd never expected to be on the receiving end of his thoughtfulness.

"Thank you." Turning the laptop so he could see it, she pulled up the list of open houses and the address of their next stop.

He started the engine, checked his mirrors. She kept an eye on her phone, wishing for contact, while they chatted about the house they'd walked through and the neighborhood up next.

"We worked two blocks over last year." She glanced around, recalling the gridlock commute had been a challenge for her in the afternoons.

"Yes, we did," he said. "You came in an hour early most days."

She wasn't sure which startled her more, that he knew or that he remembered such a trivial detail. "How do you know that? You were only there once a week on that job."

He slid her sideways look. "I keep track of my projects." His tone as taut as a bowstring, he continued, "I'm aware of every cost and the personnel involved. That's how the job gets done right."

"Hey." She held up her hands in surrender. "No offense meant."

He blew out a big breath. "Sorry. Guess that's my problem." He parked the car, pulled the key from the ignition. "My management skills come under fire with too much regularity."

She hopped out of the truck before he rounded the hood this time. Better than being at eye level with him again. "You're a good manager. Great, actually." She knew how fortunate she was to be employed by his company.

"My family is convinced I won't realize my full

potential as a contractor until I commit to it. Go full time. It's a sore spot." He brushed her arm with his and changed the subject as they walked up the sidewalk. "I know the team that did this one," he said under his breath. "I want to see your notes when we're done."

Unsure what to expect, she tried to focus on the design, material and workmanship as they walked all three stories of the newly refurbished row house. She tried to keep her mind on the task and use it as a distraction to push her worries aside, but she couldn't change the fact that she was a mother. A mother with a missing son and a phone that didn't ring.

"Decent finishes," she said for Daniel's ears only as they cycled through the master bedroom and en suite bath. "Classic design." She ran her hand over the elegant quartz countertops that mimicked far more expensive marble.

"That doesn't sound like a glowing review to me."

She elbowed him. "Save the snarky comments for later."

"Yes, dear," he replied with a nearly imperceptible tilt of his head toward the listing agent in the hallway.

Ignoring him, she opened the closet and peeked in. The wire shelves and plastic runs of hanging space were arranged in a very basic layout. At this price point, she would have expected something with more flair.

She waited while another couple cruised through, bubbling with excitement and enthusiasm. "Normal buyers seem impressed," she murmured, giving the other couple plenty of time to ooh and ah over the next rooms.

"Don't know what they're missing," Daniel muttered. "You don't seem impressed at all."

"I'm not in the best of moods." They went down to

the kitchen and as the only people in the room, she examined it more closely. She opened a cabinet, tipped her head. "Bet he got these last month when they were on closeout," she whispered. "All of it just feels a hair off target to me."

For some reason, that put a rather tempting smirk on Daniel's face.

She waited until they were back in the truck to ask what had gotten into him.

"I lost the bid on this house," he said while she made notes and checked her phone. "I might be a little bitter. What kind of notes do you make about a house you don't like?"

"What not to do," she said, as the list she was making grew and grew. "And what I might have done instead."

"Really? Can I see?"

She handed him the laptop, her mind sliding back to Aiden as she made sure her phone was set to sound and vibrate. While working on the Jennings project in this neighborhood last year, she and Rachel had often met at the park on a corner lot at the edge of the neighborhood. All three boys loved the run of beams for climbing and balance and Aiden used them as a highway for trucks to drive and crash.

"Wow," Daniel said, gaining her attention. "These changes would have hit the target dead center, upped the asking price and the profit margin."

"At first glance, sure," she agreed. "We don't know what he found, if he had to adjust finishes due to problems we can't see."

"I walked the place, did a pretty thorough inspection. If he had serious problems, he brought them on himself." Daniel shook his head, reviewing her list again. "Your skills are wasted on paint and tile."

She frowned, focused on the laptop.

He tapped her shoulder. "Did I say something wrong?"

"No." She stowed the laptop for the ride to the next open house on their agenda. "I'm happy working wherever Ed puts me."

"Well, you've got a great head for the business side of construction." He pulled away from the curb. "And I do know that contractor cut corners, whether or not he found any structural issues. If you're looking for better work, something steadier, you should consider moving toward project manager. Not with that particular contractor, with someone good."

She gave him a long look while he drove through the tidy neighborhoods dotted with trees giving way to rich, fall color and families coming and going, enjoying the crisp Sunday afternoon. A game of street hockey took a time-out as they drove through an intersection. The quarterback of a touch football game on the grass anchoring the next block of row houses was in full throat, calling out the next play. The scent of burgers on the grill drifted through her open window.

She smiled, taking it all in, as tears burned behind her eyes. It's what she'd dreamed of, creating family and memories with a warm and loving husband. Reality had given her a jolt, and her family, small as it was, was no less precious. *Believe*, she thought, while Daniel drove.

"Shannon? Are you ready to call it a day?"

"No, I'm fine." With a deep, calming breath, she dragged herself back to the conversation. "I don't have any experience managing a project."

In all likelihood, she wouldn't be able to stay here long enough to get any. Jennings Construction was her best chance at advancement, but once she had Aiden home, she would need to run. Her mind drifted toward the escape plan she updated each year, just in case her ex or his way of life caught up to her. She'd planned and still hoped like a fool that she'd never have to use it.

"It's okay if you aren't interested."

Good grief, she'd tuned him out, tuned out the world, while she silently practiced the best ways to tell Aiden they were moving. "I zoned out, I'm sorry. What were you saying?"

"No problem. You have good reason to be distracted," he said. "This may not be the best time to bring it up. I promise I'm not expecting you to make a decision today."

Decision? She swiveled in the seat, looking for a street sign. "Where are we?"

"We're in Poplar. Last week, I picked up my next Jennings project for when the Caldwell house is done. I was just saying we could walk through it. If you're interested and we can come to terms, I'll let you manage it."

"Oh." She didn't know what to say. How could life be so cruel as to drop a dream job and a significant promotion into her lap when she couldn't possibly accept it? She was tempted to tell Daniel what he wanted to hear, but he didn't deserve that from anyone, especially not someone he was going above and beyond to help.

Growing more resentful with each minute her phone didn't light up with word from the kidnappers, she gave it a hard shake. "Why hasn't he called? I have a great signal." She gripped the door handle until her knuckles turned white, wishing she could throw the damn device out the window. "No one, *no one*, knows how to inflict the most pain with the least amount of effort better than my ex-husband."

She dropped her head back against the seat, immediately regretting her outburst. "Sorry," she said, reining in her temper. "Maybe we should call it a day." Sulking, she didn't want to walk through his next project, didn't want to fill her head with ideas when she wouldn't be around to see them come to life.

"Come on," Daniel urged. "It'll be our last stop. I know there are far more important things on your mind." He curled his hand around hers as she clutched her phone. "There is no rush on this place. Dad and I bought it for a song from motivated sellers. It could be exactly the job you need once Aiden's home again."

She had to admire his optimism. The house had good bones at first glance from the street. The stately two-story, single-family detached home looked a little down on her luck at the moment. Shannon could certainly relate.

"We're here," he said, clearly enthused about the house.

She was curious about what features put that spark in his eyes. Since he'd promised she didn't have to give him an answer today, she pushed open the door. "Might as well show me around."

Daniel wanted to take a victory lap when Shannon slammed her door of the truck and stomped up the steps to the house. He understood her mood, didn't blame her a bit. She was holding up better than he'd expected, though he knew it was costing her dearly to pretend things were fine.

Whenever he got a peek behind her dark sunglasses, he noticed the strain of fighting back the perpetual tears. Here, she wouldn't have to pretend or fight anything. On this tour, it would only be the two of them walking through a house in need of skilled labor and thoughtful design to shine again.

Daniel unlocked the door and gave it a shove. "Sticks a little," he said when he got it open. She stepped inside and he heard the swift intake of breath as her head tipped back, taking in the row of stained glass windows in the high entryway.

"Pretty cool, right?"

"Gorgeous." She turned a full circle. "And so unexpected. Can't you see this floor polished on a sunny day?"

"Want to know a secret?" His heart skipped when she looked at him, delight shining in her eyes. "It's why I insisted Jennings take it on."

As he showed her around and listened to her spitball ideas for each space, he knew she was definitely the right person to oversee this project from demo to reconstruction. This house was more than a remodel for the sake of profit, it was a borderline restoration. That was the hook that had landed his dad.

It wouldn't be easy, but he'd find a valid reason to put off the start date on this one until he knew she'd take on the manager role. Though he trusted Ed with his life as well as his houses, this one was special. Something he wasn't quite ready to put a label on made him want to share it with Shannon.

On the upper floors, her brainstorm continued. It was wonderful to hear her vision matched his in both design and layout. After reading her notes on the open houses, he knew she had the organizational chops to handle this kind of challenge, despite her lack of official experience. As a company, they were missing out on a major asset by keeping her on tile and paint.

He wouldn't press her now, he'd promised not to. It was evident from the drive over that she wasn't hearing half of what he said today anyway. He'd hold his tongue, let her do all the talking, and once she had her son back, he'd lay out an offer he hoped she wouldn't refuse.

Back on the main floor, she restarted her assessment from the stairwell, her gaze roving as she rambled about how people would actually use the house. He knew that, like him, she saw more than the faded, peeling wallpaper, scuffed floors and neglected crown molding.

She laid a hand on the wall blocking the kitchen and dining room and peered up to the ceiling. "Load-bearing?"

"Yes." Thank goodness his dad wasn't ready to dive in here. So far, Daniel couldn't make up his mind about opening up the space with an expensive beam or keeping walls in place and hoping it launched a new trend. Boxy-charm? Could work. If they came up with a better phrase for marketing the listing.

"You could go with columns if you wanted to save some money. Added benefit of making the job easier and faster to market," she said, moving back into the kitchen.

"Would you, as a buyer, like the columns or the, ah, boxy character of walls? Restored walls, of course."

"We've already established I'm not your typical buyer," she said absently. She stood in the center of the kitchen, shaking her head. "All of this needs reconfiguring for modern flow. Especially if you don't take out any walls."

"Open concept or old character?" he pressed.

She met his gaze once more. "Lovely as it is, however you handle it, this place would be out of my price point. I make a habit of not dreaming quite this big."

The declaration irritated him. She had as much right as the next guy to lay claim to the American dream. "Why not?"

"Pardon?"

"Aren't dreams supposed to be big?"

Her eyebrows snapped together over her nose and he wasn't sure if she was glaring at him, the awkward kitchen layout or the idea of a big dream. He opened his mouth to ask when she spoke over him.

"Who's your market?"

"With good schools nearby, the plan is to target families looking to upgrade from starter homes."

"Smart. You'll need finishes that won't intimidate on the maintenance side."

"Good point." He hadn't thought of that. Being in construction and working with a wealth of experts on any facet of a home, maintenance didn't intimidate him as it did others. "You're avoiding my question," he said.

"I am," she admitted. "If you push me, I'll cry and I'm really tired of crying."

How the hell could he argue with that? "All right." He hooked his thumbs into his back pockets. "I can see the wheels turning. What do you see in here?"

In a strange and sudden flash, listening to Shannon's ideas for better kitchen workflow and open concept, he saw her here. Her tow-headed son perched on a stool at the island she was describing, one hand on a truck—a fire truck—the other holding a cookie. He could see her smiling in that relaxed way she had with the crew over lunch breaks.

More shocking, he could see himself walking in after a firehouse shift and being blessed by that same wide and warm smile.

He leaned against the cased opening that might one day be a column and let the images and possibilities roll through him. It happened on occasion as he made choices about a house. Seeing the finished project was part of the job. His dad had taught him that. Seeing with this kind of a specific vision? Well, that was new.

He followed her out to the backyard while he debated if that was good or bad. Her mind intrigued him and she had excellent ideas here, too, adding landscape, carving out a small garden area or a quiet oasis in the middle of the city. "Private green space."

"Exactly," she said, enthused. "It'll be time and labor intensive, but the upgrade should appeal and pay off. Think of the neighborhood block party they could hold here."

Yeah, he could see it all too well. "I'll make a note," he said, holding the door for her to go back in. He locked the rear door, checked the windows on the first level and then locked up the front door.

"Again, you could go the path of least resistance with the master suite," she said as they walked to his truck. "It depends on…" Her voice trailed off, her feet stopped moving and her eyes glazed over.

"Shannon?" He looked up and down the street, not seeing anything that would freak her out. "What's wrong?"

"He's not with Aiden," she said suddenly. "Not yet."

"Your ex?" He sat her down on the edge of the steps when she swayed a little. "What are you talking about?"

"Bradley isn't the type to get his hands dirty. I realize that's a no-brainer." She gripped her phone in both hands. "A little kid? He wouldn't want *any* part of that. Too messy. Yes, it was a safe bet he wasn't with the team that took Aiden from Rachel's house. But Bradley isn't with whoever is holding Aiden."

She dropped her head to his shoulder and her body trembled as her breath shuddered in and out.

"Take it easy."

"He's not here. It's a little thing that's a huge relief. The whole order to stick with my routine?" She tapped her blank phone screen. "If anyone is watching me or the house, it isn't him. A huge relief," she repeated.

He didn't know what to say, so he just listened, his arm around her until she stopped shaking.

"The house wasn't searched because he's not here in town. I'm sure he's calling the shots, I'm sure he wrote that script, but he isn't with Aiden."

"That's good news for Aiden, right?" He wondered what she expected her ex to find at her house, but he saved the question for a better time. Preferably after he shared her revelation with Grant when they got back to her place.

"Absolutely. I wouldn't wish time with my ex on anyone."

He nearly laughed. "If Stanwood isn't in Philly, who would he trust to handle the kidnapping?"

"He would have called in a favor among local talent. If Grant's detective friend isn't hearing any rumors about it, my ex applied the right pressure. He'd send the orders through his lawyers."

"Like Gary Loffler? You heard Grant mention his recent visits."

"I know why you think so." She moved away and faced him. "I don't believe Gary did this. Not with Aiden."

The look in her eyes told him she believed it. "Why do you have such faith in Loffler?"

"He helped me when I needed it most."

There was more to the story, but he'd learned not to pry. Victims often didn't want to revisit their worst days. She hardly knew him well enough to trust him with her deepest secrets. "Let's get going." He stood up, pressed the key fob to unlock the truck. "Hope you're right."

"Me, too." She climbed into the passenger seat. "I realize we're no closer to why he'd take Aiden now."

"Grant is tugging lines at Marburg," Daniel said. "We'll figure it out. I'd ask you to be patient but that seems almost cruel under the circumstances." He caught her smiling at him. "What now?"

"Somehow I have a tough time thinking you could ever be cruel."

He basked in the compliment all the way back to her place. Considering the fear dogging her, he thought the time away from her house had been productive. She'd shifted gears from construction solutions back to solving the mystery of her ex-husband's criminal decisions.

Although he couldn't do anything more than listen, her mind fascinated him as much as her strength. He knew part of her wanted to curl up and cry, but sheer willpower kept her going.

Willpower, love and devotion to her son. She was a remarkable woman.

Chapter 5

Shannon had a running tally of the hours she'd been away from Aiden ticking in her head. Like a runaway clock in a cartoon, time kept racing forward and no one seemed to know where her son was being held.

Monday had come and gone like Sunday, with no word at all, except she and Daniel went to work at the Caldwell charity project rather than touring open houses. Eating was a wasted effort, sleep nonexistent, though she put up a brave front on both efforts.

Tuesday, while she and Daniel were having breakfast, another video arrived. In it, Aiden held the morning paper as he fussed and whined about going home. Her heart soared at the proof of life. Like the first video, it gave them little to no information on where he was being held. She watched it every chance she had anyway.

None of her research into Bradley's business dealings panned out. Loffler hadn't been back to Marburg, Grant hadn't been able to speak with him and no amount of prompting or review of past or present headlines in New York left her any clues to her ex-husband's current motivation. It had to be business; nothing else mattered to him. If only one item lined up, they would have a lead. Despite long, secure email exchanges with Grant and his detective, she couldn't come up with anything helpful.

She feared she'd lose her mind before they rescued her son.

On Wednesday afternoon, as her nerves continued to fray, Daniel told the crew he was taking her to lunch. Ed raised an eyebrow, but no probing questions. They'd wound up at the Escape Club to hear Grant's update that the organized crime unit was working a tip that Bradley was in Philly. They had nothing more on Gary Loffler or Aiden's location.

That night after work, she found the lock on her back door had been broken. They reported it to Grant, though none of her valuables were missing. Her bedroom had been searched, though the laptop she'd left on her dresser was still there. Daniel replaced the locks while she installed a wireless home security system. When her room was back in order, she gave in to the despair and collapsed on the bed, crying herself to sleep.

It was getting harder and harder to believe she'd ever see her son again. She still felt the weight of the threats that if she didn't continue with her life as normal, her son would come back in pieces.

By noon Thursday, Shannon was only going through the motions and everyone around her knew it. She couldn't keep her focus on anything for more than a few minutes at a time. They cared about her and, naturally, asked how to help. She was tired of giving everyone white lies about Aiden feeling poorly.

Hearing a saw going outside, she peeked out the

bathroom window. Below, Daniel and Lou were rebuilding the porch, adding a ramp.

She knew Daniel planned the schedule to the hour, counting on his best team to complete the project on time. He needed her to keep it together, to help the team knock out the work before he returned to shifts with the PFD next week. He never said a word about it, though he had ample opportunity, but they both knew he'd shortchanged himself and jeopardized the schedule by not replacing her.

Yes, with her ex reportedly in town, she understood why Grant wanted someone watching over her. Daniel refused to let anyone else take over the task or even trade off. He refused to let her out of his sight. Even without the kidnappers' demand that she maintain her routine, she might as well be doing slow work here rather than force him to try to manage the project from her place.

Every minute turned into another battle to stifle the scream building in her throat. It was agony to be home without her son. Too quiet, too lonely, despite Daniel's constant presence. If, *when*, Aiden came home, she'd never get grumpy about his incessant chatter and questions again. Her heart ached every morning when she drove by the sitter's house on the way to the Caldwell house. Although Daniel was always right behind her, it made her skin crawl thinking Bradley could be watching. The word *routine* had quickly morphed into a foul oath in her vocabulary.

"Have a routine day," she muttered, treating the word like a curse.

In an effort to practice the belief Daniel kept hammering into her weary heart, she kept Aiden's favorite pullback racer in her purse. His favorite dump truck, a change of clothes and the blue rabbit occupied a backpack she carried around at all times, ready for the moment he was found and they were reunited.

She glanced at the backpack now, sitting just outside the bathroom she was supposed to be finishing. *Believe*, she coached herself silently, struggling to hold back another wave of tears.

Crying on the job would only raise more questions she couldn't answer honestly. Lying to her friends on the crew was tough, but since she hadn't brought Aiden by as she might have on a normal week, she had to stick with the latest fabricated excuse that he wasn't feeling well.

Her hands moved with slow deliberation as she tiled a shower wall. Yesterday she'd had to take out the bottom third because she'd messed up the pattern and hadn't noticed. If Ed hadn't pointed it out when he'd brought her lunch order, it would've been a whole day lost, plus materials and time. Daniel, in true saint form, had shrugged it off when she'd told him, though she'd felt horrible.

The last vestiges of pride drove her to do better today. She didn't want to be the reason they fell behind. She knew what this meant to him and he deserved to be on hand when the Caldwells saw it for the first time. The delay she'd caused—no matter the reason—only put that goal in jeopardy. Keeping an eye on her was enough of a burden for him. The least she could do was manage her work in a timely manner, per the job she'd been hired to do.

"Knock, knock."

She glanced up and over to see Ed in the framed-out doorway. If she ever finished in here, they could hang the door and finish it off with fixtures. "Hi." Suddenly fearful she'd messed up the pattern again, she studied the shower wall.

"It's looking good," he said, as if he'd read her mind. "I just came by with the lunch order."

"Oh." She stood, wiped her hands on her jeans. "Thursday. My day to pick up." She could do that. Had to jump through the hoops of her normal routine for Aiden's sake. Her smile must have come off as a grimace based on the way Ed eased back a little.

"Before you go, I ah, couldn't help but notice, um."

She resisted the urge to cut him off. Normal Shannon would keep it together, keep it friendly. "Spit it out, Ed. We're friends."

"That's just it." He stepped into the bathroom, sparing a look over his shoulder. "You left the site last Saturday really upset."

She nodded. "I overreacted to that call from the sitter."

"Right. You told us at the club. But, well..." He glanced at the open doorway again and lowered his voice. "I've been giving this some thought." His gaze slid away for a moment. When he looked at her again, the determination was clear. "I talked with Toni. If Daniel—or anyone else on the crew—is giving you trouble, speak up, all right? I don't care who it is or what he owns, this needs to be a safe workspace for everyone."

Startled, she stared at him, searching for a reasonable response.

"I mean it, Shannon." He fisted his hands at his sides. "If you need to leave, I'll help you out. Don't give me any song and dance about providing for your boy or anything else. I can get you work with another contractor. Someone good. Someone who offers benefits."

"Ed." She wanted to hug him. "I appreciate all of

that. You're the best." She paused when he started blushing. "Toni, too. Tell her thank you. I promise Daniel isn't the problem."

Ed squinted at her. "He's been hovering since he took you out last weekend. We've all noticed. It would be different if you were acting happy about it. Plus his micromanaging is making your work suffer," he added, clearly unconvinced. "Usually on a job he's easier—"

Shannon couldn't let Daniel's reputation on the job site suffer because of her problems. "I swear to you, Daniel isn't giving me grief. Aiden…" Her voice cracked on his name and she had to pull herself together. *Believe!* "Aiden's been under the weather," she managed, "but he'll be fine. This big cough he has now, after the crazy mix-up thinking he was hurt the other day, has me on edge and preoccupied. You know how it is. The doctor assures me this isn't serious. He ordered the tests anyway. A precaution."

The worry in her voice came naturally, just not for the reasons she'd given Ed.

"All right." His hands relaxed. "Waiting for results is the worst when they're small."

"Exactly. Daniel's been so understanding as a boss and a friend," she said honestly. "You, too."

"I didn't want to think he was harassing you, but y'know. Had to ask. Ignoring the behavior changes leads to bigger trouble down the line."

"It does. I appreciate you asking." She nipped the list of lunch orders from his shirt pocket. "My focus will improve, I promise."

Cheesesteaks, she noticed, reviewing the order, already hearing the inevitable debate over the proper cheese protocol for the famous Philly sandwiches. She picked up her phone and checked the app for food trucks in the area. "I can grab everything at Cheese Wheelies. They're nearby today."

Ed pointed to an item she'd overlooked at the bottom of the list. "Lou has been going on all morning about the hand-cut chips at Jack's. It's taken supreme will-power not to staple his lips shut."

She laughed. "Jack's it is. I'll call it in and head that way."

"*You* are my hero," Ed said with heartfelt sincerity.

Daniel met her at the car. "I'll ride along."

She shook her head, noticed Ed watching from the front window of the house. "I can manage the short drive to Jack's without an escort."

He arched one dark eyebrow. "We're not giving anyone an opening," he said. "Besides you know these guys. You'll need another pair of hands to carry it all." He reached for her door. "Grant called," he said at her ear.

"Great." She plastered a smile on her face, gave Ed an okay sign behind Daniel's back. "Did they find Aiden?"

"No. They found Loffler."

Hope swelled, nudging aside the pervasive discouragement. "That is something. Do they know where he's staying?"

"Should I make you turn back so I can drive?" he asked as she zipped in and out of traffic.

"You should talk." Days of so much nothing had drained her patience. "Tell me what you know."

"According to Grant, Loffler went into the Marburg building this morning, had a meeting with an attorney who has done work for Stanwood as well as a few shell corporations. As far as we know, today's visit addressed personal business for Loffler."

"Personal." Her mind spun, trying to make that piece fit. "What can that mean?"

"Wills and trusts was my first thought," Daniel replied.

"Isn't Marburg primarily a criminal defense firm?"

"They have fingers in plenty of pies," Daniel said. "Would Loffler handle the personal legalities for Stanwood?"

"Well, yes. Gary had a good handle on how Bradley did business. He didn't leave things as important as what happens to the money undone. Those details were adjusted before we exchanged vows," she mused, remembering. "As his wife, I was initially the main beneficiary."

"You had a prenuptial agreement?"

"That, too." She parked in one of the carryout spaces in front of the restaurant. "Does the source inside Marburg know if Loffler's been married recently?"

"No idea. Sounds like they're still working to find out exactly what he did during his visit."

"Do you think there's any chance I can speak with him? If I told him what Bradley's done, I think he'd talk, if only about Aiden's kidnapping."

"Assuming he knows anything, would he really hand over his boss without hard evidence? We don't have anything directly linking your ex to Aiden's disappearance."

Frustrated and exhausted, she glared at the steering wheel. If Daniel gave up on her theory, gave up on rescuing Aiden, she was lost. How quickly she'd adapted to having someone on her side to listen, to support, to keep her hopes high in the face of such ridiculous odds.

"I believe you," he said. "All I'm asking is if your ex's attorney will believe you."

"He knows what Bradley is capable of. I have that old cell phone number." Determined, she opened her car door. "Tell Grant I want to meet with Loffler." She got out and slammed the door. "We need to get the food before Ed loses patience with Lou."

"Hand-cut chips are his weakness." Laughing, Daniel opened the restaurant door, held it for her. "Give me your phone," he said as she passed him.

"Why?"

"Because you want to make that call whether or not Grant approves. You probably should." They joined the carryout line. "I'd only ask you to take an hour and think about what you hope to get out of the conversation."

"Assuming the call is answered."

"Assuming so," he agreed with a wry smile.

He had a point. Considering the extreme stress and ongoing shortage of sleep, she needed to be as deliberate about her decisions as she was about the tile work. She pulled her phone from her pocket but didn't hand it over. "You'll keep it on?"

"Yes."

"You'll tell me if anyone calls or texts?"

"Absolutely."

"You'll give it back after lunch?"

He raised a hand as if taking an oath. "I solemnly swear."

She surprised herself by putting the device into his palm. It was more trust than she'd placed in anyone other than Rachel since settling in Philly.

"I won't let you down," he said, tucking the phone into his pocket.

She believed that, too. "You haven't yet." She caught his hand in both of hers. "I'm grateful beyond words."

She gave his hand a squeeze. "The past few days would've been unbearable without you."

Mary Ellen, cofounder and wife of the restaurant's namesake, bustled forward to the counter, sliding hot, foil-wrapped sandwiches into long, white deli sacks. She'd gone to school with Daniel and others who worked for Jennings Construction. Calling Shannon to the register, she spied their joined hands and beamed at Daniel. "Well, it's about time. Good for you, Danny."

She rang up the order, swiped Shannon's credit card. "You couldn't do better than this one, he's our local hero. I want to hear all about it when we're not slammed." She gave them a card for two free dinner plates. "Bring the little one in, too."

"What was that about?" Shannon asked as they carried the haul back to the car.

"Nothing." He hid his eyes behind his sunglasses as they stepped outside. "She looks at the world through rosy glasses. Bad as my mom with the matchmaking habits," Daniel said. "You were holding my hand. She misunderstood why."

"Guess we'll clear the air for her later."

"And when we do, we'll lose the free dinners."

His dramatic disappointment made her laugh and kept her grounded when she might just as easily dissolve in a puddle of obsessed grief.

Lunch with the crew was friendly as usual, but after the conversations with Ed and Mary Ellen, she started picking up on the small glances and silent exchanges as the crew watched them. It seemed unlikely that Daniel had a thing for her before he'd been sucked into his role as her babysitter.

Even if he had been interested once, that would surely be extinguished after living with her during this constant nightmare. On her best day, she could be stubborn and prickly, hardheaded, too, according to Rachel, and these last few days were far from her best.

He'd been patient with her persistent searches to connect Aiden's capture with something from Bradley's past deals. Night after night, he let her explore and vent theories until they fell apart, never judging or steering her to a more productive task. He'd thoughtfully encouraged her to talk about her son and about what she'd do as soon as he was home.

After years of living with only her son, she felt Daniel's presence equally reassuring and disconcerting. She couldn't forget why he was there, and still she caught herself wishing that someday she could have a real relationship with a man of Daniel's integrity and character. Yes, his face might be the one she pinned on the "someday" man of her dreams, but she was far too practical to believe that could happen.

He had a life, two careers, family and dear friends. She had good friends, none of whom knew she was raising the son of a mobster. There were too many question marks in the shadows of her past to take a chance on love.

While the obligatory discussion on the most authentic cheese for a cheesesteak sandwich swirled around her, her thoughts were centered on Gary. If the phone number she had didn't work, how could she track him down? Assuming she was right and he had no idea what her ex had done with Aiden, maybe Gary would have a better idea of why Bradley would fixate on the boy at this particular time.

She grabbed her purse and the backpack and as the crew parted ways to return to their respective tasks, her phone rang. From Daniel's pocket.

Ed noticed as Daniel handed over the phone. She ignored his quizzical look in favor of the phone display, which listed a plumbing company she'd never heard of. She walked toward the sidewalk for some privacy as she answered.

Daniel followed and tapped his ear. With a nod, she hit the record app and held the phone so they could both hear the caller. "I know where your son is," the caller said in a low whisper. "Be at Old City Hall in an hour."

She'd been expecting the mean, gravelly voice from previous calls or Bradley calling to finally make his demands. This caller surprised her. "Gary?"

"No cops or they will kill your son," the caller replied. "You're running out of time, Shannon."

"Gary, wait!"

The screen flashed that the call had ended. She looked up from the phone to Daniel's intense gaze. The tip from a trusted source was almost too good to be true. "I have to go," she said. "It could take as long to find parking as it will to get across town."

"Loffler?" he asked. "You're sure."

"Definitely." She glanced at the clock on her phone, waiting for him to point out she'd been wrong about Loffler's involvement.

"You're not going alone," he said. "I'll go tell Ed we're leaving right now."

It took her a few seconds to realize he wasn't lecturing her about her lousy judgment. "Yes. Okay." Heart racing, she rubbed her palms against her work jeans as he started toward the house. "Hurry."

He gave her a long look and surprised her again by coming back, taking her hand. "If I let you out of my sight, you'll go over there alone."

She didn't think it was fair that he knew her so well after such a short and awkward acquaintance.

"Ed!" he shouted, picking his way through the half-finished front porch. "Ed, where are you?"

"Up here." Her supervisor appeared at the top of the stairs. "What's going on, boss?"

"Shannon found us a deal on cabinets for the next house. I'm taking her with me to pick them up. We won't be back today. Can you see her car gets back to her place?" He looked at her. "Give him your keys."

She didn't waste time arguing or worrying about the blush heating her face as the crew stared at her holding Daniel's hand.

When they reached his truck, he blocked her attempt to open the passenger door.

"What are y—"

He silenced her with a kiss. Shocked by the move, she stood there and let him cover her lips in a soft sweet touch. "What was that?" she asked, dazed.

"A kiss." He stroked a hand up and down her arm. "For luck."

His vivid blue eyes held hers, curious and expectant. She wasn't sure she what he wanted, only what she wanted. With that clock ticking loudly in her mind, she grabbed his shirt and tugged his mouth back to hers.

Full of promises, she indulged in a kiss from her fantasies, a kiss that would fuel her dreams for years to come. His lips, warm and firm, muted the fear pulsing through her for a delicious, timeless moment.

She eased back, breathless, happy to discover he appeared equally affected. "For *good* luck."

"Amen," he muttered, opening the door for her.

He jumped into the driver seat and handed her his phone as he started the car, put it into gear. "Forward that recording to Grant and let him know we're headed that way."

"Gary said no cops. Won't Grant call his detective pal in organized crime?"

"He also said time is short." Daniel's jaw clenched as he bullied his way through a yellow light. "I'm not having this argument again. Don't you trust me by now?"

"I do." She took a deep breath. "I do." She sent the recording of the phone call and, as a precaution, used Daniel's phone to dial Grant at the club.

"Put it on speaker," he said.

"You don't trust me?"

He shot her a baffled glance. "Saves time," he said.

"Right." All this time focused on her ex, waiting for him to negotiate for Aiden, had made her paranoid.

By the third ring, she was sure Grant wouldn't answer and her mind sprinted with the pros and cons of going into the meeting without anyone else knowing where they were. When Grant's voice filled the truck, she hesitated, having braced herself for his voice mail message.

"Hello? Hello? Daniel?" Irritation had turned to worry in his voice.

"It's Shannon," she said. "And Daniel. Gary Loffler just called. I sent you the recording."

"From a number listed as a plumbing company," Daniel added.

"He didn't try to hide who he was," Shannon continued. She went ahead and gave Grant the details of the call, including the no-police rule, and the time left on the hour they'd been given.

"I'll alert the uniforms in the area and we'll send a plainclothes team in closer to protect and support the two of you. Not enough time to set up a proper surveillance. We have plenty of cameras in that part of town. We'll tap into them."

"Thank you." This was really happening. Her stomach cramped around her lunch, as excitement, hope and fear coalesced.

"Shannon," Grant said, "your focus has to be on Loffler. You know him better than we do. We're counting on you to know if he's lying. Don't let anything distract you or spook him. Ignore everything but him. We'll cover you. Did he say Aiden would be there?"

She replayed the phone call in her mind even as Daniel answered the question. "No."

"All right. Damn it. I'll factor it in," Grant said, his frustration filling the car. "Be safe out there.

She understood the sentiment, appreciated it and knew she'd take any risk to have her son back again. "Loffler knows something. I should have called him days ago," she said when the call ended.

"Hindsight does you no good," Daniel said. "Every move you've made has been to protect Aiden and get him home. Keep that in mind and keep believing we'll make that happen."

"Did you minor in psychology? I can't decide if your utter calm in a crisis is comforting or annoying."

"A little of both." His lips twitched in a smile. "Or so I've been told."

When they were stopped at a traffic light only blocks away from Old City Hall, she caught her knees bouncing impatiently. "I don't know how cool and calm I can be with Loffler. I want Aiden back so desperately."

She hadn't felt this frantic since those last days in New York. Gary had hidden her in a motel in Jersey City until the details had been finalized. Uncontrollable fear for herself, for her baby, twisted every footstep and voice passing by her room into Bradley's men coming to drag her back under his horrible control.

"If Loffler is a friend, he'll understand love for Aiden is behind any distraction or desperation."

"Grant said not to spook him." She picked at the dried thinset mortar on her jeans. "What if I make a wrong move before he tells us where Aiden is being held?"

"Are you sure he didn't know you were pregnant when you left New York?"

"Yes. No." She shook her head, eyed the traffic light, willing it to change. "Maybe? I don't know. I was having a tough morning when he brought by the final papers. He might have seen through my hangover excuse." Thinking about those grim days only made her more nervous right now. She changed the subject. "Why did you tell Ed we were going out for cabinets?"

"It was the first thing that came to mind. While you've been researching your ex, I've been tracking down materials and options for the kitchen in that next house. I want to make it something special."

"Well, that raises all kinds of red flags."

"Why?"

She glanced his way, certain he was teasing her. He couldn't be this obtuse. "First, he knows that isn't my job. Second, what next house?"

"The one in Poplar that we walked through on Sunday," he said. "I think we should get moving on it as soon as possible. That one is really going to shine when we're done."

She gave herself a minute to enjoy the fairy tale of having her son home and working a project of that caliber from start to finish as a Jennings Construction project manager. She'd report to Daniel at least once a week, probably more often. And he'd come by to check the progress, pitch in, exchange ideas.

Fairy tale. She couldn't afford to indulge that dream. When they rescued Aiden, she would need to get out of town, out of Bradley's reach, fast.

"I'm not trying to rush you," Daniel was saying. "I know you'll want some time with Aiden before we dive in over there. And we need to wrap up the Caldwell place before I go back to the firehouse." He checked his mirrors and changed lanes to get around a delivery truck. "Guess I'm just excited as it was the first explanation that popped into my mind."

Regret knotted in the pit of her stomach, tangled merrily with the fear and anticipation of what Gary would tell them. How had she become so attached to Daniel so quickly? Leaving the job should have been simple, but she enjoyed her friends on the Jennings crew. They'd become the family of her heart. Leaving town to better protect Aiden should have been straightforward.

Silently, she heaped more curses on Bradley's head for robbing her of happiness all over again.

Daniel found a parking space and reached across the seat, covering her hand with his. Warmth seeped in, chasing away the chill that had come over her. Leaving him wouldn't be as simple as learning how to work with another boss.

"Thank you," she said. "For everything."

"It's going to work out, Shannon."

The determination in his eyes bolstered her belief and hope. "I believe you."

"Has Loffler ever been violent with you?"

"No." That had been Bradley's specialty.

"Good. Anything else I should know?"

"He's a wealthy lawyer. Arrogant. I'm guessing he won't be happy I brought you along."

"Too bad for him." Daniel's eyes flashed with determination. "Let's go get what we came for."

Hands linked, they walked up the block toward the historic landmark and she skimmed shapes and faces along the way, finally noticing Gary lingering near an information plaque that gave him a good vantage point of people coming and going around the building. His dark jeans and rumpled ivory, button-down shirt were unexpectedly casual. The shoes, Italian leather, were his classic style choice despite the lack of his normal tailored three-piece suit.

When she tensed to rush forward and demand answers, Daniel anchored her. "Easy."

He was right and she was grateful to have him beside her. "I'll make it." Aiden needed her to hold her nerve here.

"Never doubted it," he murmured.

Gary sat down on a bench, raised his chin a fraction to invite her over. "He should go," he said when they walked up.

"He stays," Shannon replied. Questions ping-ponged through her mind, but she stuck with the most vital. "Where is Aiden?"

"Not here. Your son is safe," he added hastily. "I didn't have anything to do with this, Shannon. Please believe me."

She supposed she shouldn't be surprised that Gary knew about Aiden. He dealt with all of Bradley's secrets, hers wouldn't pose a challenge. She sat down beside her old friend. "No games, Gary. Where is my son?"

"I'll tell you everything, I promise. You need to know Bradley set it all up."

It confirmed what she'd known, yet it still didn't make sense of Bradley's scripts about trading the father's cooperation for the son's life. "He's lost his mind, Gary. Go to the police and turn him in."

"On what grounds? With what evidence?" Gary snorted. "The man is as slippery as oil."

"Kidnapping is a start," Daniel suggested. "I'm sure with the right informant the cops could find plenty to work with."

"But never the evidence to *keep* him locked up." Gary looked to Shannon, his eyes clouded with worry and sadness. "The only resemblance to ransom was to get Aiden's father to cooperate, right?"

She nodded. As a friend, she wanted to care about whatever was troubling Gary since he'd cared about her welfare during her brief marriage. Aiden was more important.

"Let's walk," Gary said, donning his sunglasses. "Being out here in the open makes me nervous." He stood up and moved along the path, away from the building.

"Why are you playing games with my son's life?" she pleaded. It was all she could do not to take him by the throat and shake him. For a few seconds, she indulged herself in that scenario.

"That isn't what's happening here," he insisted.

"Then quit wasting my time and tell me where to find him."

"I will, once you promise you'll hear me out." His head might have been on a swivel the way he craned to see everyone moving though the area.

"Who are you looking for?" She stopped under a

tree, squeezing Daniel's hand as a fresh fear skittered down her spine. "He's looking for Bradley."

"I'm not." Gary shushed her. "He's had people watching me for a long time, you know how he is. I swear I'm here on my own."

Shannon glanced to Daniel while Gary shifted nervously. A breeze swirled, tugging colorful leaves off the tree overhead and sending them across the pavement like oversized confetti. "What do you want?"

"Forgiveness," he said, in a bone-tired tone. "Bradley hired a team to take your son. I had to make some calls and some threats. I found out they're holding him on the waterfront."

"That doesn't narrow it down much," Daniel said.

Gary tossed out a business name she didn't recognize along with a street address. "It used to be a holding company under one of the shell corporations. They managed warehouse space and self-storage units."

"On it." Daniel had his phone out, already sending the information up the line.

Gary led her a few paces away, his nerves obviously worsening as he spoke. "Now, about that make-the-father-cooperate demand."

Her breath caught. Gary knew too much not to be directly involved.

"He thinks I'm the father. I'm sorry you and your son were caught in the crossfire."

She gaped at him. She'd never been unfaithful to Bradley. Trying to put it into context, she failed. "That's insane."

"*He* is." Gary nodded vigorously. "He's gone over the edge."

"Why? What set him off?"

"The divorce was the beginning," Gary said. "He lost

face when you got away. Last year, one of his enemies here in Philly recognized you. I don't even know where or how. I happened to be here on business for Bradley. It was pure coincidence."

"You know how he is," Gary continued, his tone low and urgent. "He started putting two and two together and coming up with five. Over the last year, a couple deals failed and he's unraveled a little more each time."

"He has no right to Aiden."

"Legally he does. A simple paternity test would prove it."

"No," she breathed as her heart clenched. "He wouldn't. He never even wanted children." If she'd stayed, he would have made her terminate the pregnancy, by choice or by force.

"He always wants leverage. Power. Once I learned you'd had a baby, I took measures to protect you and your son and put an end to his paternal rights. It was less than a year after the divorce when I realized he was having second thoughts about letting you go."

"What do you mean?" She needed to know and yet didn't want to hear it. She'd broken free of Bradley and she refused to get sucked back into his life again.

"I tried, Shannon. Please believe that I tried," he pleaded. "Instead I made things worse." He crowded her, the regret rolling off him in waves. "When you rescue Aiden, you plan to run?"

She glanced at Daniel, her gaze drawn to him as unerringly as a magnet. "Yes," she whispered.

Gary followed her gaze. "But you love him."

Hearing such an assessment from Bradley's oldest friend startled her. "Doesn't matter." A little voice inside her head called her a liar. "Aiden's safety trumps everything else." Even the broken heart she would leave here in Philly.

Love. She couldn't pinpoint a specific moment when her heart had tumbled eagerly to Daniel, free of the walls she'd built around it. She'd been infatuated with the man since she'd met him, a healthy feminine attraction had sprung naturally from there. Spending time with him and getting to know him this past week had become a strange and uplifting counterpoint to her worry and fear over her son.

"It matters," Gary said. "You never looked at Bradley that way."

"That's a relief." Daniel had turned, gave a thumbs-up while he kept the phone to his ear.

"Don't leave town," Gary said abruptly.

"I have to," she said, forcing her gaze away from Daniel.

"No. Stay in town at least a few days. I've—" Gary went quiet as Daniel joined them. His mouth thinned into a hard, pale line. "Are they moving in on the warehouse?"

"They're sending a team to check out your lead." Daniel slid an arm around her waist. "We should go," he murmured to Shannon.

Gary agreed. "Take care," he said to Daniel. "Stanwood won't give up easily." Suddenly he pulled Shannon into a fast hug. "You were a light," he whispered. "And a wake-up call. Thank you."

The overwhelming sadness and resignation tugging at his features left her uneasy. She chalked it up to the strange meeting and the things he'd opted to keep to himself. "You should get out of here," she said. "Thank you for helping me." She backed away, with Daniel. "Then and now."

"But I didn't."

The reversal had her digging in her heels. "Wait." She looked around the park as a fresh wave of panic crashed over her. Had he really set a trap for her after all? "What are you saying?"

Gary took off his sunglasses and stepped forward. "I waited too long." His voice cracked. "Too long to get out of that life."

"Not her problem," Daniel said. "Good luck to you."

"Listen." Gary grabbed her arm hard enough to make her gasp and wince.

"Careful," Daniel warned. He extended an arm, holding Gary away from her. "You need to go on about your business."

"I've only made things worse for you." His gaze, previously so erratic, zeroed in on her now. "To protect you and your son from any claim, I've confirmed his wild accusations."

"What's he talking about?" Daniel asked her.

"I never cheated on him," she said. "You know he would've killed me."

"My commitment to the hasty divorce, my advice on the settlement." Gary raised his hands in a helpless gesture. "He twisted it all into supporting facts."

She knew what happened when Bradley slid into a blind, irrational rage. If he learned the truth about Aiden, there was no telling what he'd do to her or her little boy. "Coming here, involving me was your exit strategy?"

"Not exactly." Gary studied his shoes. "I was going to leave you word, so you could be prepared. He changed my timeline with the kidnapping."

Daniel's phone chimed with a text message. "Site looks promising. They're taking a closer look, getting into tactical position," he said, checking the text message. He nudged Shannon closer to the edge of the park. "We need to get going."

"Remember they're experts," Gary said. "You'll hear from me."

"Why don't you come with us and fill her in on the way?" Daniel suggested. "The reunion may do you good."

Gary took a step toward them. A thundering bang tore through the pleasant autumn afternoon, followed by another and one more. Three gunshots, she realized too late.

Someone shouted, "Gun!" as people scrambled for safety. She watched, horrified as blood bloomed over the center of Gary's shirt.

"No!" Shannon's scream joined the swell of those around her, and what had been an idyllic setting devolved into chaos. Daniel pushed her down behind the meager shelter of a bench, covering her with his body as the gunman fired again, hitting the bench, the tree behind them.

Gary slumped to the ground, his face gray with shock and pain. A few paces away, Shannon saw the gloating, familiar face of the shooter. "Bradley!"

Her ex-husband tossed the gun toward his victim, her friend, and gave her a sarcastic finger wave before he pulled a hood up over his head and joined the others fleeing the park.

"Oh, Gary." Shannon pressed her hands to his chest, praying she could slow the bleeding. "Hang on." She looked at Daniel. "It was Bradley. I saw him."

"I'll call it in."

"Too late." Gary coughed, blood sputtering at his lips. "F-forgive me."

Daniel had his phone to his ear, rattling off information and a request for an ambulance. Uniformed officers approached at a run from all angles, guns drawn.

"I saw the shooter," she said when the first officers were close enough. "It was Bradley Stanwood who shot this man." Good thing her ex had left. She felt like she could kill him with her bare hands.

"Hang on, Gary," she ordered fiercely. She could feel the life draining from him. "Hang on. I mean it."

"Cold."

Daniel, on his knees opposite her, checked Gary's pulse and gave her a grim look.

She heard sirens. "You hang on. Help is coming."

"Shan—" Gary coughed. "Cold," he rasped. His eyes fluttered open and when he met her gaze, his vision cleared and he seemed completely lucid. "Case. Don't let him walk."

"I won't, I promise you," she said, though she had no idea what he meant.

Daniel jumped up, waving over the paramedics.

"You know."

"Shh. Save your breath," she pleaded.

He grabbed her hand, his grip tighter than she expected. "You know." His eyes fixed, unseeing, on a point beyond her and though the paramedics rushed in, she knew he was gone.

Daniel guided her out of the way as more authorities moved into position to secure the area. She buried her face in his solid shoulder, but she didn't cry. "He was my only friend during my marriage."

He stroked a hand up and down her spine, soothing her.

"I think I'm out of tears," she murmured. "It was Bradley. He was in a gray hoodie."

"You'll give the police the description, let them handle it."

His easy touch, that calm, calm voice settled her. "What's happening at the waterfront? Do they have Aiden?"

Daniel showed her his phone. "Still working on it." He raised a hand, signaled a nearby police officer.

It took more time than she wanted to spend, giving her initial statement of the murder and a description of the shooter. How she knew both the shooter and the victim. How they knew each other. Why they were in the park to begin with. Why they needed to leave.

Finally, after a call came in from someone up the food chain in the police department, they were released. She still couldn't shed any tears as the shock set in, making her muscles quiver as they walked back to Daniel's truck.

"He killed his friend," she stammered. The blood on her hands startled her as Daniel opened the passenger door. She caught her reflection in the side mirror and refused to get into his truck. "My murderous ex still hasn't gotten his hands dirty. No, he put it on me."

"*Shh.*" Daniel reached behind the seat for a bottle of water, pouring it over her hands and rubbing away the worst of the blood. He dried her hands with a work towel and rummaged around for a jacket to cover her ruined shirt.

"He tried to tell you something at the end," Daniel said, checking his mirror so he could pull out of the parking space.

"I didn't understand all of it." She would need some time for Gary's words to sink in. "I think he said something about a cold case. He said I knew, but I don't."

Daniel reached across the seat and rubbed her shoulder. "Leave Bradley to the cops. They'll track him down. Let's focus on making sure Aiden comes home with you tonight."

"I believe it," she said, earning a smile.

She thought it would be bliss to stick around and see that smile frequently, if only on the job site. Could she stay here in Philly with her son once this was over? Much as it irritated her, she knew the answer was dependent on her ex. If the cops caught him, she could rest easy, unless he slipped through their grasp.

Her phone rang and her hands tensed. The caller ID showed the number blocked. "It's him. Bradley." Who else would it be? The kidnappers had their hands full with a looming attack.

"Speaker," Daniel said.

"And the record button." She was a pro by now, though she'd happily have gone a lifetime without needing to develop this particular skill.

"Good afternoon, Shannon," Bradley's voice filled the truck cab. Now she could hear the foul canniness behind the smooth, polished tones. "How's your day?"

"You won't get away with murder," she said. "Or kidnapping."

"Darling, I already have. Everything that matters to you is under my control. You said so yourself."

"I did." It shamed her to admit it in front of Daniel, but she had said those words shortly before she married a nightmare of a man.

She expected him to be right. He *was* right in reference to Aiden. Still, she glanced at Daniel and knew her ex was wrong. Over recent days, she'd come to care for the man tasked with keeping an eye on her. Daniel mattered. Gary had called it. She was in love with Daniel, and Bradley would never have him.

More than that, she mattered. She'd changed, learned the hard way to value herself. She wasn't the mousy, timid wife Bradley Stanwood had neatly pinned under his thumb like a butterfly to a display board. Her real journey had started that day in the hospital. Her ex had no idea who she was now or what she could accomplish.

"Would you like to hear how you can win back your son?"

"I'm not negotiating with you."

"You don't have to," he said. "He served his purpose for me."

She could hear the sneer in his voice and her memory pushed the image to the front of her mind. In the past, she would have cowered. Today it pissed her off and made her ready to fight.

"You'll rot in jail for kidnapping *and* murder. This time the charges piling up around you will stick." She paused, making sure her voice wouldn't crack. "Bring me my son and turn yourself in."

"No can do, my darling. What if I told you I sold your son to clear my escape route?"

The barb struck true and she had to work to hide it. "An ugly story told by an uglier man," she managed.

"I was everything good for you." His tone slithered over her skin, leaving a clammy chill in its wake. "You were nothing until I married you."

Again true. She'd let him swallow her identity in one quick wedding ceremony and paid the price every day of their marriage. She was too angry to care that he was airing all of her failings in front of Daniel. "I can only be happy I'm no longer the wife of a murderer."

"You know, I didn't expect your greed," he said in a tone gone thoughtful. "Or your cleverness."

Daniel gave her a look, arched an eyebrow. *Greed,*

he silently mouthed the word. She shrugged, unable to immediately put Bradley's nonsense into any sensible context.

"Give it up. I want my son back."

He gave a harsh bark of laughter and she bobbled the phone. "We all want something, don't we?"

"It's over," she snapped. "Give the order to release Aiden and let your lawyers handle the rest."

"Lawyers." Bradley cursed. "They can't be trusted. Greedier than wives, every last one of them. Your son—" he snarled the word "—is out there for the taking." The line went dead on his awful laughter.

"You okay?" Daniel asked after another few blocks. "We're almost there."

"I hate him."

"He is hateable," Daniel agreed.

"I won't dwell on it, I promise. It just needed to be said." She forwarded the recording to Grant as she struggled to make the conversation with Gary fit with Bradley's taunts.

"Also sounds a little crazy."

"Another facet he hid well before we exchanged vows."

"And after?"

She appreciated the gentle invitation in those two words. He would listen, let her vent and steer her back on track. She shook it off. A minute spent thinking about Bradley was a minute wasted.

"That's in my past," she said defiantly. "I have to focus on Aiden and our future."

What would that look like? She still hadn't decided how far she would need to run to escape her ex-husband's reach.

"Someday I suppose I'll have to tell him who fathered him."

Daniel gave a low whistle. "*If* that day comes, you'll find the right words."

Three blocks from the address Gary had given them, a policeman in a yellow safety vest stood by a detour sign in the middle of the intersection. Behind him, others were setting up barricades.

Daniel rolled down his window, refusing to make the turn. The cop stalked up to the truck window, aggravated. Seeing Daniel, his expression cleared. "Leave it to you, Jennings, not to follow the rules."

"Got the mother of the kidnapped boy here," Daniel answered, as if he reunited mothers and missing boys every day.

Well, yes, she supposed he did just that, without the extenuating circumstances of kidnappers most of the time. The policeman radioed ahead before sending them through.

"Almost there," Daniel said.

Her heart was in her throat as they pulled over, adding Daniel's truck to the long line of police cars and emergency vehicles with lights flashing. An ambulance waited half a block closer to the warehouses. She closed her eyes, praying no one would need treatment here.

She stopped right there on the street, caught Daniel's hand. Bradley's words were ringing in her head and she had a sudden fear this would go down all wrong. She didn't want to leave anything unsaid.

"Thank you." She pushed her sunglasses up to her hair, not wanting any barriers between them, no room for misinterpretation. "I wouldn't be here in one, sane piece without your help and compassion."

"Not true." He shook his head. "Shannon, you're the strongest, bravest woman I've met."

If anyone had ever said those words to her, she couldn't recall it. "I must be a late bloomer."

He grinned. "Let's go get Aiden."

"One second." She pressed up on her toes and set her lips to his. "For luck," she whispered aloud while her heart whispered, "For love."

Chapter 6

Daniel kept her hand in his as they carefully walked closer to the convergence of emergency and tactical responders. Regardless of the hell she must have endured in her marriage, he knew these days were the darkest of her life. Yet her resolve seemed to deepen with every hour of the ordeal.

Belief could do that.

He understood death, had brushed against it too often. He'd lost friends and coworkers. In high school, a beloved classmate and varsity baseball teammate had committed suicide, sending a shock wave through the community. The first fatality he'd dealt with as a candidate with the PFD had been a motor vehicle accident, the driver dead on impact, long before the truck and rescue squads had arrived. He'd even lost a mentor on the job when a fire had shifted on them while they cleared an apartment building.

That day had been a personal hell for him, and it still didn't come close to what Shannon had just survived. What could possibly be going through her mind after her ex shot and killed her friend? Daniel didn't know how close she and Gary had really been, but in that moment, hearing she was out of tears, he'd wanted to strangle her ex with his bare hands.

"There's Grant," she said, pointing up ahead.

The nightclub owner met them halfway and pulled Shannon into a big hug. He held her at arm's length and studied her. "You holding up?"

She swallowed, her gaze darting to the warehouse at the end of the pier. "I keep telling myself there are cameras all over the park. Daniel and I are confident the police will find him."

"That's exactly right. You've gotta believe."

She reached for Daniel's hand, laced her fingers with his. "So I've been told."

"This is a fast response," Daniel said. "More units than I expected."

"Detective Hertz and I were ready. We've been running down rumors right and left searching for Aiden. We had a tip on this location yesterday and PPD put more units in the area for us."

"Anything definitive?" Daniel asked.

Grant flicked a hand toward the pier. "The self-storage place makes great cover for anyone coming or going. Based on what Loffler said, they're about to go into that warehouse at the end of the pier. They just scanned with infrared and saw three adults in the office above the warehouse floor."

"Bradley told us he sold Aiden," Shannon said.

Grant's jaw dropped. "When?"

"He called shortly after the cops cut us loose from Old City Hall. Shannon sent you the recording."

She pulled her phone from her pocket to verify the message went through, even as Grant pulled up the message on his phone. Grant listened, his face going pale.

Hearing the conversation again, Daniel had plenty of questions about Stanwood's sanity. Something in those last words pricked his instincts. Stanwood was gloating, not at all worried about being caught for murder or kidnapping. Sure, the bastard had been trying to upset her with that crack about selling the boy, but the infrared equipment was good enough now to show the difference between an adult and a little kid. If Aiden wasn't in the warehouse, where had they moved him?

Daniel looked around, caught sight of the engine and ladder companies standing by at the close end of the pier. "Give me a second? I want to have a word."

"She's safe with me," Grant promised.

"Take your time." Shannon's smile was understandably tense.

He tried not to read anything extra into that tight expression as he jogged away. This wasn't about him or his baggage. It was about Shannon and Aiden and making sure they both got home safe tonight and stayed that way for a lifetime.

The last video from the kidnappers showed Aiden increasingly unhappy with the situation. Bored, asking for his mother, refusing to eat more fast-food chicken nuggets, the boy couldn't be making life easy on his captors. Daniel thought that little furrow between his eyebrows could become a permanent fixture if they didn't get him home soon.

Although the companies attending the call weren't from his house, working with the PFD made Philly feel like a small town. He greeted a few friends on his way to speak with the battalion chief, a little startled by the ache deep in his chest. He felt homesick for the PFD. The Caldwell house was important to him, Shannon's situation more so, but he was ready to get back into the rhythm of his shifts at the firehouse.

"You got something for me, Jennings?"

"There should be a child inside. The son of a Jennings employee."

"Suspected kidnapping." The chief nodded. "We heard. No sign of a child on the premises."

Daniel knew the chief's direct look was encouragement to speak up or move along. At the moment, he was technically a civilian and should be staying out of the way. He stopped stalling. "Sir, I'm concerned the kidnapper has the place booby-trapped."

"That's why the tactical teams are taking the lead," the chief replied. "We helped evacuate the pier and now we're on standby."

Something was off. "The suspected kidnapper called the boy's mother on the way over." He continued at the chief's urging, "After he committed murder right in front of her. The men inside may not know the building is sabotaged. This is all gut instinct, sir. I can't give you anything solid. Don't mean to waste your time."

"You're suggesting someone is nipping loose ends."

Loffler's dead body flashed to the front of Daniel's mind. "Yes, sir."

The chief studied the warehouse thoughtfully, turning as he took in the other facilities on the pier. "Get me the blueprints again." He snapped his fingers at a candidate.

"With all of us out here, their best escape is out to the water," the chief said. "The tactical team knows that. They moved to cover that position."

"Good," Daniel said absently. He was thinking about Stanwood's contradictory comments of selling the boy and leaving him "there for the taking." The equipment said Aiden wasn't in there.

Everything Daniel had seen so far indicated they were facing a man capable of anything. No apparent conscience or morals. Could he have double-crossed the team holding Aiden? It seemed well within the realm of possibility.

"I want to talk with someone from the city planner's office," the chief said. "Jennings, do you know if he has the right skills to booby-trap the warehouse?"

Daniel shook his head. "I only know he has nearly endless money and mob connections."

The chief's nostrils flared. "No one mentioned the mob."

"Speculating here," Daniel said. "It's not like I can hand you a file full of proof."

"They had a fire in Camden two days ago. Old warehouse, abandoned. No casualties or additional property loss. Building was similar size and age to this one. Collapsed and burned."

"Only exit to the river?"

"Yep."

Daniel swore. Not the first time an arsonist took time to practice technique before the main event. Daniel studied the warehouse, trying to see it as a criminal intent on creating a distraction in order to escape.

The chief reviewed the blueprints. "Wouldn't take any real expertise to knock this thing down. A kid with a cherry bomb and a knack for geometry could do it."

"We're not dealing with a kid." He'd washed Loffler's blood off Shannon's hands himself.

The radio on the chief's shoulder crackled and Daniel heard the tactical team report the all clear at the front, side and rear exits. He itched to get closer and see for himself even though he wasn't on duty.

If he'd had any doubts about getting back to work, they were gone. He wasn't ready to settle into life as a civilian businessman. Once the Caldwell house was done, he and his dad were going to have to talk it out. Hopefully with less shouting.

"Sold your son."

"There for the taking." Daniel knew it was vital they decipher what Stanwood meant by those conflicting comments about Aiden's fate.

The tactical team moved in as directed, covering the exits. Police snipers assigned to high-ground positions on the nearby structures had scopes aimed at those exits while a police helicopter maintained an overhead view of the area where the pier and river met.

No one inside would get away unnoticed. Logically, he should've been happy. Instead he was restless. Maybe it was fallout from the murder in the park, but he wouldn't be content until Aiden and Shannon were safely home behind her new security system.

Farther up the line, about one hundred yards closer to the warehouse, Shannon rocked side to side, her arms wrapped tightly around her middle. He should be over there, lending support. He'd done all he could, warning the chief that something could be off. Like everyone else, now he had to stand back and wait for the experts to manage the heavy lifting.

He felt the pop and rumble of the first explosion under his feet. The chief spun on his heel and as the first flames shot up the short side of the warehouse, he gave orders to his firefighters.

Radios all over the scene started crackling, snapping with voices and reports from inside. Daniel heard something about missing stairs and a blocked egress. Then came the strange news that no one other than the tactical team was inside. Reports from the helicopter claimed no one had exited to the roof.

What the hell? Before they'd gone in, there had been three people on the second level. They hadn't levitated up there. Or down again. Where had they gone?

Suddenly the window in the wide front door blew out with a flash and black smoke flowed out, billowed up, a vicious scar against the blue October sky.

Daniel fell in with the firefighters surging forward.

"Jennings! Not your day," the chief called after him.

He skidded to a stop, adrenaline pumping through his system with no outlet. If he felt this helpless, Shannon would be losing it by now, with or without the reports of disappearing people. He hurried back over to join her.

"I'm sure Aiden's fine." With his arm around her shoulders, he felt the uncertainty quivering through her body. She wasn't crying, but the shock was catching up to her. "They've got this," he said.

"Grant and Detective Hertz went off to chat." She jerked a thumb in their general direction. "I heard *manhunt* mentioned."

"Someone must have called from the Loffler scene. They'll be pulling out all the stops to find Stanwood," he assured her. He rubbed at the tension in her neck, into her shoulders while the firefighters started guiding out members of the tactical team overcome by the black smoke.

"A lot of resources are focused here and dedicated to bringing in your ex. You heard Grant say they were working the warehouse on a tip from an informant even before Gary shared the address."

She looked away from the burning warehouse to others in the area. "Something isn't right. You know Aiden's not in there."

"No one is in there according to the most recent reading," he said.

"Even so, the fire renders the infrared tool useless."

"Firefighters use other variations," he began, stopping when she shook her head. "Aiden wasn't in there and the best way out is the water."

"I haven't heard any boats," Daniel said. "The coast guard is close if we do."

"No." She turned her back on the burning warehouse, pulled him around with her. "He's had Aiden for nearly a week," she said, talking it out. "He sent professionals to take my son from the sitter when they might as easily have taken him from my house."

"If they had grabbed him from your place, they would lose the two-hour lead time," Daniel said. He started examining the other buildings as well. She'd told him more than once her ex enjoyed lording his advantages over others. Without sharing details of her personal low points of her marriage, she'd given Daniel enough to create an unpleasant picture.

The man used his advantages, made examples of people who crossed him. Loffler came to mind once more. Something as big and flashy as a warehouse fire during a child rescue diverted men who might be added to the manhunt for a killer.

"He's convinced he's in the clear," she murmured, her voice barely audible amid the rush of responders around them. "He wouldn't have called so soon after killing Loffler if he'd been worried about getting away."

Daniel had to defer to her expertise on the bastard. "You don't think he really sold Aiden?"

"Bradley is capable of anything. He's been planning this for longer than I realized."

She drifted farther from the warehouse. "Gary pointed us here. He wouldn't have lied to me."

"He was Stanwood's best friend."

"And betrayed by him through the years. There was no friendship or trust at the end. Bradley can't manage those life skills."

Her prevailing calm painted a spotlight on Daniel's rising frustration. Had she slipped into shock? Watching a friend die could do that.

She broke into a run. Daniel followed, certain she'd finally snapped. "What are you doing?"

"Gary gave us the holding company. He didn't give us the warehouse."

"He gave us an address."

"Look." She stopped, pointed up. "Do you see it?"

"The offices." Although a fresh company logo was on the front door of the smaller, two-story office building, on the side in peeling, faded paint was the now defunct logo that matched the name of the shell company Gary mentioned. At first glance, it seemed deserted, though the sign said they were open. "I see it now. The fire department evacuated everyone on the pier."

To clear an area like this in a hurry, teams probably knocked on doors, gave a few shouts and moved on if no one answered. It would be the perfect place to hide and wait out the search for Aiden. When the authorities gave up or responded to another distraction, the kidnappers could waltz away at their leisure.

With no more than a look, he and Shannon started for the front door of the office. A spray of bullets rained down from the roof of another building between the warehouse and the office, and they skidded to a stop.

Daniel looked around, but there wasn't enough cover to safely make it to the front door. The shooter had the high ground. High and to the left, he realized, craning his neck. Another rapid-fire burst chased them back the way they'd come, between this office and a row of the self-storage units.

He did fires, damn it, left the gun fights to the cops. At the moment, the police were preoccupied. This was up to him. Shannon wouldn't back down until she was certain Aiden wasn't inside.

"He must be in there," she said, anxiously leaning forward.

"Whoa." He drew her back. "Something is," he agreed. "Give me a second here."

Judging the angle, he waited a few more seconds to make sure the shooter was done. When the only noises he heard were those coming from the warehouse, he propelled her across the open space to the darker shadows at the side of the guarded building. The whole way, he prayed there was only one shooter up there on Stanwood's payroll today.

"Definitely in the right spot," she said, her chest heaving as the echo of another burst of gunfire died down. "How can we get in?"

He'd wanted an outlet for the adrenaline. "Good odds." He peeked around the corner, looking for a clear path. "Unfortunately whoever's inside knows we're coming now."

She held a finger to her lips, tilted her head toward the building.

He caught the sound of voices, too, and the crying of an unhappy child on the verge of an all-out tantrum. That was all he needed. Better to try now and make a mistake than dawdle and let the kidnappers escape the area with Aiden.

Despite the strength Shannon had shown through all of the terror of this ordeal, he knew if they didn't save her son she'd die. Not physically and not all at once. No, her heart would keep beating, and her lungs would function, while the loss of her son ate away at her soul day by day until only a husk of the woman remained.

He couldn't imagine her eyes without that fiery spirit, the wry humor, the affection she held for the friends close to her. The idea of that light going out of her eyes ignited something deep inside him, something inherently more significant than he'd ever felt on the job. A wave of protective determination rolled over him. His goal on every call was to save lives, but this had become personal.

He scanned the area, searching for anything he could use as a weapon. The best option at the moment was a chipped brick. He grabbed it, hefted it and drew his finger carefully across the sharp edge. It would do.

"What are you doing?"

If he went to check for a back door, he'd likely be facing brick against gun. If they had a shooter guarding the front door, they surely had someone at the back. Around front, he might get through the plate glass window before the sniper tagged him. Better long odds than none, he decided.

"Call Grant," he told her. "They probably can't hear the gunshots over the fire and rescue at the warehouse. He'll send backup."

Daniel slipped away from her grasp when she reached for him, asked him to wait. "No time," he said. "Call Grant."

Inching toward the front of the building, he stayed

out of sight as long as possible. On a deep breath, he turned the corner and slammed the brick through the corner of the window, shattering the glass. The shooter started firing as Daniel leaped through the opening.

He stayed low, waiting out the spray of bullets. When it was quiet, he tracked the sudden rise of voices, all adult this time, and all of them barking out conflicting orders. Keeping to the long shadows near the wall, knowing Shannon was listening on the other side, he picked his way through the front office until he was tucked back behind the stairs.

He ignored the shouts for him to come out, listening instead to this side of the conversation between the kidnappers and the shooter outside.

Two men were here, plus Aiden. He had no doubt of it now as the debate for how to proceed raged on. Probably mob and probably local hires, he thought. It fit with Stanwood's methods.

"Leave the kid." One of the men sounded as weary of the situation as Aiden. "We have to get out of here."

"The kid's the only ace we got left," a deeper voice shot back.

The radio was garbled and the two men upstairs swore. "What's that? Police incoming."

Mentally, Daniel gave Shannon a high five. Though more swearing and bargaining followed, it became clear that the deeper voice, the leader on this team, wasn't going to budge.

"We ain't getting enough cash for this crap," the whiner said. "I'm leaving the kid."

Daniel heard the unmistakable sound of a gun being readied to fire. "That's fine by me. I'll count your share as a bonus for mental aggravation."

"Put that away."

"Shut your mouth and pick up the kid."

A child shouted and squealed. Cried for his mother.

"Where is the guy who came through the window?" A pause. "He's got no idea."

"Maybe he's dead."

"We should be so lucky."

Daniel held his ground as a stair tread creaked overhead.

"The woman?"

Daniel held his breath.

"Well?"

Daniel was as impatient as the whiner, wanting an answer on her status.

"Doesn't matter," the leader rumbled. "The covered route is out and left, left again."

In his head, Daniel saw the path they were planning. They'd take Aiden around the building on the side opposite Shannon's position. He didn't need verbal confirmation that the shooter would take her out if she showed herself.

Aiden whimpered about going home.

"Got him?"

"Yeah."

"Stay right behind me and don't let him go."

Outside, the shooter suddenly started up again in three round bursts. Cover fire, Daniel and the kidnappers realized at about the same time.

The men came down the stairs, boots pounding. If they made it out the door, the odds shifted back to their favor. Daniel didn't care what happened to the kidnappers; he only wanted the boy.

Holding the brick, he slammed into the leader, taking him out at the knees and rolling with the impact into the far wall. The man tried to raise his gun and

Daniel used the extra weight of the brick in his hand to knock the gun away. He plowed his weighted hand into the man's stomach and, standing up, moved toward the man holding Aiden.

The man had frozen, staring at the scene from his vantage point on the last step. With Aiden wriggling in his grasp, he couldn't get to the gun at his side.

"Put him down," Daniel ordered. "Gently."

The man cooperated. "Take him. He's a pain in the ass."

"Come here, Aiden." Daniel held out his hand. Smart, the little guy darted away from his captor. He hesitated there, lower lip quivering, rather than run straight to Daniel. "It's all right, buddy. Your mom sent me. Let's go see her."

Aiden scrambled to Daniel's side. From the corner of his eye, Daniel caught the first man moving again, heard more shouts coming over their radios. He saw the gun rise and take aim.

Scooping up Aiden, he ran down the hallway toward the back door as the police stormed the front of the building, buttoning up the planned escape route.

The narrow hallway filled with light as the door slammed open. Tucking himself to the wall, he cupped Aiden's head, turned the little face to his chest, protecting the boy from what he expected to be tear gas or some other technique used to suppress suspects.

"Jennings?" Two silhouettes in tactical gear came through the door. "Call out!"

"Here! I have the boy."

"This way."

Squinting against the bright sunlight, he let the team move around him, putting themselves in the path of any remaining threat. They kept him surrounded, escort-

ing him away from the office building as shouts and
cheers rippled across the pier. Just as loud as the panic
earlier in town, but he heard the relief and joy in the
noise this time.

Removed from the immediate danger, Daniel took
stock of the little boy in his arms. He smelled of cig-
arettes, beer and the salty grease of a fast-food joint.
"You're safe now," he promised. "Did they hurt you
anywhere?" he asked as they walked along the pier toward the cluster of emergency vehicles.

Aiden shook his head, his eyes wide in a face that
needed a bath, his small hands clinging to Daniel's shirt.
"Where's Mommy?"

He scanned the faces for Shannon, marveling that
anyone had managed to pry her from her post near the
building while she believed her son was inside.

"Where's the mother?" he asked the group in general.

"Safe," the nearest man replied. He wore a sergeant's
rank on his shoulder. "We pulled her back for her protection."

Daniel didn't find much comfort in the answer. He'd
left her out there with an active shooter. To save her son,
but still. "What did she do?"

The sergeant cocked an eyebrow. "Sounds like you
know the woman."

He did and was proud to say so. "She's had a tough
week."

"I bet." The man smiled at Aiden. "You doing all
right?"

Aiden dropped his head to Daniel's chest and nodded in the affirmative.

"She's right over there," the sergeant said to Aiden.
"And she can't wait to see you."

The police department had circled an ambulance

with other vehicles, much as they'd circled him on the walk over. There in the middle of it all, Shannon stood, rocking impatiently from foot to foot, her hair glowing in the sunlight. Someone had given her a clean shirt and a windbreaker to ward off the brisk air.

At her side, Grant held up a police radio between them, and Daniel knew he'd been giving her every update and assurance.

And none of it would matter until she held her son again.

"Mommy!" Aiden pushed hard against Daniel's chest, eager to get down. "Mommy!" he shrieked.

Shannon turned, her face alight as she saw her son.

"One second." Daniel barely avoided taking a foot to his crotch as he set the boy gently on feet that were ready to run. "Easy."

The protective circle split for Shannon at Aiden's first call. Running forward, she dropped to her knees and let him barrel into her, those small arms wrapping around her neck as she held him close.

Joyful tears rolled down her face, into Aiden's platinum hair as she rocked him back and forth, said his name over and over. When she raised those wide brown eyes to Daniel, he thought he'd never seen anything so beautiful.

Grant clapped him on the shoulder. "Nice job."

"Happy ending's all that matters." Daniel swiped away a tear with the heel of his hand. "What happened at the warehouse?"

"A mess. Fire was showy, but no one is badly hurt. The three men inside slipped through a hatch to the river. Coast guard caught them. We'll soon figure out if they were connected to Stanwood or just in the wrong place at the wrong time."

"They'll get no sympathy from me."

"Boy looks to be okay," Grant observed.

"Told me nothing hurts." Daniel cleared his throat as he watched mother and son. Aiden would chatter, then bury his head in her neck, then chatter some more. "They'll take him to the hospital anyway."

"You, too, by the looks of it." Grant lifted Daniel's wrist so he could see the slice on the back of his forearm. "There's a reason they issue protective gear."

"Left it in my other wallet," Daniel quipped. "I'll get it cleaned up," he promised, only now noticing the sting of the laceration. "What the hell happened out here?" He didn't think he'd been in the building long enough for all of this.

"The shooter tried to clear a path. Didn't end well for him," Grant said.

"More good news." Daniel watched Shannon settle Aiden on a gurney while the paramedics started the evaluation. She kept smoothing a hand over his hair, around his ear, an endless cycle of comfort. His mother had done the same when he and his little brother were sick or hurting. "Do you think he's hurt?"

"No. She's soothing herself as much as the boy. Daniel, they took the men who held Aiden alive, but we don't have Stanwood. Can you keep an eye on her until we do?"

"No problem." He started forward as they loaded Aiden into the ambulance, stopped. "Do me a favor?"

"Sure."

"Send the cops to the hospital. Get the statements there. She won't want this coming into her home if she can help it."

"I'll do what I can. Better get moving." Grant raised

his chin in the direction of the ambulance. "Looks like she's not leaving without you."

"Get my truck to the hospital?" He tossed Grant his keys and turning quickly, nearly plowed into Shannon. He caught her, and she melted against him with overwhelming gratitude. Much as she'd done with Aiden, he just hung on for a long moment.

"Thank you. Oh, God, Daniel." She stepped back and gripped his hands hard, her gaze steady. "There just aren't enough words."

"He's safe. You're both safe now." Daniel intended to keep it that way.

Her bright smile wobbled as more happy tears threatened. "They said you could ride with us." She noticed the blood on her hand. Daniel's blood this time. "Looks like an excellent idea."

"Just a scratch," he said, pulling himself into the back of the ambulance.

Aiden's eyes were so like his mother's Daniel couldn't help feeling as if he'd known the kid for more than the past few minutes. "You doing okay?"

The little boy bobbed his chin, took his mother's hand as the ambulance started rolling.

"Mommy?" He crooked his finger to ask her to come closer. "He saved me," he whispered. "He's a good guy. Like Superman."

"Yes, he is." She kissed his hair and reached back for Daniel's hand. "His name is Daniel."

Aiden peered at him over his mother's shoulder. "Hi, Daniel."

"Nice to meet you, Aiden." Daniel stuck out his fist for a bump. "I hear you like trucks."

"You did?" Aiden's face lit up with excitement under

the smudges of dirt and grime. "Dump trucks are the best!"

"Ever ride in one?"

"No." He stretched out the word.

"It's cool," Daniel admitted. "Bouncy when they really get going. What do you think about fire trucks?"

Shannon burst out laughing, her grin infectious as they all talked trucks for the entire ride to the hospital.

Daniel knew it had been a dreadful week for all of them, but he had high hopes that the joy of this moment would be what they remembered most.

Chapter 7

Late that night, Shannon stood at the open doorway, watching her son sleep. In the watery moonlight spilling through the window, she reveled in the miraculous opportunity to enjoy each gentle rise and fall of his chest. With the floppy blue rabbit clutched to his face, he sighed a little and snuggled deeper under the covers.

Oh, how she'd missed the sweet smell of innocence that clung to his skin, the silk of his hair right after a bath. Thanks to Daniel's support she had believed to the best of her ability, though she'd never quite banished the fear that she'd never have the chance to savor these small, amazing moments again.

"Doing okay?" Daniel whispered at her shoulder.

"Never better," she whispered back. "I might stand here all night."

She breathed in the spicy scent of the man as well as the boy. Gratitude filled her, hadn't stopped since he'd walked out of that combat zone carrying her son in his arms, the last traces of gunfire and smoke an ominous echo behind him.

"Maybe you should save that for tomorrow. You could use some sleep, too."

They both could. Even with the police watching her house, she was grateful he was willing to spend another night on her couch rather than in a real bed. "Daniel, I can't ever thank you enough. You walked out with him and saved us both."

"Team effort."

He'd said the same thing at the hospital, waiting with her while the doctors examined Aiden and confirmed he hadn't been seriously injured.

Aiden had been mildly dehydrated, sported a nasty bruise on his shin, a black-and-blue handprint on his upper arm and a scraped knee. All in all, not a bad outcome considering he'd spent nearly a week with two violent men unaccustomed to caring for a four-year-old.

Daniel had survived the rescue remarkably well. The gash on his arm had been cleaned and closed with a line of butterfly bandages glowing white against his tanned skin.

She'd kissed every boo-boo, Daniel's included, while doctors administered fluids to Aiden and Detective Hertz took statements from the three of them. He showed Daniel and her son pictures and they both identified Aiden's captors. To her immense relief, her son showed no recognition of Bradley, Gary or the men captured by the coast guard.

"I want to put every mark they put on my boy on Bradley," she said, through a clenched jaw. "With a little more emphasis."

"You may have to wait in line," Daniel said darkly.

She shouldn't have been amused, definitely shouldn't have been aroused, by the comment. She dragged her gaze away from her sleeping son and smiled up at Daniel. "And here I thought I'd be first in that line, should the chance present itself."

"I'll let you go first," he allowed, "if you promise to let me bat cleanup."

"It's a date."

"It was supposed to be," he said under his breath.

She laid a hand on his chest, nudging him back into the hallway, drawing Aiden's door not quite closed. "Care to explain that?"

He shook his head, shoved his hands into his pockets. "Another time. Maybe."

"You know, now's good for me."

He sighed. "You've got that mom voice down pat. All I meant was the day he was kidnapped I was planning to ask you out. So I think I should be first in line," he said. "Since your ex wrecked my plan."

"All right." She thought back to that conversation over pewter touch-up paint and smiled a little. "You get first crack. I'll bat cleanup."

"I'm sure you can," he said, lips tipped up at the corner. "I'm convinced you can do anything."

If only that were true. If she could do anything, she'd stay right here with him.

Before the melancholy could take root, she kissed that sexy corner of his mouth, rubbed her lips along his to kiss him fully.

His mouth opened over hers and she gripped his shoulders as his hands stroked up her spine in one fluid motion. Heat burned away the last chill of her fear, left only desire pooling low in her belly.

She thought she could stay just like this, exchanging hungry kisses in the dark forever. If only. She broke the kiss and enjoyed the struggle to catch her breath as much as the feeling of being breathless.

"I probably would have said no," she said. "To the date."

"I probably would have let you," he replied. "Then."

The answer shot another thrill through her system. "Things are different now?"

"Now?" He smoothed his hands over her hips. "Oh, yeah. We've been living together for almost a week. I may have to insist on a date. I'm thinking a predictably calm dinner at an above-average restaurant followed by a movie."

"What kind of movie?"

"Chick flick," he said, grinning at her. "We've had enough action and drama."

She smothered her laughter with her hands. What a joy to be home and able to laugh and joke about it already. She thought dinner and a movie with Daniel would be a wonderful experience before she had to move on and change her name again. She couldn't stay in Philly unless they caught Bradley and managed to keep him in custody.

The reality seeped in and put a damper on the pleasure. As of the time they were released from the hospital, no one had seen him since the Loffler shooting.

"We could start that dating ritual with a beer downstairs," she suggested.

"Sure." He brushed her bangs to the side, traced the line of her jaw with his thumb.

If they didn't get downstairs soon, she'd drag him into her bedroom, to hell with consequences and regrets. She held the rail tight and deliberately moved to the stairs.

Maybe another woman could sleep with Daniel and still walk away. She wasn't sure she had that in her, not after so many months idealizing him, thinking about what it might be like to know him better. To have someone special in her life, a man who could be her friend and lover, a man willing to stand as a role model for her growing son.

She wouldn't deny her heart the wishing, though her mind knew this was only an interlude. No matter the circumstances that had thrown them together, no matter how his kisses set her off, this was temporary. Had to be. As supportive and solid as Daniel had been through her crisis, she couldn't lead him on. She wasn't free to promise him a lasting relationship while Bradley was in the wind.

In the kitchen, he opened a beer while she poured herself a glass of wine, taking a seat at the table. She couldn't sit on the couch with him as they'd done on other nights, didn't trust herself to keep her hands off him with so many emotions swirling through her. Gratitude, love and relief with a beautiful joy layered over all of it. Unable to separate one from the other, she thought it best to maintain a safe distance. No sense muddling up things now that Aiden was home and might pick up on any weird vibes.

If they ever wound up in bed, she didn't want any doubts between them about why. Sex wasn't a weapon or a gratitude tax in her mind. Between two healthy, consenting adults, intimacy and pleasure should stand on its own merit, a private sanctuary apart from the outside world.

"After all my fussing about keeping to a routine, I can't wait to get Aiden back on his schedule," she said. "It's going to be a challenge not to just spoil him rotten for the rest of his days."

"You wouldn't do that and ruin your good parenting record."

"Hope you're right." She sipped the wine, letting the cool flavor roll over her tongue. "I'm hoping being normal will settle him and assure him the worst of that nightmare is over."

Daniel walked over and turned the chair backward, straddling the seat. "You're not thinking of being on the job tomorrow?"

She shrugged, avoiding his gaze. She'd gone back and forth with the decision since they'd left the hospital. Going to work would be perfect for her, except she'd have to drop off Aiden. She wasn't ready to let him out of her sight. And what if the police needed to speak with her about Aiden's case or Loffler's death? On top of that, the doctors had warned her Aiden might become distressed or agitated, returning to the place where he was taken. All of those added up to instances where she'd have to leave the crew to cover for her.

"I hope the kidnappers cooperate," she said, changing the subject.

"My opinion?" he asked.

"Please."

"We take the day, maybe two, to relax and regroup. Everything else can wait."

So much for the subject change. "You don't need to babysit me," she said. "And you definitely need to go to the site. The crew will benefit," she added as he started to argue. "I feel bad enough for setting you back on a schedule that was tight to begin with."

He reached over and covered her hand. "Let's take this a step at a time. First, we get through tonight. If Aiden's feeling good tomorrow, we can all go by the Caldwell project together and check on the progress. We'll make a list and adjust the timetable while the crew gushes over Aiden. They will, especially now that they know what really happened. He needs that full circle affirmation as much as they do."

Guilt nipped her conscience. "I hope they understand why I lied about it."

"We both lied," he reminded her. "They'll get it. They all love you both."

Shannon debated the wisdom of a second glass of wine. Daniel simply got up, found the bottle and poured more for her.

"He'll want the park," she mused, breaking the silence at last. "Rachel and her boys will want to see him." Her palms went damp on a rush of nerves. "It's not her fault, I know it up here." She tapped her temple. "The idea of leaving him there scares me." She drew her knees to her chest. "I can never say that to her."

"She probably knows." Daniel patted her knee. "It's okay to feel everything you're feeling. We'll go by and you'll reconnect with your friend while the boys play for a while."

He seemed so easy with it. "How is it you're so understanding?"

"Not my first crisis." That small smile came back, and his blue eyes twinkled. "Not even my first crisis with you," he teased. "Give yourself time to recover."

"Right."

"You said pancakes are his favorite breakfast." Daniel asked.

"Yes."

"Think you can make enough to keep up with both of us?

She considered how happy it would make her to try. "Pretty sure."

"Cocky. I like it." One dark eyebrow dipped low with skepticism. "You'd better get some rest then. We'll have a boys-against-the-girl test of your pancake power first thing." He polished off the beer. "After that, we'll make sure he has time with his buddies, run by the Caldwell house, then hit the park.

"Sounds like a full day."

He sent the empty bottle into a brief spin. "Think it would be too much for him if we go by the firehouse? Give him a tour?"

Too much for Aiden? Not at all. "He'd be thrilled." She was fairly certain that would prove too much for her to resist. "Were you really trying to ask me out? Last Saturday," she clarified.

He pushed the longneck bottle aside and lightly outlined each of her fingers. "It wouldn't have been much of a date," he admitted. "I was supposed to tend bar and close up after the concert." He stood up and tucked the chair back into place. "I hoped you'd come out, sit at the end of the bar and let me buy you a drink. Let me flirt with you a little."

"That's…" *Startling. Crazy. Tempting.* She couldn't pick one.

"Flattering?" he supplied with a grin.

His answer was better than hers so she nodded. "Yes." She cupped the wine glass in both hands while the lovely scenarios of potential dates with him flitted through her mind.

"Are you going to let Stanwood drive you out of town?"

His question hit too close to the real reason she kept her distance from him. She left her wine glass on the table and walked out to the front room, searching for a reasonable answer. It wasn't gratitude or joy swamping her now, but frustration. The only choice she could make was the one that safeguarded her son. Couldn't he see that?

"You left New York."

"Yes, I had to." Staying would have been emotional suicide, not to mention the danger to Aiden. "To protect myself and my baby."

"I get that. I'm just making sure you see things are different now. You don't have to leave Philly. You have friends, support and stability here."

All of whom her ex would happily mow down or use against her. "I also have an ex-husband skulking around, twisting up my life and hurting people. Killing people," she added. "Aiden's been a pawn once. I can't stay here and let that happen again."

Detective Hertz had specifically directed her not to leave town. Grant had said the same thing. Hell, Gary had, too. None of that kept her here in town tonight. Only Daniel. Given a choice, she would have left a number for the detective, packed the essentials and bolted on the first bus headed west.

Exhaustion hit her in a brutal sucker punch. The murder, the rescue, the week of unthinkable stress catching up with her, she sank onto the couch and dropped her head into her hands.

"I do see that side of it." His voice was soft, compelling. "Impossible not to. You're a wonderful mother." Daniel eased into the chair across from her. "Fierce, devoted. Never doubt it."

She looked up. "But?"

"No buts, Shannon. I'm only asking you to trust the people who care about you and Aiden. There's no weakness in leaning on a friend through a crisis."

"I've been leaning all week," she said, exasperated. She wanted to feel like the woman he described. If she had to run to reclaim her independence and shake free of the skeletons of her past, she'd do it.

"Which is a good start," he said with a heart-melting smile. "Go on up and get some sleep. We have a big day tomorrow."

It should have been easy after nearly a week of restless, sleepless nights. Up the stairs, turn right, crawl into her bed and sleep. Her mind and body were happy with that plan, but her heart stopped her at the top of the stairs. She turned toward Aiden's room and eased the door open. Tiptoeing, minding the creaky floorboard, she double-checked the lock at the window and the security status of the house with the app for the wireless system on her phone.

Brushing a kiss to her son's head, she sank to her knees beside the small bed, breathing in her son as she offered up more prayers of thanks. For Daniel, Grant and everyone involved with Aiden's rescue.

And there, her head pillowed on her arms at the edge of his bed, Shannon slept at last.

Daniel told himself he was happy she'd gone upstairs, that he'd done the right thing letting her go up alone without stealing more of those amazing kisses. He made his bed on the couch, his mind sifting through recent events. Pushing his hands through his hair, he sat down hard, staring at the dark stairwell, wondering why he was still here.

Technically, his job was done or nearly so. Despite Grant's request, he didn't have to stay every night, not with the police watching outside and the new security system to protect her if her ex showed up again. He'd lived all his life in Philly and he trusted the police to catch Stanwood. Her son was home safe and the men who'd snatched him from the sitter were in custody.

Like her, he hoped they cooperated and threw Stanwood under the bus. Quickly. So Grant would officially release him from this assignment. Living with her was becoming an unbearable temptation, a reminder of what he wanted and what he couldn't hang on to. He was stuck on her, even knowing she'd run, take Aiden and disappear, the minute she had a window.

That was the real reason he stayed, sleeping on her couch and helping her make plans for tomorrow. He wanted to keep her, them, in his life just one more day. He had tomorrow and he'd come up with something for the day after that. He wasn't ready to let go.

On the cushion beside him, his phone vibrated. He answered without looking at the display. At this hour, it could only be Grant with news. Probably bad news.

"You sound weary, Mr. Jennings."

Not Grant at all. "Stanwood." He hurried to find and activate the call recording app. "How'd you get my number?"

"She's playing you," Stanwood said, the sneer coming across loud and clear. "Didn't think she had it in her," he said with a tone resembling admiration. "Do you fancy yourself in love?"

"You put your hands on that boy." Daniel flexed his good hand, imagining the satisfying crunch of fist meeting face.

"I did no such thing," he replied, indignant.

"Go home, Stanwood." Daniel had to work to keep from shouting. "Crawl back under your rock and leave her and the kid alone."

Stanwood made a dry, rasping sound that might have been a laugh in Daniel's ear. "Once again she's found herself a champion. I take full credit for teaching her that skill."

Daniel wanted to argue, managed to hold his tongue. Shannon had made all of the effort, the sacrifices and the decisions to become the mother, employee and woman he respected and yes, *loved*. It wasn't any of her ex-husband's business.

"She didn't pull the trigger, but she killed Loffler. You were there, you know. I saw you send the boy back to her warm embrace. You won that battle, my friend. Enjoy it, because you're outgunned in the war ahead."

While Stanwood carried on, Daniel moved to the front window, half expecting the man to be out there on the porch, watching from a car. The porch was clear and the parked cars within his view of the street were empty. "Do you always talk this much?" he asked.

Another rusty laugh. "Ask her, champion. Ask her where she got the money to move to your fair city."

That wasn't any of Daniel's business.

"She won't tell you. When she digs in her heels and refuses, when she looks at you with those big eyes, ask her who she is willing to sacrifice to keep what isn't hers."

He glanced behind him, making sure Shannon wasn't on the stairs. "Cut your losses and leave town, you bastard." Daniel kept his voice low. "If you stay, I'll make sure you go down for murder."

"I'll stay, thank you, until that bitch returns what's mine," Stanwood snarled. "And if I go down, I *will* take her with me."

The call ended and Daniel sat there, staring at the blank phone as fury pumped through him. If Stanwood stuck around, Shannon would run. He'd seen it in her eyes, heard it in all the words she didn't say about having a future here in Philly. She would run, with good reason, and never look back.

He thought he might be sick.

He'd offered her a better job, a role that could benefit everyone involved from his dad right down to Aiden, and she wouldn't commit. He had a fresh understanding of why. Stanwood's tenacity, his reach and his vile way of making the irrational sound reasonable could get under anyone's skin.

Daniel flopped back on the couch, staring at the ceiling and rubbing a hand against the ache in his sternum. What he didn't know was why the bastard thought Shannon had something of his. He couldn't mean Aiden. The man was too crazy to be seeking parenthood.

Ask her, Stanwood's voice ricocheted through his head. Daniel shook it off. He'd go out himself and buy two bus tickets and send her away before he took any orders or guidance from her ex.

That ache in his chest burned now. If Shannon had something Stanwood needed or valued, she'd taken it for good reason to escape an abusive husband and unthinkable circumstances.

He got up and went to the kitchen for another beer. What did he really hope to gain by sticking around, playing house with her and her son? *Everything.* What a dumb answer. The day had been too long, too tumultuous for rational thinking at this hour.

Yes, he wanted to kiss her again. He wanted more from her—body and soul. It was okay if she didn't want him in return; he knew how to exit a relationship gracefully. He wouldn't let Stanwood, of all people, force them apart, deny them a chance to find out what they might be to each other. No, he wouldn't accept that without a hard fight.

Oh, she trusted him, though there was still a wall she wouldn't let him breach. It was as if he could see her living her life behind a pane of frosted glass, but nothing he did brought it down, brought her out or let him in.

His phone rang again and he set down the beer to grab it before it woke up Shannon or Aiden.

"Listen, you sli—"

"Daniel?"

At the sound of his mother's voice, he held the phone back, confirmed the call. "Mom? You okay?"

"Better than you, it seems. We just saw you on the news."

Daniel heard his father grumbling in the background, didn't need to know the precise words as the disapproval came through just fine.

"You were involved with that trouble down at one of the piers?" she asked. "Are you back on shift already?"

"Not yet." Daniel knew she'd be waving a hand to hush his dad or walking to a different room. He started laughing. Blame it on the adrenaline or frustration, he couldn't stop.

"The reporter said you were integral in saving that boy."

"Did they use my name?" Maybe that was how Stanwood got his cell phone number.

"Not that I recall. You looked good, sweetheart. We were just worried."

"I'm fine, Mom. No injuries." Aside from the cut on his forearm. "My shirt was the biggest casualty. Long day is all."

"Your dad went by the house where you said you were staying. He fussed about the lack of progress."

Fussed, his mother's way of saying his dad came

home and yelled for half an hour about Daniel's lack of commitment to the business.

"That's just a favor for a friend. No timeline on that one yet," he said. "The Caldwell house takes precedence."

"As it should." He could hear her smiling. "We're so proud you got involved for that family. It's looking great. Your crew is handling it perfectly."

"You've seen it?"

"Your dad took me by this afternoon."

He stifled the groan. Of course his dad would come by on the one afternoon he was off the site.

"What's this I hear about a place in Poplar? I don't want you stretching yourself too thin. You don't need to prove yourself to anyone."

In this instance, he knew *anyone* meant his dad.

He might not like lying, might not be good at it, but he could be glad he'd given Ed a better reason for walking out early today than the truth that he'd been dashing off to help an employee with her kid. His dad would have had a fit. The last thing he wanted as the heir apparent to the company was to send the man to an early grave.

He gave his mom a few more minutes, finished off his beer while they chatted. He promised her he'd be back on the Caldwell project in the morning and wished her good-night.

Careful to move quietly on the steps, he went up to the bathroom. The bright, juvenile jungle theme of the shower curtain and wall art made him smile every time.

It was as natural as breathing to turn and check on Aiden before he went back down. Doing so, he found Shannon sound asleep half on and half off the boy's bed. He stepped closer and noticed she was holding Aiden's hand.

Couldn't blame her for wanting to stay as close as possible after the harrowing week they'd had. She needed good rest as much as her son did. If he left her here, she'd wake up miserable and sore.

He gently jostled her shoulder and softly called her name. She was out. He scooped her up and carried her back to her bedroom, pulling the covers over her so she wouldn't wake up cold.

"Sleep well." Unable to resist, he kissed her forehead.

She nestled into the warmth of the bed, her face relaxed in sleep. Something about her contentment sank into him, too, and when his head hit the pillow on the couch downstairs, he slept soundly, as the day's troubles gave way to more pleasant dreams.

Chapter 8

Shannon woke absolutely certain this was the best Friday morning of her life. She didn't remember dragging herself to bed, but she rolled out and crept down the hall to peek in on Aiden. Though he often rose early, today he was still sacked out. Better for her, she thought as she rushed through her shower and dressed in yoga pants and her favorite sweatshirt.

She had a pancake contest to win today.

Downstairs, she made coffee and prepped pancake batter while Daniel went up and showered. With half a cup of coffee in him, he called Ed for an update.

"All set over there?" she asked when he finished.

"Crew is making progress. They can't wait to see you both."

She drank her coffee, apprehensive about facing everyone today. "Maybe we shouldn't put so much on his agenda today."

"You're nervous."

"A little." She didn't like that he knew her well enough that he could see it, much less call her on it. "With good reason," she added.

"You should be," he said.

The reply caught her off guard. Where was the easy-going, thoughtful Daniel? It was like he'd flipped a switch overnight. Old nerves tried to take root and she nipped them, ready to stand her ground. This was her house and she could make him leave.

"You don't stand a chance of keeping up with the pancakes Aiden and I will put away."

It took her several seconds to realize he was teasing her. Rattled, she poked at the double batch of dry ingredients for the pancake batter.

"Shannon?"

Before she could answer, the floor creaked overhead and a few seconds later the bathroom door slammed. "He's up," she said as her heart fluttered. "He slept through the night. No nightmares." She did a quick victory dance.

"So did you," he pointed out.

"About that." She felt heat rising in her face. "Did you tuck me in?"

"Guilty as charged."

She was processing that information when Aiden raced into the kitchen, his blue rabbit in one little hand as he made a beeline for Shannon. "Good morning, Mommy!"

She lifted him up, gave him a big squishy hug and then pretended to smother him with kisses until he giggled. The ritual over, he noticed Daniel, laid his head on her shoulder.

"Good morning, Aiden."

Her son's big eyes moved from her to Daniel and back. "Say good morning," she whispered.

"Good morning, Daniel," he said shyly.

"Good job," she said, letting him wriggle out of her

arms. As much as the idea appealed, she couldn't stay in the house and hold him forever. She opened the fridge and poured him a cup of juice. "Daniel had a good idea for breakfast."

Aiden sipped, staring at Daniel. "Does he live here now?"

"He stayed with me and helped a whole bunch while you and I were apart," she answered.

Aiden stared at Daniel, the furrow between his eyebrows digging in. "You helped Mommy while the bad guys had me?"

"I did. It was hard on her while you were gone."

"You helped me, too." Aiden waited another long second, then walked over and pressed himself to Daniel's knee. "You're the good guy."

Daniel stroked her son's hair. "Back at ya, bud."

Shannon blinked away happy tears. "Tell him your idea," she suggested, ignoring the crack in her voice, buying time for her heart to settle back to its normal rhythm.

"Your mom tells me you like pancakes."

"Mmm-mmm." Aiden perked up. "They're my favorite!"

"Mine, too," Daniel said. "What if we play a game?"

"With pancakes?"

"Yup. The two of us—" he wagged a finger between them "—will eat all the pancakes we can while your mom tries to cook enough to keep up with us."

"Yes!" Aiden bounced up and down. "Pancake game!" he chanted as they set the table, prepped butter, syrup, plates.

They gave her a run for her money and called it a tie when everyone was stuffed and there were two pancakes left on the griddle. "You can have them tomorrow," she said to Aiden as they finished cooking.

"Or dinner?" he asked.

She laughed at the hopeful tone. "We'll see. There's a lot to do today."

"Like what?"

"I thought we'd go see Rachel and the boys. They missed you."

Suddenly Aiden's eyes filled with tears. "I don't want to go there. I want to go work with you today."

She gathered him close, rocked a little as she rubbed his back. "We're all going over for a visit." She kissed his hair. How were they going to get through this? "Rachel's my friend," she said. "She and I want to talk about girl stuff while you and the twins play."

"The bad guys are gone? They were mean."

She wondered if Daniel could hear her heart cracking at her son's worry and fear. "No. No bad guys ever again." Shannon gave him another hug, aimed a pleading look at Daniel over Aiden's head.

"I'm going, too," Daniel said, stacking up plates.

"Will you stay while Mom and Rachel talk like girls?"

"I'll stay."

"'Kay." Aiden's pouting lip retracted a bit.

"After that," Daniel said, "I thought we could go by the construction site where your mom's been working."

"All of us?" he asked, his hands working over the poor rabbit's ear.

"Yes," Shannon replied. "Why don't we go up and get dressed?"

"'Kay." He hopped like a rabbit to the stairs.

"We'll be right back," she said, following her son.

In the bathroom, Aiden showed more signs of worry.

"I didn't get to see houses with you on Sunday," he said while Shannon helped him wash the remnants of breakfast from his face.

"You'll see the house we're working on today," she said as he brushed his teeth.

The answer mollified him as the conversation turned to trucks while she helped him change out of his jammies and into clothes for the day.

"No socks," he said, kicking his feet.

"Socks," she said. "It's October." After a short scuffle for form, he let her put on his socks and shoes.

When they got downstairs, Daniel had the kitchen cleaned. Even the griddle and mixing bowls were washed, dried and put away. She just stared at him.

"Did I do it wrong?"

"No." They'd cleaned up after themselves all week. She just hadn't expected him to take the brunt of KP. "Thank you."

"You have to wash your face," Aiden pointed at Daniel.

He pressed the towel to his face, raised his eyebrows at Shannon.

"Daniel's face looks clean to me," she said. "Let's get your coat."

"Is not." Aiden patted his own smooth cheeks. "Mine is clean."

Catching on, Daniel took a knee and motioned to Aiden to come closer. "This isn't dirt, it's a beard. Come feel." The boy giggled as Daniel's scruff tickled his palm. "I know you've seen whiskers before."

Aiden laughed and patted Daniel's jaw.

"Tell you what, tomorrow morning I'll make it disappear like magic. You can help me."

"Really?"

She stood back, watching the man and boy talk beards and razors and shaving and felt her heart wishing once again. She couldn't interrupt them, it was too adorable and there wasn't a firm schedule today. Savoring the moment, she knew it would be a happy memory she and her son could carry forward. Could she stay? Was there a path that kept them in Philly if her ex escaped the police?

She was still debating it when they were parked at Rachel's driveway fifteen minutes later. Before the kidnapping, Aiden would have sprinted ahead, truck of the day in hand. Today, his little hand gripped hers and held on tight.

"You're staying." Not a question this time.

"We're all staying," she said gently. "And only for a few minutes."

"'Kay."

The brief visit had a rough start, with Aiden nervously clinging to her at the gate. He settled in better when the twins came out in a mood to play hard. In the kitchen, Shannon and Rachel caught up over a cup of coffee while Daniel played outside with the boys. He pushed swings, drove cars through the sandbox and looked for all the world like an overgrown five-year-old having the time of his life.

"You landed a good one there," Rachel said, a gleam of feminine appreciation in her eyes. "I thought your boss was amazing the day…well, the day it happened. And now? That man is a keeper. Five stars, my friend."

"You might be reading too much into it," Shannon said. Recalling the kisses, her lips tingled at the denial. "He's been a rock through all of this but he has a life."

"A life with plenty of room for you and Aiden, I'd bet."

Rachel was only making what Shannon needed to

say more difficult. "I may not be in Philly much longer," Shannon blurted. "Aiden and I may be moving."

Rachel gave her a cool stare.

"We may not have a choice," she added. "You're my best friend. Family really."

"In my book, family sticks," Rachel said quietly. "We haven't had any more trouble here. Even if we had, I'd say running away is the wrong call."

No, it was the *only* call until Bradley was behind bars and she had some assurance he'd stay there.

"It can't be just you and Aiden against the world forever," Rachel said. "I heard they caught the kidnappers." Rachel's gaze drifted to the window again. "The news had great coverage of Daniel carrying Aiden back to you."

"What? We haven't seen that." If her ex had seen it, Daniel might be more of a target. Suddenly the coffee burned in her stomach.

"I should've taped it for you. Then we could play it at your wedding reception."

"You're making too much of it." Her heart pirouetted in her chest at the idea, despite all the other factors. Factors that, if ignored, would end with others getting hurt.

After promising Rachel she wouldn't do anything rash or leave town without a proper goodbye, they went outside. Oh, how she hated lying. Gathering up Aiden, his cheeks bright pink from the crisp air and raucous playtime, she handed Daniel the car keys while she settled Aiden in the booster seat.

"Did you have a good talk?"

"We did." Parts of it were good, she thought when it felt like a lie. "Looked like you were having a grand time yourself."

"Couldn't help noticing Rachel's boys have a fire truck."

"I'll rectify the error immediately."

He reached across the console and took her hand. "Hold that thought a bit, okay?"

Realizing he was up to something, she nearly offered a lecture on bribing children. Except that would be rude. And incorrect. Daniel and Aiden were carrying on as if they'd known each other for years rather than hours.

At the Caldwell house, the crew stopped everything to come out and give Daniel a standing ovation and Aiden a big welcome home.

"We have cupcakes!" Lou ducked back into the house and returned with a lavender bakery box. With Aiden right there, Shannon and Daniel glossed over the particulars of the kidnapping situation.

"I knew you weren't right," Lou declared, aiming a finger glazed with sawdust and chocolate frosting at her.

Ed kept a watchful eye on both of them and Shannon hoped that, unlike Rachel, he'd keep his thoughts or theories on their personal involvement to himself.

Riding a sugary high, Aiden ran up and down the new ramp while Ed caught them up on the progress they were making.

"The flooring should be here later today," Ed told them. "We've got this under control."

"Daniel can come back this afternoon," Shannon offered. "We'll all be back tomorrow."

"Maybe," Daniel corrected. "It depends on what Aiden needs."

"Take the weekend," Ed said. "You've all been through hell. It's Friday. If you don't celebrate, what good is it being alive and together?"

His words followed Shannon, pressing at her, as the

three of them stopped for lunch at the diner Daniel had taken her to for brunch last Sunday.

"What do they have here?" Aiden asked. He was preoccupied with the picture on the child's menu and the small box of crayons the waitress had given him.

Shannon read him the menu, noting the distinct displeasure on her son's face when she mentioned chicken nuggets. A week ago that had been his favorite.

"Everything is good here," Daniel said. "I think I'll have mac and cheese."

Aiden's jaw dropped. "You can't. You're a grown-up."

"That's a dumb rule," Daniel said.

They had a brief, laughter-filled debate about foods appropriate to various age groups, and when the waitress returned with drinks, the ordering process went more smoothly than she expected.

As did the meal. Aiden wasn't a picky eater, though his appetite seemed a bit off and she could see he was running out of steam. Although he didn't nap much anymore, he didn't get kidnapped, either. Thank God. She knew better than to coddle him, but she didn't want to push him, either. He'd been scared, stuck with strangers for nearly a week.

"Maybe we should go home and chill out," she suggested when they left the diner. "He's asleep."

Daniel checked the rearview mirror and chuckled. "Fresh air and good food will do that. We could just drive for a bit."

A good compromise as her son would probably wake up as soon as they stopped. With the sky clear and sun shining, it seemed like a perfect day. She planned to enjoy it, since in her mind they were overdue. With only the occasional sharp reactions from her son as any indication of what he'd been through, she felt confident that he'd bounce back without much trouble.

"I know I'll have to keep an eye on him going forward," she said. "But he seems generally happy and content. It gives me hope that this won't have a lasting effect on him."

"He has a loving mom, great friends. He'll be fine," Daniel said, taking her hand. "Seems like a break in the routine is what we all needed."

Words like *we* and *all* were addictive and she basked in them, drinking them in as she might turn her face to the sunshine after a week of rain showers.

Aiden woke up after an hour's nap, groggy and a little grumpy as they reached the firehouse. They'd skipped the park, planning to make that stop after the tour if Aiden was up to it.

Here, too, Daniel got an ovation for his heroics, though he tried his best to wave it off. He introduced her and Aiden to everyone and she did her best to keep names and faces together as they walked around the firehouse.

Aiden, little legs tired, asked Daniel to carry him as they toured the kitchen and lounges, the sleeping areas and all three stories of the building the firefighters called home. It was a vantage point she hadn't seen before, a sense of family she hadn't expected. The commitment rested well on him, on all of the people she met.

"Want to see the trucks?" Daniel asked Aiden.

"Yes, please!" Agog at the size, the shine, the tools, her son asked question after question about everything in sight. With extraordinary patience, Daniel answered them all.

"Normally we have an ambulance, too," he said. "It's out on a call right now."

"We rode in an ambulance already." Aiden nuzzled into Daniel's embrace, yawning. "I don't want to do it again."

"That's understandable." Daniel rubbed his back. "You think you can handle one more surprise before we go home?"

"Uh-huh."

"I don't know," Daniel said.

"Please?"

"Jennings, a word?"

At the sound of his chief's voice, Shannon turned with Daniel to see Chief Anderson standing at his door watching them, a smile on his face.

"Won't keep him long, I promise, Ms. Nolan."

"No problem." Shannon opened her arms for Aiden and gave Daniel a smile.

"Hey, bud." Daniel looked around, pointed to another firefighter. "Direct all your questions to Mitch, okay?"

"'Kay," Aiden replied.

Shannon, her sleepy son on her shoulder, felt something slide into place as she watched Daniel stride down the hallway. Not an elusive wish, more of a peace and contentment for what was here and now. Daniel was a fantastic boss on the construction side of his life. Seeing him here? She felt honored that he'd shown her he was a firefighter in his heart.

A confident man in any arena, there was a happiness to him here at the firehouse that she hadn't seen before. He might not define it that way, but it was evident to her. Whatever happened between them, it gave her an inexplicable satisfaction to have this priceless glimpse of him.

Her phone rang, pulling her from the reverie and she shifted Aiden to her opposite hip so she could fish it out of her pocket. She felt a wave of hope when she saw Grant's name on the display.

"Grant, hello!"

"Hi, Shannon. How's everyone doing today?"

"We're doing great," she said, looking down at her boy's soft cheek. "Did you, um, find the man you were looking for?"

Mitch, the firefighter Daniel had pointed out to Aiden, motioned for her to take a seat on the couch. He murmured something about cookies to Aiden and when her son grinned, he guided him over to the kitchen. "That okay?" he whispered.

She nodded, grateful for the help amusing her son. She didn't want him overhearing anything that would raise more fear about his ordeal or more questions she wasn't ready to answer.

"The manhunt is ongoing," Grant said. "The cameras lost him about an hour after the shooting."

Her heart sank.

"We did get some interesting news about Loffler's business at Marburg."

"That seems fast. Don't attorneys usually drag things out?"

"Seems Loffler broke that mold, starting with your divorce from Stanwood."

"Fair point."

"Because my source knew we were looking, when the 'upon death' action popped up this morning, she told me first. Knowing I could reach you. I hope you don't mind."

"Not at all." It felt as if her poor judgment in husbands was practically public knowledge, having to share so much about those dark days with Grant and Daniel directly. Once they caught her ex—she had to believe it would happen—he would likely try and drag her name through the mud with his. She needed to get used to a lack of privacy. At least until she could hit the reset button on her life.

"Upon death, his Marburg attorney was to contact you immediately. You and Aiden are named as his beneficiaries." Grant whistled. "From the looks of this, you won't need to worry about Aiden's college expenses."

Shock wasn't a big enough word for the sensations coursing through her. "Pardon me?" She pressed a hand to her forehead. "Why would he do that?"

"According to the paternity test I'm looking at, he's providing for his son."

"That's impossible," she whispered. "I never, we never." She cleared her throat, lowered her voice. "I didn't cheat." Suddenly Gary's comments started to fit together. "Oh."

"Oh?" Grant echoed.

"Yesterday Gary asked my forgiveness. He said he'd made things worse while trying to protect Aiden from Bradley. He must have meant the, ah, test." Her heart started racing and her skin felt cold. "He must have called in favors at the lab his law firm uses to fabricate that report."

And Bradley must have discovered the test results and kidnapped Aiden to punish them both. He'd killed Gary for the betrayal. She would be next. Her stomach rolled. She had to breathe through her nose to keep from getting sick.

"I can't have this conversation here," she said, her voice hoarse.

"That's fine. You'll need to speak with his attorney, sign some documents, that kind of thing. I have the relevant highlights from the file here for you, so you don't have to go into it cold in front of strangers at the law office. Call me when you can talk, or come on by."

She fumbled with the phone, ending the call. Tremors rattled through her.

Aiden's sweet giggle caught her attention and she forced her lips into a smile as she watched Mitch and another firefighter help Aiden decorate slice-and-bake sugar cookies. She would miss the life they'd built here, miss the friends who had become her family.

No choice, she told herself ruthlessly. Bradley wouldn't quit, wouldn't give up, once revenge settled into his mind. They had to leave, had to run. It might already be too late.

At Chief Anderson's encouragement, Daniel entered the office first. "Sorry to interrupt the tour," the chief said, closing the door.

"No problem," Daniel said. He knew Mitch would get a kick out of Aiden. "Did you get the truck for him?"

"Yeah, sure, we've got that ready to go." Chief Anderson sat on the corner of his desk. "Even got it wrapped."

"Great, thank you." Daniel reached for his wallet. "He'll love it."

"Put that away. Everyone was happy to pitch in for the boy."

Daniel didn't argue, though he wanted to. "What's on your mind, chief?"

"How are things at the Caldwell house?" the chief asked.

"Coming along," Daniel replied. "We'll be coming down to the wire, but I think they should get moved in a week from Sunday." It was the last day of his leave. He was looking forward to coming back on shift with that project completed, if for no other reason than his dad would have one less thing to nag him about.

"Little guy looks to be holding up after the ordeal."

"He's tough as his mother. We had a little glitch at the sitter at first. He'll get through. His mom is smart about it. She wants to coddle him, but she won't. Not too much." Daniel thought about how well she'd defused the signs of stress throughout the day. "Trucks seem to overcome just about every crisis he has."

"Good news on all fronts."

"I appreciate you letting me give them the full tour today." Daniel sensed something else at play, pushed a little. "You could've said all of this in front of them."

Chief Anderson tipped his head. "We've missed you around here." He worked his thumb into an old burn scar that creased the top of his hand. "I'm looking forward to having you back on shift."

"Right there with you. If anything, the extra time away has confirmed this is where I need to be."

"Not in a week," Chief Anderson said. "I know the time off was approved and you're due. Any chance you'd be willing to come back early?"

Yes. No. Daniel crossed his ankle over his knee and tapped the heel of his shoe. "I really need that week," he said. Torn between two commitments, three counting Shannon and Aiden, he wasn't sure how to answer his chief. "What happened?"

"Structure fire." Chief Anderson rubbed at the old scar again. "Minor injuries left us short. I can call in someone else, but I want you, Lieutenant. We need you."

Ed and the crew on the Caldwell house needed him. And Shannon's situation was hardly resolved. Daniel resisted the urge to look around for her. He couldn't just come back on shift tonight or even tomorrow without talking it over with her. Not a conversation he was eager to have. With Stanwood on the loose, he couldn't leave her unprotected and Grant would need more than a few hours to find someone to watch over them.

"Are you asking for today?"

"Tomorrow?" his chief asked hopefully.

Daniel sucked in a breath, thinking it through. "I need to be at the Caldwell site in the morning." In his mind, he calculated who among the crew could keep an eye on Shannon if he came in. "I can be here overnight Saturday to Sunday," he decided. Between Shannon's new security system and Grant's resources, they could cover that much. "After that, I'll have to make some calls. I really need the week."

"I'll take whatever time you can give me." The chief stood and extended his hand. "Want to tell me what's really going on with her?"

No. "Not much to tell that hasn't been all over the news," Daniel evaded.

"Uh-huh." The chief stared him down, hands at his waist. "She's pretty."

"True, but it's not like that." Except it was exactly like that.

"You're a lousy liar." Chief Anderson laughed. "Is she good for you?"

"Yes," he said, realizing it was true. Crisis or not, Shannon was good for him. Her son, too. The challenge would be convincing her she could count on him for the day-to-day stuff. He supposed a surprise shift would be a good first test of whether she had it in her to put up with the danger and weird hours of his career. The job had proven too much for his previous relationships and he'd rather know now, before he grew any more attached to Aiden.

"I'm glad to hear it." His chief pointed through the glass. "I wish you luck, Lieutenant. Let's see if the kid likes your present." He handed Daniel the long rectangular box wrapped in superhero paper.

When Daniel and the chief reached the kitchen, everyone was admiring a plate of cookies, apparently baked by Aiden with Mitch's guidance. When Daniel's eyes met the boy's, his heart just leaped as the little guy rushed him. "Come look, Daniel! We baked cookies."

"Awesome."

"This one is yours." He pointed to a cookie resting on a napkin with his name on it. "It has Superman sprinkles," he said. "Red and blue and yellow."

"Nice. Thanks, bud. We've got something for you, too." Daniel held out the box, watched the boy's eyes go wide. "Go on."

Over his head, he caught Shannon's eyes going misty, her teeth nipping her lip. Suppressing a laugh or more tears? Asking had to wait as Aiden ripped wrapping paper and gave a whoop of delight. "A fire truck! Mommy, look!"

The elated reaction Daniel hoped for got even better when Aiden wrapped his arms tight around his neck, then dashed around the room, giving high fives and big thanks to everyone in turn.

Chapter 9

Shannon laughed, surprised it was possible, as Aiden made siren noises all the way back home, rolling the big fire truck back and forth across his lap. Once they got in the house, he took it straight to his corner and started a new game with all of his trucks.

"That was pretty awesome," she murmured as she and Daniel watched him play.

"Boy needed a fire truck."

And she would be sure it came with them when they relocated. She offered him a beer, took one for herself.

It drew Daniel's attention, the opposite of what she'd planned. "Aiden wants his pancakes for dinner, " she said. "Should I order pizza for us?"

"Sure, if you add a side of conversation." He tapped his forehead, then pointed to her. "What's on your mind?" he asked.

She didn't want to tell him. Knew she'd regret it for years if she just walked away without an explanation. For the moment, she convinced herself to send him a letter once she was gone. "Laundry," she said. "I'll go get it started if you call for pizza."

"Deal," he said with a smile.

Sorting clothes, she clutched the shirt the police had given her at the pier. The shirt she'd worn to work had been stained with Gary's blood and no one wanted her son to see that. Her mind replayed the image of Daniel striding toward her, holding Aiden. She closed her eyes, frustrated beyond measure with the situation. He'd done so much for her and her son. She couldn't stay and put more lives at risk, yet she couldn't go with a clear conscience.

Examining the jeans she'd worn yesterday, she searched all the familiar stains and tears from work. When she found more blood soaked into the seams and stitching where she'd knelt beside her friend, she rolled them up to pitch them.

Something dropped to the floor with a light clatter, skidding out into the kitchen.

Daniel, on his way in with his own dirty clothes, picked it up. "What's this?"

"I don't know. It fell out of a pocket." She looked at the small black rectangle resting in his wide palm. "Looks like a flash drive, but I've never seen it before."

"Where'd you get it?" he asked.

"I just told you," she snapped. Immediately contrite, she held up her hands in surrender. "Sorry. I have no idea where it came from." She turned back, added his clothes and started the washer.

He turned it over a couple of time until he found the slide that exposed the USB connection. "Don't you think we should take a look?"

"Probably." She swallowed, tried to smile. "Did you order the pizza?"

"Forty-five minutes," he replied. "I tacked on a plain cheese for Aiden."

"Great. Thanks."

"Hey." He stepped in front of her as she tried to get around him. "You've been on edge since the firehouse. Did being there upset you?"

"No." Looking into his stunning eyes dark with concern, she realized he expected the answer to be yes. There was too much on her mind to even start digging into that issue.

"Then…"

"My bad mood has nothing to do with you or the firehouse." She'd never find a man like him again, a man who could see through her, a man who connected with her son on a lovely, intangible level. "I could love you," she said, squeezing the words through the grief gripping her throat.

His chin dropped and his hands fell away from her arms. "Pardon?"

She knew he'd heard her. "I could and, and I c-can't." She hated Bradley with something darker and more intense than she'd ever felt before. His twisted obsession would drive her away from Daniel before they had a chance to see what might happen. "That's not fair and I'm sorry."

"To hell with fair." His eyes went wide as he remembered Aiden in the other room.

"Not the first time he's heard that one," she admitted. She noticed he didn't return the sentiment, or give any hint to his feelings for her. Frankly, she was grateful he let that subject go.

Daniel pulled her into a hug. "Talk to me, Shannon."

"I don't know where to start." She listened as Aiden started making siren sounds again. "Grant called me while you met with Chief Anderson." She peeked around the corner, made sure Aiden wouldn't hear her, lowered her voice anyway. "Gary faked a paternity test so Bradley wouldn't ever make a claim on Aiden."

"Good Lord."

"Exactly." The tension in her shoulders melted at the understanding in his gaze. "He left instructions with an attorney and, papers, and he gave us money. Significant money according to Grant."

He held up the flash drive. "Do you think Gary slipped this to you yesterday?"

She didn't care. With a shrug, she focused on the worst piece of the situation. "I have to leave town. Aiden and I are sitting ducks if I stay."

"Not tonight. Not until you talk with that attorney and look over those papers."

She rolled her eyes. "Bradley is insane, Daniel. He's probably staked out day and night watching the law firm."

"Good point." Daniel pulled out his phone, sent a message to Grant. "Detective Hertz can send someone over to check."

"Daniel, don't make this harder than it is."

He pulled her close to his body and claimed her mouth. She hung on as her body went pliant against him, reveling in the heat and need arcing between them. When he raised his head, she whimpered for more. He obliged. His hands slid over her hips, pressed her closer, his arousal unmistakable.

"It's pretty hard on me, too," he breathed against her throat. She trembled in eager anticipation. "You're not leaving. Not tonight. Give me that much."

She nodded, her voice useless.

"If it comes to it, I'll help you pack." His voice was as rough as sandpaper. "Promise me."

"I promise."

The doorbell rang and Aiden shouted, "Mommy! Pizza guy is here."

"I've got it," Daniel said.

Alone in the kitchen, she managed to pull herself together. After dinner and a cartoon movie, it took both Shannon and Daniel to get Aiden upstairs and settled into bed. When she was sure he wouldn't call for one more story or glass of water, she pulled out her laptop so they could check the flash drive.

"Better do a backup first," Daniel suggested. "In case something on it tries to eat your files."

"I doubt Gary's goal was to trash my computer," she said, though she ran the backup.

She opened the files on the drive, finding electronic documents confirming what Grant had said. Daniel blew out a breath through pursed lips. "Damn."

"What?" She shot him a look.

"Now if I say I love you, you'll think I'm after your money."

She elbowed him, not willing to revisit that conversation. He just took her hand and pressed a kiss to her knuckles. "Keep going."

They opened and read each file and by the time they were done, Gary's last words made sense to her. "He wasn't cold. Well, maybe he was. But he was definitely saying 'cold case.'"

Daniel leaned forward, squinted a little as she scrolled through the document. "An affidavit?"

"This is a statement that he saw Bradley commit murder in New York." She sat back and read it once more. "We'd been married about three months and he'd taken me out to the Hamptons." She remembered the victim Gary mentioned. "I'd been hoping to find something that linked Bradley to a crime back then. Gary did it for me."

"And Aiden." He stroked her back, massaged her neck in a way that left her wanting to purr. "You need to give this to Detective Hertz."

"Yes." She copied the files, saving them to the cloud. "I don't want to send it by email in case Bradley has someone in the police department feeding him information."

"Okay, but I'm letting Grant know we'll be by to see him tomorrow afternoon."

She shook her head, closed the flash drive, then shut down her computer. "Another day away from the Caldwell house isn't good for business."

"We'll manage. For tonight, I have an idea to get your mind off all of this."

"Oh, yeah?"

He turned her chair, dragged her up into his lap and kissed her. With his hands roaming over her body, learning her, he proved pleasure was an effective distraction against the trouble outside these walls.

Breathless, needy, her heart stopped at her son's sharp cry from upstairs.

"Nightmare," she said, sliding off Daniel's lap. "Give me a rain check?"

"Count on it." He caught her chin, gave her a quick kiss before she darted away.

Daniel closed his eyes and leaned forward to rest his elbows on his knees while he waited for sanity and self-control to return. He couldn't let her run. These documents had to give Hertz something to help them find Stanwood. Find him and lock him up for a lifetime.

He listened to her singing softly to her son, the lullaby soothing him, too. When the dryer buzzed, he dealt with it, folding and sorting clothes in three distinct sizes. When did it become natural to do these things for someone else? The answer didn't matter, only his resolve. He wasn't letting her run.

The thought followed him as he made his bed on the couch, kept him awake for too long as he worried about tomorrow's shift. He'd meant to talk to her about it. Now it would have to wait until morning.

And morning came too soon, waking him with the rich aroma of fresh coffee, the sound of her in the kitchen. He stumbled up the stairs, doused himself with a cold shower. When he made it back to the kitchen, he immediately resented her for looking so fresh when he felt like hell. "Morning."

"Good morning," she said brightly. "We're going with you today," she said, handing him the full coffee mug. "You need all hands on deck to finish the Caldwell house."

Still bitter about the flooring delay, he gulped down the hot, smooth coffee. "You aren't ready to leave Aiden at the sitter," he replied as the caffeine cleared the cobwebs from his brain.

He'd dreamed about her all night. Dreamed of shaping those soft breasts with his hands while she moved over him, took him deep. Dreamed of finding a way behind that frosted glass wall. He'd dreamed of days in the park, watching her son jump fearlessly from a swing. Teaching him to measure, cut, build as he'd been taught. To have a hand in raising that wild, free spirit into a man. His heart simply wasn't his anymore. It seemed a lifetime ago he'd been wishing to know her better. Now he did and he couldn't bear the idea of walking away.

Of letting her walk away with the boy.

If Hertz and his team didn't haul in Stanwood soon and throw away the key with the affidavit from Loffler, Daniel would keep his word and help her pack. Hell, he'd drive the getaway car himself, as long as she planned an escape for three rather than two.

She'd fight him on his choice to go, point out all the reasons he should stay. He'd fight back and find some way to counter those arguments. He knew how to build a strong foundation, one strong enough for her dreams, his and Aiden's, too.

"You're looking rather…fierce this morning." She turned away, starting on breakfast. "Did something happen?"

"It's about to," he said. He put his hands on those sweet hips, turned her around. With a fingertip, he lifted her chin, laid his lips on hers. "There. Now it's a good morning."

Her smile, the slightly startled happiness in her big brown eyes, transformed his day.

He grinned at the sound of the slamming bathroom door upstairs. Water rattled in the pipes as the toilet flushed, the sink faucet turned on and off again. Then the deliberate footfalls of Aiden coming down the steps.

Daniel counted each sound, took another gulp of coffee and set the mug on the counter a split second before Tornado Aiden raced around the corner, his eyes bright.

"You learn fast," Shannon murmured.

"Yes, I do." Daniel caught Aiden as he leaped, gave him a bear hug and tickled his neck with the stubble on his jaw.

Aiden squealed in delight and grabbed his face. "Good morning, Daniel."

"Good morning, bud."

Aiden rubbed his hands back and forth along the whiskers. "Can we go shave?"

Daniel ran his hands over the stubble. "It should probably grow while we eat some breakfast. Give Mommy a kiss so she'll cook for us." He gave him a little toss, then handed him to Shannon.

After Aiden gave her a big hug and a smacking kiss, they decided on eggs and toast. Using the step stool, Aiden put bread in the toaster while Shannon cracked eggs into a hot skillet and Daniel set the table.

He sat back with his coffee, enjoying the domestic tableau more than he probably should. "Better eat up," he said when Aiden got distracted with the fire truck he'd brought to sit with them in the extra chair. "Mom says we're going to work today."

Aiden mashed a bite of scrambled eggs with his fork and looked up at Shannon through his long eyelashes. "All of us?"

She nodded. "I'll need you to be a good listener today. We have lots to do before the Caldwells can move in."

"Will Ed and Lou be there, too?"

"Yes." She nipped a bite of her toast. "Would you rather play at Rachel's house?"

His pale eyebrows furrowed as he propped his chin on his hand.

"Elbows off the table," she said.

The lower lip jutted out, storm clouds brewing on his face, but he obeyed.

"We need all hands on deck to get Mr. Caldwell's house back in shape," Daniel said. "Your mom is a big help to me. Think you could be?"

"Can I bring my new fire truck?"

"You bet." He spread jelly on his toast and folded it,

would have put the whole thing in his mouth if Aiden hadn't been watching. He took a decent bite instead, caught the jelly with his tongue.

Aiden scooped jelly out of the jar and plopped it on his toast. Folded it and, taking a big bite, had jelly squirting out, dribbling down his chin.

"Finish up, now," Daniel told him. "We have shaving to do."

The kid cracked him up, patting shaving cream on his face, mimicking the motions with his finger rather than a razor and making faces. Shaving done, they brushed their teeth. Aiden managed to talk at the same time. Yeah, the kid cracked him up and slipped right under his defenses.

They decided to drive both her car and the truck over to the site and he laughed as Aiden hauled out a giant tote. He'd packed as if they were moving in rather than staying a few hours.

Eventually the kid would need to go back to the routine of the sitter, but it didn't have to be today. If Daniel didn't need Shannon's help wrapping this one up, he would have given her a week off paid, assuming Grant could assign someone to stay with her and keep her lousy ex at bay.

Daniel had to go back to the firehouse tonight and still hadn't told her about the surprise shift. They needed to make a plan and he didn't want her to think she wasn't in the loop. He knew the hang-up was that he wasn't any more ready to have Aiden and Shannon out of his sight than he had been yesterday.

Calling out cheerful good mornings, Ed greeted Aiden with a high five and sent both mother and son off to deal with the bathrooms.

"What's wrong?" Daniel asked when they were alone. "All this perkiness scares me at this hour."

"You noticed?"

"Ed?"

"We almost had it," his lead said, patting his hammer. "I know you wanted to wrap this up before you go back on duty."

"We still have a week. What happened now?"

"No flooring," Ed explained. "It's like the order disappeared. I can't get what you wanted for another two weeks."

He looked at the completed ramp, the wider porch. Lou would stain those today, paint the doors and window trim. He'd been making calls for help with the move-in, aiming to have the family back in the house next Sunday afternoon. "Two weeks?"

Ed nodded.

"Let's keep moving on what we can do." Daniel pulled out his phone. "I'll figure it out." He paced away and started making calls.

No one could give him a good explanation for why his order had disappeared. Worse, no amount of cajoling or bargaining could put a rush on the replacement order.

Frustrated, tired of banging his head against the proverbial brick wall, he went inside to check on Shannon and Aiden. He was pleased to see the little guy playing with the fire truck on a canvas drop cloth just outside the bathroom they'd enlarged to make it more accessible.

"I've got a problem," Daniel said. "Care to consult?"

He walked her through it, flipped through the project binder where he kept track of everything from the opening bids to design to the finished product.

"I've never seen this." She looked up at him as if he'd invented binders and dividers. "Nice job."

"Thanks. Our flooring is delayed." He flipped to that section of the binder. "I ordered it in plenty of time. Should have been here Thursday and it didn't show up yesterday per the reschedule."

When he said it, he realized his mistake. That glassy fear had settled over her eyes as she met his gaze. "Stop it. This is not related to *that*."

She arched her eyebrows. They both knew he meant *him*. He refused to go there.

"I'm asking for an alternative. The suppliers say I can get something closer to this." He tapped a picture of white oak and her nose wrinkled. "Exactly. Help me out?"

She carried the samples out into what would be the family room. "You wanted this product for the durability."

He marveled at the way she seemed to live on the same page with him. "And easy care."

"Mmm." She paced a little, came back to the binder.

"While you're thinking, there's something else I keep forgetting to mention." Maybe she'd take it better while she was distracted. "The chief needs me to come in tonight, work overnight."

Those big eyes met his over a handful of floor and paint chips. "For a shift?"

"I'll be back by Sunday brunch. We can go out, tour a few houses." He braced for the disapproval, the trepidation, even that flash of excitement that she'd been kissing a man who ran into burning buildings.

"Are you going back early?" she asked, looking at the samples again.

"Not if I can help it." He hooked his thumbs in his

tool belt. "I want to be on hand for the rest of this. Assuming we can get the floor done."

"If Chief Anderson asked you to cut your time short, it must be important. Ed and Lou and I can wrap this up."

"Floor pending."

She flipped the binder to a blank page in the back. "Can you give me a list of who you've called?"

He wrote it down. "What are you thinking?"

She closed the binder and stepped close to him, ran her hand up and down his arm. "I'm thinking you tempt me." She pulled back. "We both have work to do. If you need the challenge and camaraderie of the firehouse, if they need you, don't let us stop you."

Her acceptance seemed too easy, too good to be true. Then the words crashed over him like a bucket of ice water. "Shannon. You wouldn't…" He couldn't finish the sentence.

"No." She looked so startled it gave him hope. "No. I've been giving that some thought, too." And with a soft, sexy smile he wanted to see every day for the rest of his life, she walked back to her tile work.

Daniel dug in, working up a good sweat, determined to make the most of every minute. Just before noon as he was taking lunch orders for the crew, Detective Hertz called, requesting an emergency meeting with Shannon at the Escape Club.

Daniel swore, wishing the detective had sounded more upbeat and less miserable about the meeting. Instead, he handed the order to Ed, along with cash to cover delivery and tip, and went to tell Shannon and Aiden they had to leave.

When Daniel parked her car in front of the club, the butterflies in Shannon's stomach took flight again.

Please let them have good news. News that would let her stay.

They walked up to the front doors and she heard the drum set. Had to be Grant. She'd never considered percussion lyrical, but Grant was doing far more than keeping time or pounding for the sake of noise. She glanced down, smiling at Aiden's wide and curious gaze.

"That would be Grant." Daniel listened and rapped hard on the door between the beats. "He considers the drums a workout."

"Do you like it?" she asked Aiden.

Nodding, he raised his arms. "I wanna see."

"Nothing much to see yet." She let him lean forward to trace the letters on the door, though the shades within the glass panels were down. "You can ask Mr. Sullivan to show you the drums before we leave."

As if he'd been waiting for his cue, Grant opened the door with a big smile. "Welcome, welcome," he said brightly. "Come on in." Once they were inside, he closed the door and reset the security system. Then he held out a hand to Aiden. "I don't believe I've had the pleasure. Are you Aiden Nolan?"

The boy nodded, leaned into her shoulder, uncertain as he took in the high ceilings of what had been a warehouse.

"I'm Grant. Daniel and I are friends." He pulled Daniel into a one-armed hug.

"You were there," Aiden said. "When Daniel found me."

"I was. I'm glad you're here. Your mom's told me so much about you. She says you're really brave."

Aiden's grip on her sweatshirt relaxed. "Were you the one making all the noise?"

"Noise?" Grant laughed. "That was me. Do you want to help me make more noise?"

Shannon let Aiden wriggle out of her arms to go with Grant. It would be the perfect distraction while she and Daniel spoke with the detective.

Daniel tipped his head toward the end of the bar where Hertz waited, just out of Aiden's view.

"I appreciate this," Hertz said.

Unable to help herself, she slid a look back at her son. Grant had everything under control. The place was locked up, the system set against intruders and still she couldn't quite relax.

"Have the kidnappers turned on Bradley?" she asked when they reached Grant's office.

"No. Both men were found dead this morning." Hertz closed his eyes as if saying a prayer before he continued. "They didn't give us anything. It won't be long before the news stations hear two inmates died overnight."

Shannon sank back into the closest chair. With Gary dead, the kidnappers were—had been—the last link to Bradley. There would be no stopping him despite the affidavit Gary left behind.

"Guess that means you didn't find him hanging out around the Marburg offices." Daniel's voice sounded far away, though Shannon could see him clearly. "No leads at all?"

"Correct," Detective Hertz admitted, misery in his gaze. "Informants claim he's still in town. My counterparts in New York have confirmed he hasn't been seen there for over a week."

"He's on a revenge binge," Shannon said. Her ex-husband had murdered his friend in cold blood to satisfy his bruised ego. "And running on bad intel." She rubbed her palms against her thighs. Which was worse, having her ex on a tear because he thought Aiden wasn't his or knowing the truth that he'd fathered a child? "I'm next."

"Hang on," Daniel said, his hand solid on her shoulder. "That's not going to happen."

Suddenly she regretted letting Aiden out of her sight, no matter that she could still hear him banging on the drums with Grant onstage. "He won't stop," she whispered. She dug deep for courage. "There were times, when I was married," she clarified. "He could become obsessive over the smallest offenses. He won't stop," she repeated. With the benefit of time and hindsight, she could look back at their dating life and see the moments Bradley had hidden his true nature with rigid control.

"On the surface, I'd have to agree," the detective replied. "We believe Gary was cutting ties, trying to get out."

Shannon nodded. "He said as much."

Hertz continued, "So Stanwood flushed Gary out by kidnapping the child he believed Gary fathered."

Though she hadn't faked a paternity test, she would always carry that guilt with her, knowing Gary died for nothing more than being a decent human being.

"Is it possible he's learned the truth and wants his son after all?" the detective asked.

Icy dread trickled down her spine. She stared at the floor, wishing she'd known then what she knew now about Bradley Stanwood. "He doesn't want Aiden. Not for the sake of being a father. If I hadn't left him, he would have forced me to abort the pregnancy." All these years later, with a healthy son, it still hurt her heart to say the words aloud.

She heard Daniel mutter an oath. "He'd take Aiden to punish you."

"No." She forced herself to say it. The detective

needed the harsh facts. "He's more likely to kill us both to tie up loose ends." She peered up at Daniel, already grieving for what they'd never have. "We need to leave."

He shook his head, mouth set and tears in his eyes. "There's another way. Another reason he's in town."

Sorrow gripped her. Her only hope was if Bradley self-destructed before he destroyed her. "He's only after revenge and suffering."

"Do you have any idea who might be helping him here?" Hertz queried.

Shannon lifted her gaze to the detective. "I've been out of his life for nearly five years. It wasn't as if he discussed business with me while we were together."

"You have to know something to help us find him," the detective insisted. "Properties, assets, anything."

Her mind was focused on one thing: survival. She knew it was time to move on, to leave Philly and start up somewhere new. Her gaze drifted to Daniel and slid away. Regrets would follow her, despite her best effort to keep her heart safe from wishful thinking and sweet dreams of happy-ever-after.

From this point forward, to survive and save Aiden, she had to run. Fast and far. Every hour she delayed gave Bradley an advantage.

Bradley had always considered her disposable. She'd known when she signed the divorce agreement that running would always factor into her life. She'd prepared for it.

"Give me something," the detective pressed. "Try."

"How about you do your job," Daniel snapped. "She can't give you what she doesn't have."

Ignoring Daniel, the detective pleaded with Shannon. "Come down to the station and we'll show you what we have. It could spark something. You might not realize how much you know."

"Is protective custody an option?" Aiden had just escaped his role as a pawn. She wouldn't put him through it again.

"Yes, if we get something solid, hard evidence we can use to prosecute."

"What about the affidavit Loffler gave her?" Daniel said. "That has to count for something."

Hertz looked at her. "Were you there?"

"Yes. It was out in the Hamptons as Gary stated."

"Did you see anything?"

She shook her head. Gary had said that she knew, but even after going through the files, she didn't understand what she was supposed to know.

Daniel swore again. "She's an eyewitness to Loffler's murder. That must be worth some protection."

"I'm keeping a patrol car in the area."

"Gee, thanks."

"It's okay." She reached for his hand. "He shot and killed his friend, convinced I was unfaithful. None of us should have expected him to let me off the hook. If I carry on with my life, he loses face."

It was how she'd escaped the marriage. Under Gary's advice, she'd threatened to destroy the man's public image while she had plenty of witnesses to back her up. With his coaching, she'd managed to get into Bradley's head long enough to get out of his reach.

"You weren't unfaithful," Daniel pointed out, ever the champion.

Her heart warmed at his automatic defense though it didn't change the dire circumstances. "When Bradley gets this way, the truth is irrelevant." She closed her eyes, listened to the steady beat of the drum set.

"You're watching the luxury hotels? He wouldn't sacrifice comfort on his mission to punish me." *To kill me.*

"I've got people combing the city. My informants are talking about him being here. No one claims they've seen him since Loffler was killed."

"House rentals would be the next guess," Shannon said. "He could give orders without being inconvenienced."

"Nothing like that is popping."

The idea of starting from scratch put a knot in her stomach. Where could she go that would ever be out of Bradley's reach? His resources would always outpace hers, even if she claimed the inheritance from Gary. "Have any of your experts found anything helpful from the files Gary gave me on that flash drive?"

"Nothing that helps us pin him down," Detective Hertz said.

"You want to run." Daniel folded his arms over his chest.

Her heart pinched at the accusations in his eyes, the disappointment. "*Want* isn't the right word," she replied.

He moved, taking a knee in front of her. "Don't." He took her hands. "You run now and you're running forever. Run and Loffler died for nothing."

She kept her gaze on Daniel. "Go for the jugular much?"

"It only hurts because you know it's true." He tried to smile and failed.

She sighed, wishing with every fiber of her being that she could just curl into his strength and forget everything else.

"I'm here for you and Aiden, sweetheart. You're not alone."

She wasn't sure when she'd heard sweeter words.

There had been plenty of loneliness in her life before Daniel. Then it hit her. "The bastard." She gripped Daniel's hands. "He could have killed me when he shot Gary."

"What are you saying?"

She swore again, pushing a hand through her hair as it all clicked. "He wrote that stupid demand to keep the normal routine so he could figure out who was important to me." She should have seen the tactic sooner. "He tossed the house that day just to be an ass."

"But he said you took something from him."

She stared at Daniel. "What?" The detective echoed her question.

"Oh, crap." Daniel pulled out his phone. "Stanwood called. After we rescued Aiden. I meant to send over the recording and Mom called. I'm sorry."

He played it for them, had Shannon laughing bitterly. "I only took the settlement Gary negotiated. I even left my ring." She gave herself a mental shake. "It doesn't change anything. He's likely to kill you next just to torture me."

"Not going to happen."

"Not if I leave." As she said it now, mad as hell, a new idea sparked. "Hear me out," she said as both men protested. "Let's say I try to bolt, make it obvious I'm leaving because I'm panicked. That means I'm not here to see my friends die. He would follow me."

"You're sure?"

"For a man like Bradley, saving face is as vital as air and water."

"And if he's just being an ass, as you say?"

"He's not. This is a classic Stanwood game of cat and mouse." She saw Daniel's deep blue eyes turn hard, his jaw set. "If you want to get your hands on him, I should guide him away."

Neither man said anything so she pressed on. "Waiting only drags this out," she said, willing them both to understand. "The longer Bradley stays here, the more of a threat he is to everyone who knows me."

Daniel folded his arms over his chest. "Lay it out for me. How do you see this going?"

"I go back to my place with Aiden. We pack up fast, essentials only, and load the car with a couple of suitcases. Drive by the construction office, take a minute to quit and ask for my pay and then hit the road." She'd walked him through her actual plan, minus the truth of her fake identity, alternate bank account and the emergency fund she kept in reserve to cover last-minute airfare out of the country.

"It's a big risk," Daniel said, scowling.

She knew it, knew how she'd change it up if Bradley did take the bait. "It will only look like I'm alone," she reminded him with far more bravado than she felt.

"Better if you go to Marburg first," the detective said, warming to the idea.

She checked her watch. "How late are they open on Saturday?"

"Trust me, they'll make time for you."

"Let's do it."

She'd slipped Bradley's noose once but she wasn't foolish enough to think it would be easy to do it again. Putting herself out on a limb was a huge peril. Aiden compounded the danger exponentially. He was a person now. Though she'd loved him desperately during her pregnancy, the bond and her devotion to him only strengthened with each day. "We have to try or Aiden will never have a chance at a normal life."

"I don't want him in the car," Hertz said. "I won't put a child in jeopardy."

"If Aiden stays here, I guess that makes it look like you'll turn around," Daniel said. "Let's work it so I meet her at a rest stop or something." His gaze held hers. "That way I can bring you back here where you belong."

How could she argue with him when he said things like that? Still, she didn't want him out there in the line of fire. "I'll turn around the minute police have him," she said.

He didn't look entirely convinced, though he relented. They spent another few minutes fine-tuning her plan and the timing, adjusting for the best route based on traffic cameras to monitor her progress and anyone on her tail.

Daniel protested once more. "I don't like her out there alone while your team sits back watching. Stanwood struck fast and close when he shot Loffler. He's got no reason to change that approach with Shannon."

"Daniel."

"Can't we use a decoy?" he asked Hertz. "Use Shannon for part of it, the decoy for the rest. Make the switch at the construction office. He's not expecting her to run, doesn't know her plan, so no one on his payroll would be watching there."

"And where will you hide Shannon?"

"She can stay at my parents' place."

The detective groaned.

"It's perfect," Daniel said, warming to the suggestion. "Gated community. An apartment over the garage," he added, ticking off the points on his fingers. "She can stay there, off the radar until you drop a net over Stanwood."

"Let me make some calls." Detective Hertz moved behind Grant's desk and picked up the landline.

Within another half hour, they had a plan they all agreed on. Feeling hopeful, Shannon and Daniel went out to gather Aiden and start putting things into motion.

Chapter 10

The decoy mission had to wait until Monday afternoon because of Daniel's shift as well as the construction office rule about no work on Sundays. The extra day gave them more time to make sure the switch went smoothly. They'd agreed that Daniel would go back to shift work once the decoy left town, presumably because Shannon no longer needed his protection.

Daniel entertained Aiden Monday morning while Shannon met with the Marburg attorney and made arrangements for the financial windfall. He had no illusions that she'd updated her will and what should happen with Aiden should Bradley succeed. The journal and other papers Gary had left her she'd brought home to read through later. Daniel thought she'd likely have time on her hands in the days to come. Though he knew Loffler's last words haunted her, she was continually frustrated by her inability to decipher what Loffler must have hoped she would see.

If Aiden noticed anything off at the construction office—they'd arrived in his mom's car and left with Daniel in his truck—it didn't seem to bother him. She'd told Daniel that Aiden's nightmare on Saturday night was shorter than the night before. Last night, Aiden had slept through without so much as a whimper. With every normal behavior from her son, Daniel noticed Shannon relaxing more.

"I know this isn't how you wanted to spend your last day before going back on shift," she said as they finally passed through the security gate at his parents' neighborhood.

He checked the rearview mirror, confirming Aiden was absorbed with his truck. "Better than worrying about you out on the road with nothing but traffic cameras," he said quietly.

"You're sure your parents don't mind?"

"Not in the slightest. You'll be lucky if my mom doesn't drive you out of town for real. She's likely to fall in love with Aiden on sight." He sure had. "All her friends are having grandkids and my brother and I hear it all the time that we need to catch up."

Turning into the drive, he heard Shannon's wistful sigh.

He hadn't looked at the three-story stone house with the warm red trim through objective eyes in years. "It's always been home," he said. "My dad didn't build this one, though he's remodeled every room to Mom's standards over the years. The garage is around back."

"Where are we?" Aiden asked from the back seat. "Can we go home, Mommy?"

The second question edged closer to a whine.

"Soon," she said, her gaze taking in the view.

"I left my best dump truck." Aiden rubbed at his eyes with a fist.

"We packed your trucks," she said. "Daniel put it in the back. You'll see when we get inside."

While her son twisted around in his booster seat, straining to spot the luggage in the back of the pickup, she sent Daniel a smirk. "Thank you. Leaving behind any of the trucks would have put a wrench in my getaway plan."

"What's a getaway?"

He laughed. Her son didn't miss much. Daniel followed the wide drive to park behind the house. He cut the engine and swiveled in the seat. "Right now, a getaway is hanging out in a new place for a couple of days. Ready for an adventure, buddy?"

"Yes!" Aiden pushed at the seat belt. "Let's go."

"Can't fault his enthusiasm."

Shannon smiled. "He was about two when I did a three-sixty trying to stop for a traffic light during an ice storm. I was all freaked out, white knuckles on the wheel, and he was in the back clapping and shouting, 'Again!'"

When Aiden and his truck were out of the booster seat, Daniel pointed to the steps at the side of a three-car detached garage. "Explore first or luggage first? Your choice."

"Explore!" Aiden jumped forward with both feet, then thrust a hand high in the air. "Charge!"

Daniel led them up the steps with Shannon bringing up the rear. He unlocked the apartment door and pushed it open. "Welcome, young squire."

Aiden raced forward. It wasn't as big as her place, but with luck they wouldn't be stuck here long. Daniel studied Shannon's face as she stepped into the apartment. He felt like a kid again, mentally crossing his fingers and hoping for a stamp of approval for a job well-done. "I'll get your security system set up in a few minutes."

He'd built this place with his father. It was where he'd

learned valuable lessons in planning a full project. His dad had let him plan the space and together they'd fine-tuned the details until it became a guest suite. Over the years, he'd lived here, then his brother and various relatives who'd stopped in for holiday, vacations or while passing through on business trips. Though it wasn't five-star by any means, it was practical and, more important for Shannon and Aiden, it was safe.

A wall with an archway in the center neatly bisected the space, leaving the living and kitchen areas up front with a view over the driveway. Two small bedrooms and a full bath were on the other side of the wall, with windows that overlooked the yard.

"It's lovely. Smart design," she said.

Pride swelled up inside him at her words. He had to remind himself he was a grown man rather than a kid. "It was a practice project. Not a ton of space."

"It's more than enough," she interrupted. "Right, Aiden?"

Daniel tried to view the space through a stranger's eyes. At first, the small apartment had been a hodge-podge of furniture phased out of the main house. Over the years, his mother had systematically updated the furnishings and decor into a cohesive style and she'd made it a comfortable space. One he knew she used for herself occasionally.

Aiden ran straight to the mission-style couch and scrambled up, bouncing a little on the cushions as he shrugged off his small backpack. "You can read me a story."

"In a little bit," Shannon said. "Mommy and Daniel need to talk a minute first."

"Not you." Aiden's pale eyebrows dipped into a frown over the brown eyes. "Daniel."

"How about we get the luggage first?" Charmed and more than a little pleased the kid asked for him, he wanted to do it.

"'Kay." Aiden hopped down, ran for the door.

When they had the luggage up, Aiden went right back to the couch. Waved the book.

"On my way." Knowing it was foolish to get attached, he couldn't seem to unhook himself from the boy or his mother. Didn't want to.

"You don't have to," she whispered. "You know he understands work and obligations."

"It's fine. Things won't fall apart in the next fifteen minutes." He sat down beside Aiden and opened the book about a bear having fun at school.

The boy snuggled into him while he read and he heard Shannon moving about in the bedrooms. The moment was so comfortable, he decided to analyze the feeling later and just let himself enjoy it. The polite move would have been to help her unpack, except she managed that task with the same efficiency she managed everything else.

As he reluctantly closed the book, the story over, a knock drew his attention to the front door.

"Who's there?" Aiden asked, a little fear creeping into his voice.

Daniel held out his hand. "Let's go find out."

Together they opened the door to his mother's smiling face. "Hi, Mom."

He introduced her to Aiden and she crouched down to shake the boy's smaller hand.

"Pleased to meet you, Aiden," she said. "You can call me Tess."

Aiden smiled shyly, gripping Daniel's hand tightly. Retirement agreed with his mom. As did her new painting hobby she'd left behind to come check on him. Her shoulder-length sandy brown hair was pulled back in a high ponytail, secured with a soft blue scarf. She wore faded jeans smudged with paint and similar paint colors stained her fingertips, but her open yellow button down and white T-shirt were spotless.

"Am I interrupting?"

"No." She wouldn't have let him turn her away if he'd tried. He invited her in and when Shannon came into the front room, he caught the sudden flutter of nerves when her eyes went wide and she fluffed her bangs. He made the introductions, wishing he could ease that perpetual worry she carried around since Loffler died. "Thanks so much for this, Mrs. Jennings," Shannon said. "I hope we won't be underfoot for too long."

"Nonsense. And call me Tess. Daniel built this place with his father ages ago and I'm happier when it's getting good use."

That notorious mom look slid over the three of them and Daniel could practically hear the gears clicking along in his mother's head. She'd have the wedding invitations planned by morning if he wasn't careful. "I need to get back to the site and Shannon—"

"Shannon and I can get acquainted while you're gone," his mother finished for him. "Why don't the three of you join us at the house for dinner tonight?"

Daniel bristled, wary of the way she'd worded the invitation to make them a unit. He glanced at Shannon, but she replied with a gracious acceptance before he could offer a believable excuse.

"Wonderful." His mom crouched again to speak to Aiden. "Do you like fried chicken? It was Daniel's favorite when he was little."

Daniel managed to smile, though he wanted to roll

his eyes like a teenager. "Sounds great, Mom." He turned to Shannon and Aiden. "I'll be back in a bit. If you need me to pick up anything on the way over, just send a text."

Taking his mother's elbow, he steered her out of the apartment and down the steps.

"She's pretty."

"Pretty tough," he said as casually as possible. That toughness under the pretty surface kept pulling him in deeper and he didn't want to surface for a lifetime.

"Single moms often are."

At the bottom of the steps, he pulled out his keys. "No matchmaking," he warned her. Shannon had said she could love him. He wanted to give that "could" a chance to grow without any nudges or interference.

Tess gave him an arch glare. "When have I ever?"

She hadn't, not really, though she made no secret of the fact that she wanted him to settle down and give her grandchildren. He wasn't opposed to the idea of a wife and family, he just hadn't found a woman willing to step into the role with him.

"I'm just making it clear."

"Mmm-hmm. Have you known her long?"

He didn't care for the sly glint in her eyes. "She's been with the company for three years or so. Does great work."

"And you always help out our employees with housing?"

Now he did roll his eyes. "Things haven't been going well for her, Mom," he heard himself say. "I can't talk about it, but she needed an assist."

"She needed you." She reached up and patted his cheek in that way mothers had. He'd seen Shannon do the same with Aiden. "You're a good man, Daniel, and whatever the situation with Shannon and her son, I'm sure you're doing what's best for them. It's who you are." Clearly sensing his discomfort, she opened his truck door for him. "Just make sure you think about what's best for you, too."

Thinking of what was best for him circled through his mind all afternoon as he walked the job site and caught up with the progress. He wasn't happy to still be wrestling with the absent flooring. He needed to get a final answer out of Shannon, because on this one he didn't like anything as much as his first choice.

"Will we get Shannon back on site soon?" Ed asked. "No one's faster at the finishing touches."

"I can hope." Everyone knew he'd wanted this one done and fast. It wasn't the first time a remodel had slipped past the target deadline. Unfortunately in this case, his dad was keeping a running total of loss numbers for every hour of delays. If the project stalled out for another few days while he was on shift, Daniel would never hear the end of it.

"I'm not sure if she'll be back tomorrow." It all rested on whether or not the police could catch Stanwood. "We're not at finishing touches without a floor."

"No, but having her around would get us there faster," Ed pointed out. "The crew worries about her and her kid."

Daniel did a double take. He should have expected it, especially from this crew. They were his best and he'd invited them into this charity effort because of their skill as well as their interest and willingness. Shannon had a way of drawing people together.

"She and Aiden are doing fine," Daniel said. He didn't elaborate. Sharing anything more could jeopardize what they were trying to do. "If she can swing by she will. You know how she loves the work."

"All right." Ed shuffled his feet, clearly debating his next words. "We wouldn't let anything happen to her." He laid his hand over the hammer in his tool belt as if it were a gun. "If you've gotta be back on the job, you could trust us to look out for her and her boy."

"We've got too many moving pieces to have Aiden underfoot right now."

Ed scoffed. "That settles it. Now I know the rumors are true."

"What rumors?"

"You got a thing for her and the kid."

Daniel swallowed the immediate protest that would only prove Ed's point.

"It's good." Ed aimed the steely gaze he saved for straight edges and perfect corners at Daniel. "Good for both of you, not that you asked."

"I'll tell her you're all worried," Daniel allowed. "She'll appreciate the concern." He didn't need the entire crew taking an interest in his personal life. He tried to shove his feelings into a box and they wouldn't go.

He'd lived with her, they'd exchanged more than a few hot kisses and he still worried she'd run. Maybe she should. He sure as hell shouldn't get clingy if staying meant danger. More than anything he wanted her and Aiden safe, secure. Whatever he felt for her, she had more pressing, lifelong matters of doing the right thing for her son.

On his side of it, he was a firefighter to the bone and unwilling to give it up. Not even for the sake of family harmony. As much as he loved—liked—Aiden, being a dad required as much commitment as the PFD. There was only so much of him to go around.

"I could love you." The words annoyed him as he wrestled with all of it on the drive back to his parents' house. It was like looking at life through a leaded glass window, the facets catching and refracting light of what could be, not what was.

Everyone he knew enjoyed both the firefighting career and the side jobs. If he made his dad happy and took over Jennings Construction, what would that look like? Could he dial back the schedule so he wasn't working himself to death on his days away from the firehouse?

Dialing back meant cutting back personnel and hours. That wouldn't work. He wasn't about to put that kind of stress on the families that relied on Jennings Construction income. No way did he want to lose his best people to other contractors or the challenges of juggling two jobs to maintain the status quo. Good as Ed would be as second in command, Daniel knew he didn't want more responsibility than he had now, even if it came with a hefty pay boost.

Exasperated with the lack of insight or answers when he arrived at his parents' house, Daniel parked around back and climbed the stairs to the garage apartment. Something told him he'd feel better, would be better able to cope with a family dinner, if he could have a minute or two with Shannon first.

He knocked before he opened the door, feeling unreasonably awkward. They'd been muddling through the strange living arrangements. No reason to develop a hang-up now. Only the location had changed.

Walking in, the apartment was too quiet and Daniel snapped to attention. Had Stanwood managed to get to them here? He stepped back outside, looking for any signs of a struggle he might have missed.

The back door of his parents' place flew open on a

wild shout. Daniel's heart leaped into his throat before he realized it was a happy sound. Aiden raced across the driveway, shouting the obvious, "We're over here!"

Daniel's gaze moved past the boy to find Shannon standing in the open doorway, smiling as she watched her son. When she offered a small wave, he returned it and felt the frustrations slide to the back of his mind.

Who was he trying to fool? He already loved her and Aiden. Completely. They were the place his heart called home. She said he learned fast, but he'd fallen for them even faster. But he couldn't tell her, couldn't ask her to stay until he knew they would be safe.

With a wild giggle, the boy climbed the stairs as fast as possible, giving up on the railing and scrambling forward with hands and feet in an accurate impression of a gamboling puppy. He was talking a mile a minute and Daniel only caught about every third word.

Hearing *cake* and *favorite*, he assumed his mother had invited Shannon and Aiden over early. Hard to be aggravated with that, under the circumstances. While her ex was in the wind, Shannon really shouldn't be alone. It's why he'd brought her here.

Maybe he could plant the seeds for his mom to stick by Shannon tomorrow while he was on shift.

When Aiden reached the top of the stairs, Daniel plucked him up. "Did you say cake?"

"Yes." Aiden patted Daniel's face. "The kind of cake you made when you were small." He scrunched up his face. "Were you really small?"

"Once upon a time," Daniel replied.

"That's like a story." Aiden laughed again as he squirmed to get down. "Dinner's waiting on you."

"Uh-oh." Daniel bent to drill a finger into the kid's

tummy. "If I didn't know better I'd think you were hungry."

"I am." Aiden's head bobbed vigorously. "Come *on*."

The boy babbled in a constant monologue all the way to the door, passing by his mom with a loud declaration that Daniel had arrived and they could eat.

Tess met the boy in the hallway and handed him a basket of rolls. "If you put this on the table, we'll be all set."

"'Kay." He took the bread basket, his little face serious. "How is the cake, Mimi?"

"Baking perfectly."

When Aiden was out of sight, Daniel gave his mother a hard, quizzical look.

"Mrs. Jennings is a mouthful, Tess didn't feel right once I heard him say it," she whispered. "Go get your father." Her gaze drifted to his hands. "On second thought, you wash up. Shannon can—"

"I'll tell Pop it's time." Aiden streaked by them all.

"Pop and Mimi." Daniel shook his head. It wasn't a big deal. Or it wasn't until he caught the wistful shimmer in Shannon's eyes. Had her parents ever met Aiden? She never mentioned them. Another layer of mystery to her and he wanted to solve them all. He tucked the question away for now. He could ask once they got the little guy to sleep tonight.

As much as he struggled against parental expectations, he couldn't imagine his life without them in it. He could easily see Shannon making the tough choice to isolate herself and her son to protect her own parents. In his mind, it wasn't the right choice. Then again, he hadn't spent any time married to Stanwood. Praise God.

When Aiden returned towing "Pop," they all sat

down. His mother had stopped short of fine china, but everything else indicated an important occasion.

Inside, Daniel cringed. Even without the added evidence of "Mimi and Pop," he could see the designs his mother had on Shannon as a potential daughter-in-law. It might have gone just that way, if he'd asked Shannon out months ago. Now they had to shore up a cracked foundation before they could build on it.

The salad had barely made it around the table before his dad started grilling Shannon about her past. It was in these moments that all the innocuous comments about how much he resembled his father troubled him. Would running the construction company eventually turn him into a gruff and stubborn old man?

"Dad." Daniel shook his head. "Not tonight, okay?"

"What? I like to know who's at my table. She already told me she's from New York."

He arched an eyebrow at her. "You did?"

She nodded, gave a half shrug.

"She's already got the job," Tess pointed out diplomatically.

Daniel glanced at his mother as she studied her husband with exasperated affection. Her eyes held that same spark of love tonight that shined so brightly in their wedding pictures.

"It's been a long time since Ed interviewed me." Shannon smiled graciously. "I worked on construction sites through the summers in high school. My first experience with builders hooked me. It was a mission project with my church youth group."

"What did you build?" Matthew asked.

"We went to a low-income area and did repairs of all kinds. My first job was with a roofing crew."

Matthew whistled with admiration. "Hot work."

Shannon agreed.

"I'm not gonna eat the peas, Mommy."

"You are." She took a bite to demonstrate. "They're very good."

Aiden scowled at his plate. "They're green."

"Mrs. Jennings—"

"Mimi," Aiden interrupted Shannon with an adoring gaze for Tess.

"—made us a lovely dinner," Shannon continued smoothly. "You'll taste everything with good manners."

Aiden pushed the small helping of peas around his plate.

"Far cry from summer work to full time." Matthew was like a dog with a bone. "Did you go to college?"

"Give it a rest, Dad," Daniel muttered.

"Yes, sir." Shannon replied over him with the same unruffled tone she'd used with Aiden. "I have a bachelor's degree in international business."

"Seems that makes you overqualified to tile showers on our builds."

She laughed and Daniel admired her restraint. He shot his mother a pleading look and she ignored him, thoroughly engrossed with the little boy.

"You might be surprised how much it overlaps," Shannon said.

Matthew's bushy eyebrows twitched. "How's that?"

"International business requires preparation, a solid foundation, good product in the form of expertise, along with time and patience to get from start to a clean, polished finish."

Matthew cocked his head and laughed outright. "Right enough." He turned to Daniel. "I like her. You could do worse."

Tess *tsk*ed at her husband.

"It's true," he blustered.

"It's not that kind of dinner," Daniel said as color crept into Shannon's cheeks. Under the table, he tried to reassure her, rubbing her knee with his. If she'd let him, he'd be her shelter against everything unpleasant from his Dad's nosiness to Stanwood's deadly threats.

"And why shouldn't it be?" His dad reached for his glass of beer.

"Are you fighting with Pop?" Aiden asked Daniel.

"Not at all, bud. Did you eat the peas?"

Aiden scowled at his plate. "No."

Daniel speared a pea on each tine of his fork. "Bet I can eat all of mine before you eat all yours."

Aiden's brown eyes lit at the challenge and he sat up in his chair. "How'd you do that?"

"Years of practice. Go on," Daniel urged. "I'll wait." He did, then he won the first round, let Aiden win the second. Soon enough all the peas were gone.

But the game didn't derail his dad's agenda for long. He caught Shannon's eye. "We could watch the little guy if you and Daniel would like to go out for a bit."

"I've got to be at the firehouse early tomorrow, Dad."

"Another time, maybe," Shannon added.

"That's no career when you have people depending on you," his dad groused.

At this point, under the pointed gazes of both his mom and dad, it was impossible to know if they meant the construction company or Shannon and her son.

Either way, the old argument was…old. He'd made his choice and while he loved the construction work, he wasn't ready to give up fighting fires. He couldn't be what they wanted him to be, not yet, maybe not ever. "Since I'll never please everyone, may as well please myself," he said.

His father glared at him over his beer. "That's a selfish outlook."

"Daniel gave Aiden a tour of the firehouse the other day," Shannon interjected. "Well, both of us. We were very impressed."

Matthew opened his mouth, but Tess spoke first. "It's exciting isn't it?" she asked Aiden.

As the boy launched into a description of his favorite aspects of the trucks, Matthew wisely held his tongue. It was the first time in Daniel's recollection that his dad dropped the subject so easily.

He seized the moment to start clearing dinner plates and dishes. The sooner they made it through dessert, the sooner this would be over. Too bad his dad wasn't done.

"How much longer are we into that charity project of yours?"

Daniel felt Shannon's gaze on him and avoided it. "Ed has things under control." he said. He wasn't about to mention the flooring trouble, though his dad might already know. He placed slices of cake in front of each of them.

"In other words, you don't know when you'll be done."

"We're close, Dad," Daniel said with a sigh. "We won't go over by more than a few days," he confessed.

"Not at all if you would stay on site and keep up with your crews from start to finish." He was gaining steam and Daniel didn't know how to stop the runaway train of his dad's disappointment.

"I'm afraid that's partly my fault." Shannon bravely entered the fray and Daniel stifled a groan. "Due to some personal trouble of mine, Daniel's been distracted."

"That had nothing to do with it."

"What kind of trouble?" Matthew and Tess asked in unison.

"I got taken," Aiden said. "By the bad guys. Daniel did a Superman and got me back to Mommy." He stuffed another bite of cake into his mouth, blissfully unaware of the stunned silence he'd created.

No, the kid didn't miss much at all.

"I had good help with that." Daniel followed Aiden's lead, cutting into his own thick slab of cake with satisfaction at his father's dumbfounded expression.

Tess looked at Daniel. "This was the boy," she said, brushing Aiden's white-blond hair.

He rested his hand on the back of Shannon's chair, making it clear where he stood on the issue. "Yes."

"We don't expect that trouble to follow us here," Shannon explained. "Staying here is merely a precaution. If you're uncomfortable, if you'd like us to leave, we will."

Tess was already shaking her head. "You're staying," she said in the irrevocable tone that ended all arguments during his childhood. "We're happy to have you both."

"Aiden and I appreciate it very much. Thank you."

"Thank you," Aiden echoed with a chocolate-coated smile.

"Can I help with the dishes?" Shannon asked.

"We'll manage." Tess glanced at the clock in the hallway. "I imagine it's getting close to bedtime for your little man."

Daniel and Shannon gave her a few more minutes with Aiden by clearing the table before wrestling a reluctant and yawning boy out the door and up to the apartment.

Daniel did what he could to help Shannon with the bedtime routine, his thoughts in turmoil over the dinner, his upcoming shift and the sense that his dad might have a point about his decision to be a firefighter.

"Why is it called a daybed when you sleep on it at night?" Aiden asked in yet another attempt to delay the inevitable lights-out.

"Hmm? Oh. Girls give normal things fancy names." His reply earned him a light elbow from Shannon.

"Fancy names and lots of pillows," she said. "It's a daybed because it's good for day stuff, too."

"Like what?" Aiden's fingers worried the ear of his rabbit.

"Naps and reading. Maybe we'll test that out tomorrow."

"With a truck race! Naps are for babies."

"We'll see." She bent and kissed him good-night. "Sleep well."

"Now Daniel," Aiden demanded.

When Daniel came over, Aiden surged up to hug him, the little arms tight on his neck. "Are you staying here, too?"

"Sure thing, buddy."

"Okay. I like it when you stay."

When Aiden had run out of clever delays and excuses, Daniel and Shannon retreated to the front room where he immediately apologized for the fiasco of dinner.

"Don't do that." She waved off his apology. "You have nothing to be sorry for. I'm making tea, do you want some?"

"How can you say that?" He followed her. "They were rude."

"They were parents. They love you." She reached back into the cabinet for a second mug. "Someday I'll probably embarrass Aiden the same way."

"Not a chance," Daniel countered. At her raised eyebrows, he added, "They ride me to quit and take over the family business every chance they get."

She slowly came closer, as if giving him room to bolt before she slid her arms around his waist. He watched her, caught in that warm brown gaze as she pressed up on her toes and brushed her lips to his. The irritation choking him all through dinner faded under that sweet caress.

Bolt from her? Not a chance. He cradled her head and took the kiss deeper, his fingers flexing into the silky, short hair. He kissed her with all the feeling he didn't dare put into words. Yet.

Her eyes were glazed a little, her lips rosy when she eased back and returned to the tea.

Right. Aiden might not be asleep yet.

Daniel shoved his hands into his pockets and paced to the window, staring down at his truck in the dark driveway. "I should have come up with a different place for you to hide. Should've known they'd be impossible. They get that way when any woman walks within ten feet of me."

"They love you," she said again, as if that explained away a multitude of poor behavior. Maybe it did.

Behind him, he heard her tear open tea bags and the soft clink of the saucers as she covered the mugs to steep the tea.

"I've always liked your dad. And your mother is lovely."

"She did everything except call Aiden her grandson." He left the window in favor of the better view of her. She'd worn a soft, rust-colored skirt with a gold sweater over a wine-colored shirt to dinner and he hadn't even told her how pretty she looked. "You look like autumn tonight."

She stopped and stared at him. "Thank you?"

He nodded, making a note to give her compliments more often. "You're beautiful all the time, but this is really nice. I meant to say so earlier."

"Thank you," she said as her cheeks went pink.

Single parenting was challenging enough and she made it look so easy he forgot she didn't have anyone reminding her that she was amazing. He wanted to take on that role.

"Are your parents alive?"

She gave a small start at the question before regret flickered in her eyes. "Yes."

"Does Aiden know them?"

"No." She held up a hand. "It's a long story and you have to be on duty early tomorrow."

"I want to hear it." He wanted all of her secrets, wanted to take the focus off his own awkward family dynamics. "Please."

He wasn't sure she'd answer as she pulled spoons out of the cutlery drawer and honey from the pantry shelf. "I was a few classes away from graduation when I dropped out to marry Bradley," she said. "My parents hated him for distracting me from my goals. It didn't matter that he paid off my student loans as a wedding gift. Didn't matter that I finished my degree online before Aiden's first birthday. They never liked Bradley and never forgave me for marrying him."

Her overwhelming sadness put things into perspective. "No wonder my family dynamics didn't faze you." The comment earned him a small smile, so he pressed on. "I thought maybe you kept them at a distance to protect them," he said.

"I wouldn't mind having that option," she admitted. "In your shoes, I'd be irritated with the Mimi and Pop thing, too. I wasn't trying to overstep or insert Aiden where he didn't belong."

He laughed. "Trust me, I didn't think you had anything to do with it."

She handed him the tea, took her mug with her to the couch and curled into the corner, one foot tucked under her. "Are you sure about us staying here? I don't want to put anyone else in Bradley's crosshairs."

"This is the safest place I know while I have to work and the cops are trying to track him down." He studied his tea. "Maybe Dad's right about me not finishing things. I'll talk to the chief tomorrow about—"

"Don't you dare finish that sentence with anything remotely related to stepping back from the PFD."

Her intensity stunned him. Other women had yelled at him—or worse—and walked out when he chose firefighting over them. "You're the first person not connected to the PFD to say that to me."

"I don't believe you."

He shrugged. "My uncles, Mom's brothers, were firefighters. Dad always blamed them for making me think it was all ladders, hoses and calendar shoots."

She snorted. "I imagine going through the academy disabused you of any such notion."

He marveled that she got it. "Those were long, hard days," he said, remembering. "My dad would've preferred it if I'd been half as enthused about roofing at fifteen as you were. I did everything possible to hang out at the firehouse with my uncles."

He looked around the apartment and smiled. "That's about the time Dad started on this. Implied it could be for me when I was old enough."

"Was it?"

He walked over and sat on the opposite end of the couch. "Seems I'm putting it to good use at the moment. Looking back, I know Dad was trying to draw me away from a firefighter's life."

"He's so proud of you," she said. "They both are."

"Funny way of showing it."

She grinned, sipped her tea. "Parents want their kids to be safe and happy. Standard flaw in the parental design since the two don't always go together. Whatever the hang-up with the PFD, those fears and concerns are on them. Were your uncles injured on the job?"

"Nothing worse than a couple of close calls, though there have been other losses along the way."

"On them," she repeated firmly.

"Maybe it's the curse of being firstborn," he said. "That need for approval. Doesn't bother my brother at all to go his own way." He felt like an idiot, saying it like that. "I've got a great life and I'm whining about it when we have bigger concerns. Did you hear anything from Hertz?"

She shook her head. "You know, wanting approval of the people who matter most is a universal concern." She stretched an arm across the back of the couch and stroked his shoulder. "As an outsider looking in?"

"Sure, go ahead." He knew she'd set him straight. It was this basic common sense that he'd gotten used to during their days together. Her practical nature, her sincerity, generosity and humor. If he had a wish to toss out to a star, it would be that they could get through this and make it. He wanted her and Aiden to be his family.

With an idyllic picture in his head, the words were on the tip of his tongue when she spoke first.

"I think your strong will is too much like your dad's,"

she said. "It's not a lack of approval, it's a different point of view. You see your career as a service and responsibility and he sees steady work hours and weeks and completed projects in the same light."

"I think he just wants to retire and move to the Bahamas. If I'd fall in line and take over the business, he could ditch Pennsylvania winters for palm trees and ocean breezes." With Shannon and Aiden to come home to, maybe the sacrifice would be worth it after all.

She laughed softly, the sound sliding over him as warm and sultry as the ocean lapping at a sandy shore.

"Whether or not my dad and I agree on my immediate future, I appreciate you being so understanding about dinner."

"Aiden had a blast with your parents." She gave his shoulder a shove. "You got him to eat his peas." She fluttered her lashes. "You are Superman."

When the laughter died down, she dropped her gaze to her mug. "Can I ask you a personal question?"

"Apparently, it's the theme of the night."

"Why aren't you with someone already?"

I'm with you. He had to fight to keep the words to himself. It wasn't the time to put that pressure on her when he knew the idea of running still appealed to her. "Should I be insulted by the question?"

"No." Her teeth nipped her full lower lip. "Family is obviously important and a core value for the Jennings."

For both of us, he thought, but again, he kept his mouth shut.

"You can't deny it."

"I'm not." He appreciated her candor and should be focusing on that rather than how much he wanted to kiss her again. "I've shown a couple of women this mansion." He waved an arm around. "They weren't as impressed by the idea that I built it as you seem to be."

He caught her fingers and brought her hand to his lips. Better to distract himself with that kiss than put his heart under the gentle protection of her palm.

Shannon knew she was treading on sensitive issues. His attempts to make jokes accentuated with that gallant kiss to her hand only proved it. "I'm trying to ask if there is, or has been, someone specific." She plowed on as he shook his head. "Someone who makes you doubt women as a whole."

His eyebrows furrowed over those gorgeous blue eyes. "That's a severe assessment."

She kept her hand linked with his, savoring the stroke of his thumb across her palm. He had such capable hands. "I've been there, that's all. After…well, after I reclaimed control of my life, I was afraid to take another chance. Not many people want to admit a failed relationship is a tough hurdle."

"Are you volunteering to help me over that hurdle?"

The teasing tone and the subtle twitch of his lips into a smirk did nothing to quell the voice in her head screaming, *Yes, please!*

"No. I'm trying *not* to interrupt your life," she insisted. "You've gone above and beyond as a boss and a friend. You've done more for Aiden and me than anyone else. I just wanted to say if you need a friend to listen, or whatever…" She gave up before she dug herself a deeper hole. Why couldn't she make her point without sounding like an idiot? Or worse, a desperate single mom who hadn't had sex in far too long. Oh, yeah. Because that's what she was.

Daniel had opened her up, and dreams she'd given up

on were resurfacing. Did they have a chance to build a future? He'd told her to believe they'd get Aiden home and now her heart wanted to keep believing... in love.

"You don't have to stay over," she said briskly, rising. "Given a choice, I'd rather be at home. I'm sure it's the same for you." She didn't even know where he lived, only the remodel project he'd been crashing in on the day Aiden had been taken.

She took her empty mug to the kitchen sink, rinsed it and put it into the dishwasher. The gesture was so maddeningly responsible, directly opposite to the pulsing need she felt whenever Daniel was nearby.

Her rich, romantic imagination had gotten her into trouble with Bradley. While she knew how to spot losers with more accuracy now, she also had a better grip of what made a man a keeper.

Daniel was firmly entrenched in that category. It was so much more than her physical attraction to his square jaw, dark hair, vivid blue eyes and sculpted body. All of the packaging had starred in the ridiculous fantasies she'd enjoyed since his first appearance on a site. Now she knew him—his thoughtfulness and dedication, his commitment to career and community. She knew he helped her simply because she was part of his immediate circle and still she longed for something more. Something she feared was well beyond her reach.

When she'd said she could love him, it was already too late. She did love him.

"What hurdles did he leave behind?" Daniel asked.

She jumped, would have turned but he was too close. Her lips tingled, hoping for a kiss. No, being face-to-face with him right now would be a massive mistake.

"I've heard you blame yourself. I've seen the shame on your face while you accept the fallout of your choices. Tell me the rest of it, Shannon." He spoke her name in a delicious caress over the nape of her neck.

She should be shoving him away, feeling crowded and afraid with his bigger body at her back. Instead, her belly quivered with anticipation.

"Trust," she heard herself reply. "He made me doubt my intuition."

"In all men?"

She studied his strong hands, tanned skin made more perfect by the occasional scar. She wanted to know the story behind each one. "In most men. For a time."

Daniel was different, the first man she wanted to trust, to believe in. "I was blinded by what I saw on the surface."

"What did *he* do?"

It had been ages since she'd let herself put any of the blame for her foolish marriage on her ex-husband. Even if someone had been available to listen, she couldn't have explained any details without risking her, the baby or the listener. Daniel was already involved, already in the crosshairs. "He played on that advantage, preyed on my naïveté. Looking back at the way he isolated me, I want to go back and shout a warning to that star-struck girl."

His lips trailed up and down the side of her neck. She shivered, too warm, too edgy.

"Two women were important to me." His voice, low and rough, was loaded with the old aches. "Important enough that I introduced them to my family."

Her breath backed up in her lungs. It took all her willpower to stand there, caged by his arms, letting him talk when she wanted to touch, to put his mouth to better use.

"When the thrill wore off and the reality and dangers

of my job set in, they walked away." His lips skimmed over her skin, up along her neck. "My dad blamed the firehouse, hooked me deeper into the company. My mom called the women weak and said I went for shallow over substance."

Trust. He'd offered her an invaluable gift. She repaid him with the same. "On the outside, Bradley was everything I thought I wanted. Successful, handsome and charming. His interest in me was its own seduction. Once I was caught, his, he changed into someone else. Something ugly and unrecognizable."

"You gave up everything for him."

"I didn't know how else to express what I thought was love." She'd never given anyone the broken pieces of her soul she was putting in Daniel's hands.

"He hurt you." His knuckles whitened as his fingers curled into fists on the countertop.

In a thousand small and massive ways. "Life dishes out hurt to all of us," she said. "I'm stronger now." Her hips brushed against his as she turned and faced him. He needed to see her strength, needed to see her resolved in the present rather than weakened by the past. "Aiden is my joy, one I wouldn't have without those terrible days with Bradley." The muscles in his arms flexed as her palms flowed up to his shoulders. "I would have lost him without your help."

He kissed her forehead, featherlight. "I want to stay. I want you, Shannon."

Those four words, raw and packed with need, echoed the desire and cravings slamming through her system. Too many words built up in her heart, her throat, and she gave up on conversation. His lips parted and she silenced him with a kiss, pouring her own answering wants into the heated contact. Sinking deep and fast, she molded her mouth to his. Taking, giving more.

He gripped her hips, squeezed, bringing her hard against his arousal. She clutched his shoulders for balance as passion lanced through her body like an arrow. Her fingers fumbled on the buttons of his shirt while his tongue swirled across hers, invading, teasing and retreating. At last she pushed his shirt open, off, and got her hands on the hot, firm flesh of his torso.

She moaned as she kissed a path across the wide expanse of his chest, the curls of hair tickling her lips.

He tugged her sweater back, then in a slow slide, pushed her shirt up and over her head. He groaned at the sight of her breasts, released her bra.

She smothered the shocked giggle as he boosted her up onto the counter, then clamped her lips hard against the cry as his mouth closed over her breast. He nipped the hard peak gently with his teeth, soothed with tongue and lips. She arched into him, her body already primed and dancing at the edge of a climax.

She wrestled with his belt, flicked open the buttons on his jeans, desperate to get her hands on more of him, all of him.

The day's growth of beard on his jaw was delicious and rough against her skin, left her pleading as he claimed her mouth once more. Skin to skin, she was swamped by wave after wave of sensual need, longing to be filled, joined, overwhelmed by him.

Pulling up her skirt, she lifted her legs to clutch his hips and rubbed herself shamelessly against him through her panties. The orgasm shot through her in a scalding rush of delicious pleasure, but she wasn't nearly satisfied.

Neither was he, thank goodness. His hand slid under

the lace, his fingers stroking her while his mouth plundered hers until she was quivering at the edge of bliss again.

She heard the seams rip, couldn't surface enough to care as he thrust deep inside her. For a moment, it was enough to feel him, to savor the way her body gave and flowed around his.

Then he moved and she craved more. He was everything, the only thing that mattered. Long slow strokes filled, faded and filled again. His pace quickened and she matched him, hanging on and kissing him deeply to smother the cry of ecstasy as another orgasm pulsed through her. A moment later the pleasure claimed him, too, his body trembling around her, in her.

When her heart rate slowed, her breathing steadied, the absurdity of what they'd done, or rather where they'd done it, crept in.

"Are you laughing?" he asked, easing back and putting himself to rights.

"Guess I'm giddy."

He drew her skirt down over her legs, tracing the hem above her knees. When he looked up, his expression stole her breath. "In all my fantasies of you, this kitchen counter didn't feature. I won't overlook it again."

Her knees wobbled as he helped her to her feet. "Fantasies? About me?"

He jerked his chin in the affirmative, his gaze unwavering. "That sounds creepy I suppose?"

"Not from you." She took his hand in both of hers. "Oh, Daniel." Walking backward, she started for the bedroom. "Follow me and I'll show you a recurring fantasy I've had about you."

"Seriously?"

She paused, pretending to think it over. "Unless it creeps you out?"

He tossed her over his shoulder and carried her to the bedroom.

She laughed, happy to take all he wanted to share, reveling in the joy of the moment and giving back everything he would take from her.

Starstruck again, in the best possible way, she brought her fantasies to life in the safe, strong arms of the man she trusted with her body, heart and soul. The man she loved.

Chapter 11

Daniel's alarm sounded and he quickly slapped it off before gently untangling himself from Shannon's luscious, supple body. He had no regrets as he sat on the edge of the bed with the fragrance that was hers alone lingering in the air. Hard to believe she wouldn't have a few regrets, he thought, pushing to his feet. He'd just have to burn that bridge when they got there.

He grabbed a quick shower, shaved and dressed for his shift, riding the energy boost of great sex all the way into the kitchen. He made the coffee and laced up his boots while it brewed.

He'd filled his tall PFD travel mug and was reaching for his jacket when he heard the bathroom door close. Now what did he do? Wait or head to work? It wasn't like he didn't have practice leaving for work before a woman woke up. Walking out on Shannon without a word, after dumping his family issues on her and taking her to bed, didn't feel right. He checked his watch and gave himself five more minutes.

While he waited he heard his dad's truck start up. Daniel swallowed down more coffee, his dad's voice in his head scolding him for getting involved with Shannon. At least he assumed his dad wouldn't approve of his getting involved with a woman and kid with trouble as big as Bradley Stanwood and his associates. It was hard to get a read on where Dad stood on Shannon as a future daughter-in-law.

Shannon on her own merits had tempted him and starred in his more creative dreams for over a year. Now that he knew her as a woman and as a mom, he was only in deeper. With the attraction sparking between them, landing in bed was practically inevitable. What came next wasn't as clear. The incomparable, satisfying experience stirred up questions in the back of his mind.

She was already single-mom tough, but was there room in her life to be the kind of tough necessary to love a firefighter?

His five minutes were up. He went to the whiteboard on the fridge to leave her a note about when he'd be off when he caught sight of her rounding the corner.

Her hair tousled from sleep, her nightshirt falling to mid-thigh, he cursed the job he loved. "I need to get over to the house," he said. "You'll be good here today?"

"We'll be safe if that's what you mean." She skirted around him to get to the coffeepot. "I can check in on the progress at the charity house for you."

"You're supposed to lay low and stay out of sight. Ed will send me any updates."

"That works," she said over the rim of her coffee mug.

The easy reply put him on edge. "What are you thinking?"

"Have Ed keep me in the loop, too," she suggested. "My phone works. I know what you want over there.

We've talked about it enough and I can keep track with your project binder."

"You're sure?" He trusted her, he just didn't want her out there alone while Stanwood was in the wind. Every indication was he'd followed her car and the decoy north, but Daniel wasn't convinced. Worse, he knew Shannon wasn't either, though she hadn't said it aloud.

She tipped her head toward the clock display on the microwave. "You need to get moving," she said with a smile. "Have a good shift."

Might as well take the leap and believe. Surely the philosophy could apply to relationships and crises alike. He couldn't help himself. Pulling her close, he gave her a slow, sweet kiss. It would never last him through an entire shift and he hoped it would leave her wanting more as well.

"Aiden will be up soon." She smoothed her hand over his shoulder. "Go have a good day. We'll be fine."

Daniel forced himself to leave the apartment, surprised by the challenge it posed. He felt a pang in his chest that he didn't get to see Aiden before shift. The kid had wormed his way in and Daniel couldn't wait until Stanwood was in custody and they could do this right.

Was he ready for a family? He wondered as he reached the firehouse. If that family started with Shannon and Aiden, he was definitely ready and he hoped Shannon could get on that page soon. He didn't want to come home to a hollow construction zone anymore.

Striding into the firehouse, he felt a different kind of home, surrounded by men and women who were as close as brothers and sisters. Each of them had lives outside the house and the risk of their work. Contrary to his dad's grousing about adrenaline and responsibility, Daniel respected how the people he worked with balanced commitment to their families with a career serving the greater community. Although he might be a black sheep at home, a disappointment to the family business, he fit in around here.

The routine and focus required for the work pushed his personal questions aside. It felt as if he'd been gone for months rather than weeks. The firehouse wasn't as different from a construction site as his dad believed. The camaraderie, teamwork and timing were critical to success in both areas.

The morning ticked by with details and drills until finally the speakers sang out with a call. "Think you remember how it's done?" Mitch asked him as they donned gear and loaded into the truck.

"Easy as riding a bike," Daniel replied, climbing into his seat.

The driver navigated traffic, swiftly reaching a house in the heart of a rundown neighborhood. "Squatters dropped a match, I bet," Mitch said as the crew poured out to assess the situation.

"Probably." Daniel looked around the deserted street. On most calls, someone met the truck, desperate for help. At the very least they usually had to deal with curious bystanders milling about.

The lack of activity put an itch between his shoulder blades. "Stay alert," he told the crew as they started into the building.

The fire had a good head start and tried to discourage them with heat and hungry flames. Smoke gathered in heavy clouds at the ceiling and Daniel knew as well as the others the fire was running through the walls.

Not much time.

Working in pairs, Daniel and three others searched for victims trapped inside. Seeing the discarded drug paraphernalia at the door, they followed the trail of it up the stairs. Over the radio he heard the crew outside working to get the fire out before it spread.

A warning from the chief let them know they didn't have much time before the roof would drop in on them. The building groaned, underscoring the chief's assessment. Daniel and Mitch hurried to clear the rooms on the third floor.

In the central hallway, Mitch tapped his shoulder, pointed upward. "Time to go."

Over the radio, the chief ordered them out.

"I'm right behind you," Daniel said to Mitch. "One last room." He aimed for the one room they'd overlooked. Tucked behind the stairwell, with the door closed, it was easy to miss.

"It's a closet," Mitch said as a fiery chunk of the ceiling dropped down into the hallway. "Let's move."

The closed door bothered Daniel and he pounded on it. The police were constantly rousting kids out of houses like this. None of the other doors had been closed. He tested the knob, locked, thought he heard a cry. "Someone's in here!"

Mitch turned back. "What the hell?"

"It's locked." Daniel had his Halligan into the door frame already, prying at the brittle wood. "Fire department!" he shouted as he worked. "Call out!"

With a pop, the door came free and Mitch shoved it aside. Huddled in the corner, a skinny person with stringy hair and a tear-stained face coughed.

"Let's go," Mitch said, reaching toward the victim. "Can you walk?"

A bony arm and hand reached back, trembling. Daniel reported they were coming out with a victim and led the way. They hit the landing on the second floor when the roof gave out with a deafening squeal and thunder. The fire, freed from the walls, blazed anew with a ravenous, deep voice.

His radio blasted with shouts, orders and demands for status. Daniel looked back and got a nod from Mitch, relayed they were okay. For the moment.

A chunk of the roof had dropped through the stairwell, trapping them between the center of the house and the front door on the landing between the first and second floors. Daniel swiftly reassessed, watching and listening to the fire moving around them. "We can hand off over the gap," he decided.

Mitch nodded an agreement as Daniel moved into position, easing his way around what was left of the stairs. Between them, they moved the victim, a young woman, over the gaping hole in the stairs. She coughed and choked, her thin body shivering like a leaf riding a windstorm. The air quality should have been better as they moved toward the front door, but debris from the roof collapse added foul dust clouds to the smoke.

Daniel steadied the victim until at last they were free of the burning building and out in the clear air of an overcast day. Daniel shoved back his mask and inhaled the brisk, cool air. Paramedics rushed forward with a gurney for the victim. They'd covered her dirty face with the oxygen mask when a sharp, whip-crack of sound sliced through the air.

Not sounds from the fire, that was a bullet. Followed by two more.

Daniel and Mitch moved to cover the woman they'd rescued while the paramedics tried to get the loaded gurney behind better cover. One wheel of the gurney got jammed in the pock-marked sidewalk and they went crashing to the ground.

The tumble knocked the wind out of Daniel and sent pain lancing around his ribcage, up his side. Mitch swore. Behind them, the chief barked out more orders as the shooter kept firing. Policemen arriving at the scene leaped into action, calling for backup as they moved to return the gunfire coming from an equally dilapidated building across the street.

Undaunted, the shooter kept firing. Daniel glanced to the victim, wondering who wanted her dead so badly.

"Move the truck!" the chief shouted.

Daniel heard the engine rumbling, felt the truck drive up closer to the house, putting an end to the rain of bullets. They righted the gurney and settled the patient, giving her oxygen. Long minutes ticked by while they hunkered down until finally the police announced they'd found the shooter's nest, not the shooter. While they continued in pursuit, the firemen and paramedics finished their work as well.

"What kind of trouble are you in?" Daniel asked, worried for the girl they'd rescued. The track marks on her arms proved her an addict in need of immediate intervention. She shook her head weakly, sucking in the offered oxygen. She pointed to him and Mitch. "Said he wanted firemen." She worked to force out each word.

A chill slid down Daniel's spine at the statement.

"We need to transport." The paramedics started moving.

Searing pain had Daniel sucking in a breath as he stepped aside.

"You need to ride along?" Mitch asked.

Daniel shook his head. "Landed wrong on the gurney, that's all. Did you hear what she said?"

Mitch nodded. "I also noticed the gunfire was focused on us. Didn't end until the truck moved."

"Not a good sign," Daniel said. At Mitch's pointed look, he took a careful breath around the pain in his ribs. "I'll go tell the chief."

"Be sure you add the part about your girlfriend's ex being with the mob," Mitch said quietly. "Grant gave me a heads-up when I covered for you Saturday night."

Daniel couldn't argue. It might be random craziness that pushed the gunman or it might be Stanwood. Whether he'd pulled the trigger himself or hired it done, Daniel couldn't rule out Shannon's ex. Reluctantly, he said as much to the chief.

Ignoring the pain in his side, Daniel helped his crew pack up for the trip back to the firehouse. With a start like this, he feared it would be a long shift.

He wasn't wrong. They'd only been back an hour when another call came in, same neighborhood, similar fire. No one trapped inside, which was a relief, but when they rolled back into the house, Detective Hertz was waiting for Daniel.

Apparently, witnesses described a man similar to Stanwood in the area, offering cash.

"The decoy didn't work?"

"He figured it out, lost us," Hertz said. "We don't know it's him, but you need to be careful. I've checked on Shannon. She and the boy are fine."

"So he's targeting my lieutenant?" Chief Anderson asked.

"*If* it's Stanwood, and that's my bet, he isn't known to get his hands dirty."

"He has the money to hire others."

The detective nodded in somber agreement while the *if* echoed in Daniel's head. "Seems like one hell of a coincidence if it isn't Stanwood."

"Be careful is the best advice I have right now."

Hertz closed his notebook. "The patrol continues to shadow the Nolans. I'll be sure there's an increased presence here, too."

The detective walked out and the chief stared at Daniel, hands on hips. "You could stay off the truck until we know."

"Not if you're giving me a choice, sir."

The chief scowled down at the stack of reports on his desk. "We need you," he said thoughtfully. "You don't do me a lot of good if the shooter succeeds."

"I'm aware." He wouldn't do anyone any good if Stanwood managed to wound him or worse. Still, if he was drawing Stanwood's focus from Shannon, he considered it progress. "If he's out there setting fires for a chance at me, the police will have a better chance of catching him."

"Get after it, then," the chief said.

Daniel walked out of the office and pulled out his phone, checking for updates from Ed or Shannon. Hearing a commotion in the kitchen, he walked in to see what his crew was getting into now.

Shannon knew something was wrong the moment she walked into the firehouse. There was a weird undercurrent in the air. When he saw her, Daniel's smile was bright enough, but she saw the quick wince and heard the catch in his breath when he scooped Aiden up into his arms.

"Hey, buddy," Daniel said as Aiden wrapped his skinny arms around his neck. "How's your day going?"

"We saw the charity house," Aiden began. "Mimi took us." He continued giving a full rundown of the day's events from breakfast to afternoon baking as only a four-year-old could.

To her amazement, Daniel appeared engrossed by the recounting of her son's day. She scolded herself for the reaction, for expecting Daniel to get tired of Aiden. Daniel wasn't Bradley, nor was he anything like the other two men she'd dated briefly.

She stepped forward. "Here are the cookies."

"Whoa," Mitch said, taking the plate from her. He grinned at Aiden. "You really baked these? They look tasty."

"You have to share," Aiden said. "Mommy said so."

Daniel tickled a silly giggle out of her son. "Did you save any for me at home?" he asked in a conspiratorial whisper.

Aiden bobbed his head, eyes sparkling, and the two of them were obviously planning something while her mind was stuck on the idea of home being a place for all three of them. Together.

She'd ruthlessly jerked her mind back from that twisty track of contentment and possibility and future as she and Aiden had baked the cookies. Two batches of her favorite double-chocolate chip later, she hadn't quite found her way back to accepting this was temporary. Once more, sex had changed everything, but there would be no regrets. If this was all they had, she would enjoy it without putting pressure on either of them.

One of the paramedics led Aiden off to explore something else, giving Daniel and Shannon a moment alone.

She wanted to ask what was hurting him, but thought it better if he volunteered the information. A small test for both of them, considering what they'd each needed to overcome. "The house is coming along," she said.

"Great." He tipped his head, stepping back into a quiet corner of the hallway. "Any chance we gained a day or two on the schedule?"

A purely feminine part of her had been hoping he'd moved them out of sight to sneak a kiss. "Maybe half a day." She reached into her tote and pulled out the project binder.

"You're joking."

"Not at all." She opened the binder to her day's notes. "I made a couple of calls and got a workaround on the back-ordered flooring."

"I didn't want to sacrifice quality."

"We didn't. Jennings didn't," she amended quickly when his brow furrowed. Sharing an apartment, having the best sex of her life, didn't make them an enduring "we." *Live in the moment.* "It's the exact product you ordered, fulfilled through remnants."

His dark eyebrows lifted with momentary respect and surprise and then dipped into a frown. "I didn't think of that."

In reflex, she reached out to comfort him, drawing her hand back before she overstepped the boundaries. This was his place of business. "You've had other things on your mind."

His enigmatic blue gaze locked on to her. "Last night—"

The dispatch warning sounded and the call came for the ambulance only. Aiden appeared at the end of the hallway as the paramedics headed out to the job. He raced for Daniel again, barreling into his leg.

Daniel winced more visibly this time.

"Easy," she said to her son. "Did you have fun on the ambulance?"

"They call it a rig, Mommy."

"Good to know."

"Will you go out next?" Aiden asked Daniel, his eyes wide. "Are your sirens louder than the rig?"

"Definitely. You heard them on your tour."

"We need to get going," Shannon said to Aiden, reaching for her son.

"I'll walk you out." Daniel dropped down, offering his back to Aiden. "Hop on, bud."

Aiden scrambled up, his small hands gripping Daniel's shoulders as Daniel held his legs. She smiled at the two of them making plans for the end of Daniel's shift tomorrow.

At the car she'd borrowed from Tess, Daniel reached over his head and turned Aiden upside down as he put him on the ground. The delighted squeal melted her heart, making her wish once more for a life that probably wasn't in the cards.

She had to consider that she and Aiden would be in danger, even after her ex was in custody. He would use every resource to take aim at her again before he let her testify against him. Gary's last words echoed in her head again. That was why she'd resorted to baking and delivering cookies. She'd been reading the journals he'd left for her and getting nowhere on the whole "you know" deal.

A sweet, happy-ever-after family life with Daniel wasn't just wishful thinking, it was a pipe dream at this rate. Knowing it, she should cut herself off from him now, move on before Aiden got any more attached to Daniel or his parents.

A little sad, she kissed Aiden's cheek as she buckled him into the booster seat.

When she'd closed the door, she was ready to tell Daniel she'd move out of the garage apartment before he got home. Somehow she'd find the words to explain it to Aiden.

"Be careful driving home," he said, reaching up to

smooth her bangs away from her eyes. His palm cupped her jaw, his thumb cruising over her cheekbone as he studied her.

She knew he saw too much. "Daniel."

"Don't say it." He drew her face close, gave her a toe-curling kiss. "More, don't do it."

"What?" She was still processing the way he'd kissed her out here, in full view of anyone who cared to look this way.

"You're thinking of leaving again. Don't do it. The apartment is the safest place for you and Aiden." He pressed a hand to his side. "For all of us."

She waited, but still he didn't volunteer any information about what was hurting him or where this was coming from. Remembering the conversation from last night, she wouldn't push. If he was on duty, she trusted him to be fit for duty.

"Okay. I'll stay." They both heard the unspoken "for now." *Take what you can get*, she thought. *Give back all you can.* There wasn't a better approach under the circumstances. Wrapping her fingers around the car key in her pocket, she gave him a smile. "Tell everyone to be safe. I hope they enjoy the cookies."

"Shannon." He caught her hand. "If you need anything before I get off shift, go to Mom."

She nodded, not trusting her voice.

"We had an incident on an earlier call."

"Incident?" she echoed, keeping her voice steady.

"A bystander took a few shots at the truck during our first call of the day. It happens." He circled an area on his torso. "I landed on some equipment when we were taking cover. Bruised a couple of ribs."

She let that sink in, knowing he didn't want her fussing over him. He was standing here, clearly aching, but well. The time to worry had passed.

"The police are handling it. Witnesses are describing the perp in a way that makes me think of Stanwood," he added. "Hertz said the decoy failed."

Her stomach lurched, and she struggled to keep it together. "Did you see the shooter?"

"No." He sighed and scrubbed a hand over his hair. "It's probably unrelated." His shoulders shifted. "I'm only a little banged up."

"Okay."

He shoved his hands into his pockets. "You're not upset?"

"No. I admit I'm not happy you're banged up in any way, shape or form. What kind of friend would that make me?" She gave him an exaggerated once-over from head to toes and back again. "You're a grown-up and you look well enough." Giving in to impulse, she pressed her lips to his cheek and then stepped back, keeping it casual. "We'll be safe, you do the same. Deal?"

"Deal," he agreed with a nod.

She escaped around the car, grateful her smile and knees held out until she was behind the wheel. As she drove away, she kept the obscenities in her head where her son wouldn't hear them. No, she didn't care for Daniel being hurt in the line of duty, but if it was Bradley who had shot at him that made her an accessory. Not in the legal sense, on a moral scale, and it weighed heavily on her heart.

He'd been inconvenienced from the moment the kidnappers had taken Aiden. Things had only gotten worse—and better—since they'd rescued Aiden whole and healthy.

Bradley was a brutal egomaniac on the best of days. Only the obsession for revenge explained why he'd stay in town after Loffler's murder, why he'd shoot at Daniel.

"Who am I kidding?" she asked aloud while Aiden sang along with a playful and happy children's song. "He's never going to quit."

"Who, Mommy?"

"Lex Luthor," she said automatically thinking of Superman's nemesis. Where was Bradley hiding? She took the turn toward the Jennings' house with guilt nipping her heels that she couldn't decipher what Gary was convinced she knew. If the police couldn't find the evidence connecting Bradley to the recent kidnapping and murders, she had to find something else that would stick.

"What cold case did he mean?" she asked herself as she pulled into the driveway and parked the car. She dug out Gary's journal from her tote and flipped back to the earliest pages. "Oh! It took me long enough. Sorry, Gary."

"Who's Gary?"

"An old friend," she answered, suddenly in a rush to talk to Detective Hertz.

Following Daniel's suggestion, she went to his mom for help. Tess was as delighted as Aiden to have some unplanned time together, another sweet tug on Shannon's heartstrings as she left them waving from the front porch. For the past four years, she'd convinced herself she could meet all of his needs and in the past two weeks, she'd seen that conviction shredded. Aiden needed more than his mother and the sitter's family. He needed deep, stable connections that she'd never be able to give him if they had to keep hiding from Bradley.

She used the voice command on her phone to dial

Grant, relieved when he agreed to meet her at the police station.

"Did something happen?" Grant asked again when he found her waiting just inside the doors of the station.

"You probably heard someone shot at Daniel's crew as they answered a call earlier today."

"No." Grant rocked back on his heels. "I hadn't heard."

"Daniel implied it's a coincidence," she said. "He didn't see the shooter, but he told me witnesses are describing a man similar to my ex," she added.

"You think Stanwood attacked them."

"I don't *know*," she admitted. "During our brief marriage, I learned that once he goes into loose-cannon mode he stays there until whatever he thinks needs done is done."

"What do you need from me?"

"Understanding." She fidgeted with her car key. "When I left him, I took only the settlement and some investment advice from Loffler. I didn't realize he was giving me something more." She patted the journal. "He sent me away with some information as insurance, tucked into the divorce papers." She paused as his painful final moments replayed through her mind. "It should have clicked when I saw the contents of the flash drive."

"You've been out of that life for some time," Grant said.

"And I tried to block out the bad things I did see." She took a deep breath. "Thanks to Gary's clever journals, I have information that will put Bradley behind bars and keep him there. Maybe not for these recent crimes, but it will give the police a chance to arrest him for racketeering and bribery at least."

Grant reached out and squeezed her shoulder. "I hear he's between lawyers at the moment, so let's get to it."

She snorted a laugh. "Gallows humor?"

"It's effective for a reason."

Working his way through the police station, Grant guided her to Hertz's desk. She made a formal statement about how she came by the information she was handing over. Using the journal Gary had left her and pointing out the key to the coded information in the flash drive files, she gave them properties, dates and high-profile guest names. She even gave them a property address in Society Hill that she and Bradley had visited before they married, where he'd made more than one shady payoff while she'd been too innocent and oblivious to grasp the full impact of those conversations.

She could be thankful now that names and numbers naturally stuck in her head. Gary's sacrifice would make a difference and finally bring Bradley to justice. Detective Hertz was organizing a search of the property in Society Hill as she and Grant left and she hoped that tip led to Bradley's immediate capture.

"You did well," Grant said as they walked out of the station to the parking lot. "You'll tell Daniel, right?"

"As soon as he's off shift, yes."

Grant donned his sunglasses and opened her car door for her. "He'll be glad you're putting this behind you."

"For good this time."

She hadn't considered that before, that holding on to an escape plan was a tacit way of clinging to that old life and all the baggage of that tumultuous, violent relationship. Yes, she'd needed the sense of safety at first. Now she was fighting for a life she'd carved out of nothing and it was time to be bold and brave.

Proactive, she thought with a smile. She couldn't wait

for Daniel to come home. The first thing she needed to say was she loved him. Then she'd tell him she was making a new plan. A plan to stay in Philly. A plan to stay with him forever if he'd have her.

Chapter 12

She'd given in to Aiden's endless begging and stayed for dinner with Daniel's parents. They might worry over their son or misunderstand his motives for staying with the PFD, but beneath all of that they loved him.

Even without Daniel, the conversation turned to the construction business. Apparently, Aiden had shared the day's adventurous search for a flooring solution.

"Remnants." Matthew forked up another bite of pot roast. Chewing, his gaze locked on Shannon. "I would've insisted on a lesser option with same-day delivery. Daniel would've paid more or waited for the original order.

Shannon reached for her water glass, pleased when her hand didn't shake as she raised it to her lips. She wasn't sure of the ground here or what kind of response he expected.

"Say what you mean, Matthew," Tess scolded gently, "before she forgets how much she's enjoying the meal."

He cocked an eyebrow, the move so reminiscent of his oldest son, Shannon relaxed. She saw so much of both of them reflected in Daniel and wondered if they'd ever realize that was the crux of the conflict. People looked into mirrors and focused on the flaws, rather than admiring the strengths.

"Can I have seconds?" Aiden asked.

At Shannon's nod, Tess refilled his smaller plate. "I do love having a polite young man at my table." She smoothed a hand over his pale hair, her eyes a little misty.

"Say what you mean," she prompted her husband once more.

He helped himself to the green beans, then sighed. "I only meant that you found a better solution. Kept the project on track."

"Saved half a day," Aiden mumbled around a mouthful of food.

Matthew paused in the act of stabbing a green bean and gave into a chuckle.

"Chew and swallow first," Shannon reminded her son.

He did. "You did the happy dance," Aiden said, daring her to deny it. "I saw it."

"I bet she did." Tess grinned at her.

Aiden wouldn't let it rest. "Time matters, you said."

"Boy's right. I wasn't keen on taking on a pro bono project of that scope, but Daniel insisted." After a moment, he looked Shannon in the eye. "I appreciate you stepping in when he couldn't see it through."

She bit back the automatic urge to defend Daniel by pointing out he had final say and authorizations. Instead, she offered Matthew a sweet smile. "I enjoy solving problems. It's a great feeling when the solution works for everyone up and down the chain of command."

He aimed a narrow look at her and his wife blotted

her lips. Her eyes, the same startling blue as Daniel's, were twinkling with amusement.

To Shannon's relief, he dropped the issue while they finished the meal and the conversation followed Aiden's favorite topics of trucks and cookies and everything in between.

When she was finally able to make her exit, Matthew walked her home, carrying a dozing Aiden in his arms.

She'd first met Matthew Jennings at the construction office of course, but seeing him at home set her back a little. He was a gruff, no-nonsense person and she respected him as a smart and generous businessman. Now she saw him with new eyes, soaking up all the resemblances between father and son. They shared the same tough, proud framework, the critical eye and problem-solving intelligence that made them both so capable as builders, men and providers.

There was fascinating comfort in that continuity from father to son when a woman was considering the idea of creating a happier future.

"I thought you were trouble," he said abruptly.

Shannon chose not to be offended. "You wouldn't have been wrong. I hope you realize I didn't intentionally drag your son or anyone else into my problems."

"Got that much by now." He bounced Aiden gently while she unlocked the door at the top of the steps. "Plan on running off?"

That question sparked a shower of nerves across her skin. "No." She pushed the door open, followed him inside. "Not anymore."

Matthew settled Aiden in his bed, closed the door and returned to the front room. "You were thinking of running." He stared her down.

"As recently as this afternoon," she admitted.

"What changed your mind?"

"I'm in love with your son, Mr. Jennings." Saying it aloud made her feel better, stronger. It turned her hope for the future into something solid and real. "More important, I love my son. Running from trouble isn't the example I want to set for him.

"I can barely remember my parents," she told him. "Seeing you and your wife reminded me what true love looks like, what a family should look like."

Two flags of color stained his cheeks and he shoved his hands into his pockets. "You expect Daniel to step in as that boy's daddy?"

"I expect Daniel and I will work out what we need and what happens next."

The bushy eyebrows pulled together once more and she knew what he was about to say. "I would never ask Daniel to be something he's not. Mr. Jennings, you have a phenomenal son with many skills and a heart that calls him to service as a firefighter."

Matthew swiveled away from her and stalked to the door. "He got that adrenaline-loving hero complex from his mother's side. Her dad and her brothers."

Not to mention the eyes, she thought, hiding a smile. "Plus another dose directly from you." She marveled that Matthew couldn't see it.

He turned on his heel, his eyes hard and suspiciously bright as he stared her down once more. "I taught him how to measure, cut and build."

"Has your business always run well? Did you never take a risk?"

"Of course there were lean times," he answered with a huff. "Everyone has them."

"Still, you provided, raised your boys with more options than you had. It's what we want as parents."

"Of course." He relaxed a fraction and the anger in his face gave way to bafflement. "How'd you get to be an expert so fast?"

She smiled, wishing she could hug him. He looked like he could use it and yet she thought it would get awkward. "Not an expert as much as an outside perspective. Could you walk away from the business you love?"

"I'd sure as hell like to retire," he said, gruffly.

"Daniel knows you want to retire and he knows you want him to take over. He's an excellent project leader and a fair boss. Maybe there's a way to hire someone to bridge the gap as you ease back before he's ready to step completely into that role."

"If ever."

"A thousand things could happen on any given shift," she said. "Thanks to you, Daniel has the firm footing to fall back on."

"Unless he dies on the job."

He was pushing her, testing her. "A thousand things could happen on any given day on a job site," she countered. The hitch in her pulse had far more to do with Daniel being attacked by a madman while doing his job, but she wasn't about to mention that.

"A father wants the best for his children," he said, dropping his gaze to the floor. "Is it so wrong to wish him—"

He dropped to the floor and Shannon panicked. "Matthew?"

"Floor's hot," he said, pressing his palms flat.

"What?"

The small window over the kitchen sink cracked and shattered in answer. She ducked down, watching in horror as wicked flames licked up and around the frame and caught on the curtains inside.

Smoke followed, swiftly fogging over the ceiling. The light fixture over the sink crackled and went out.

"Get to the door. I'll get the boy," Matthew said, turning toward the bedroom on his hands and knees.

"I'll call 911." Her phone was in her purse by the door. Keeping low under the smoke, Shannon crawled toward the front door, the floor hot under her hands and knees. The sounds of the fire eating away at the roof pushed her closer to panic. She found her phone and called 911, hoping the dispatcher understood her through the spate of coughing as she gave the address and reported the fire. "There are three of us in here," she said between more coughing.

The dispatcher asked her to stay on the line as another light overhead zapped and went out. The flames cast eerie shadows over what had been a cozy and familiar space. The heat and fumes were disorienting, the smoke stinging her mouth and nose. Through it all, she heard Aiden cry out for her. She dropped the phone and started toward his room.

"I'm here, baby!" she shouted over the fire raging across the far wall. A moment later, she saw a shadow of her son scrambling into view. "Where's Pop?"

"Stuck," Aiden wailed with tears in his eyes. "He said come to you. He said leave."

She couldn't go back to help Matthew until Aiden was clear. Clutching him close, she tugged his shirt up over his nose as her mind sorted what needed to be done. She put a hand on the doorknob and snatched it back, her palm scalded. Terror and panic knotted her stomach. With one hand locked with Aiden's, she peered through the window to see the landing engulfed by flames.

They were trapped. She'd been prepared to send

Aiden down to safety and now her mind wheeled. What now? How to save her son? Herself? Daniel's father?

She squinted against the fire closing in around them. Looking back toward the kitchen window, she judged her chances of getting Aiden safely through the window and down the trellis. The fire department was on the way. She just needed to buy them time.

She gripped Aiden's shoulders. "All three of us will get out of here," she told him, the words scraping against her raw throat. Grabbing two coats, she tucked her son next to her and they crawled back to the sink. She soaked the coats with water, purposely ignoring the flames sliding over the ceiling. She draped one coat over Aiden and hurried on hands and knees down the hall to find Matthew. The smoke was thicker here, the flames louder.

"Pop!" she called through the closed door.

"Get out of here!" he hollered back, his voice rough.

Shannon pushed open the door, shocked to see the corner of the roof missing and Matthew pinned under a beam. Grateful for the miracle that he was still alive, she and Aiden crawled closer. She tossed the wet coat over him, ignoring his orders to leave him.

"Stay with Pop," she told Aiden. She moved to where he was pinned, searching for a way to free him. "Fire department is on the way," she told him.

"Just leave me," he pleaded.

"How bad is it?" she asked, shoving at the beam and getting nowhere.

"Go!"

"We can't." She sat down and put her feet to the beam, hoping her legs were strong enough, while she squinted through tears to find something for leverage. "Stairs are blocked."

"You can't die here."

"Same goes."

Something underneath them groaned and rocked. She turned and covered her face as sparks fell from the dissolving ceiling, cinders steaming on the wet coats.

"Forget me," he barked. "Use the access stairs under the closet in your room."

She didn't know those existed. Before she could argue about him coming with them, the glorious sounds of sirens and truck horns blasted over the destructive roar of the fire.

Moments later, a truck ladder appeared in the open corner and relief flooded through her as she lifted Aiden into the care of the firefighter. When he reached for her, she stepped back, signaling to Matthew still stuck under the beam. He relayed the message on his radio and the following pause felt like an eternity.

"You first," the firefighter said.

"He's Daniel's father."

"We know. We won't leave him."

Stuck on the ground away from the action, Daniel's heart pounded in his chest as he watched his crew work the fire. The chief had him sidelined with his weeping mother when all he wanted was to get in there and get them out. Shannon, Aiden and his dad were stuck near the center of the fire. It looked as if the whole building would crumble in on itself any second.

"Let me go," he begged the chief. "I know that place inside and out." Hell, he'd helped build it.

"Stay right there. Child coming down the ladder."

Daniel's heart skipped erratically as Aiden was handed down the ladder extended over what had been his room. Daniel could just make out the iron frame of the daybed in the light from the flames.

He and his mother moved to the ambulance waiting across the street, ready to see for themselves that Aiden was okay.

Aiden scrambled away from the paramedics and ran for Daniel, clinging like a burr. Other than a dirty face and smoke-infused clothing, he didn't look any worse for the ordeal. His brown eyes were bloodshot and his voice raspy. "Pop and Mommy are still inside," he said. "Go get them!"

Gently, Daniel sat Aiden on the gurney and put the oxygen mask over his small face. "Working on it," he said. "Look there." He shifted the gurney around so Aiden could watch. "Here comes Mommy now."

Tess kissed Aiden and returned to her place by the chief, a stoic silhouette with her hands to her mouth as she watched every moment of Shannon's descent. With every muscle in his body tense, Daniel felt much the same as he and Aiden waited for Shannon to reach the ground.

"What about Pop?" Aiden asked, his voice muffled under the oxygen mask.

"They're working on it," Daniel said. His crew was working swiftly, and he knew they were more than capable. But playing the bystander with the lives of his family on the line, Daniel understood how slowly time could move when you didn't have any control.

"See that flat yellow thing?" Daniel pointed to the firefighters on the ladder. "It's called a backboard." It kept him calm, explaining the process of the rescue to Aiden. He knew from the radio chatter his father was pinned under a beam. He could see for himself, the way they were fighting the fire on two fronts, that time was running out.

As firefighters escorted Shannon to the ambulance, she waved them back to help his dad, then rushed ahead to check on Aiden. It was all Daniel could do not to pull her into his arms and kiss her until he was sure she was real and safe and not a figment of his imagination.

"You're safe," he said, wiping soot from her cheek.

She caught his hand and held it to her face a moment. "Your dad is okay," she told him over Aiden's head. "I don't think anything was broken."

"You're safe," he repeated, his relief palpable. "The call came in and I—" He stopped as his mother joined them.

"Matthew is okay," Shannon told her as they hugged. "I told Daniel I don't think anything is broken."

"He's too grumpy to go down easy," Tess said. "You two stayed with him?" she asked, stroking Aiden's hair. "Such a brave boy." She looked to Shannon, tears spilling down her face. "Brave mama, too."

A second ambulance rolled up and she hurried over to meet her husband as they carried him over. "Damn girl wouldn't leave," Matthew said.

Daniel rolled his eyes and Shannon laughed, with a few tears of relief mixed in.

He gave the paramedics room to examine her for injury and gave her a few minutes on the oxygen before he tried to put the emotions rolling through him into words.

"The call came in..." His voice failed him. *I love you.* Too soon for that. Giving in to the need, he pulled her into his arms and just held on. "What happened?" How had they all wound up in the apartment? "Was Dad grilling you again?"

Holding her and reaching out to the little boy who

had become so vital to him, Daniel discovered it was possible to be relieved and angry all at once. Through it all was a swell of gratitude that she and her son and his dad were alive and well under the layers of smoke and singed clothing.

"No. Aiden made sure your mom invited us to dinner," she began.

Daniel groaned even as he smiled a little at the image. That wouldn't have been a challenge.

"It was fine." She smiled, leaning into him a little. "Aiden had a blast."

The boy nodded.

"He was worn out and your dad carried him up to the apartment, tucked him into bed."

"And?" Daniel prompted when her gaze drifted to the decimated garage.

Her golden eyebrows knitted into a frown. "We were talking when he realized the floor was hot."

Daniel listened, amazed by her bravery and still terrified for the near miss. He cupped her chin and laid his lips on hers for a brief, gentle kiss. "I love you." Though he said it in barely more than a whisper, he knew by the stunned expression on her face she'd heard him.

She laid a hand over his heart, her brown gaze a bit starstruck. "I love you, too," she said, her lips tilting into a smile. "I meant to say that first. The moment I saw you."

"Say it whenever you like." He kissed her. "I can take it." Maybe not the best time for such a declaration, but now that the words were out, he wanted to shout them for everyone to hear. "I love you, Shannon."

"Are we married now?" Aiden asked.

They laughed, together, as he hoped they'd do everything from this point forward. Before either of them could explain, shouting erupted from the neighbors gathered to watch the crew put out the blaze.

A gunshot parted the screaming crowd. Stanwood, his features distorted by the flashing emergency lights, looked like a madman in the midst of utter chaos.

He leveled the weapon at Shannon. "You ruined me!"

Shannon leaped in front of Aiden, and Daniel sheltered her as Stanwood pulled the trigger. He counted two, three shots and saw a corner of the gurney mattress explode in a puff of plastic and foam. His turnout gear wasn't remotely bulletproof, but it was big enough to hide Aiden and most of Shannon while he shoved them into the back of the ambulance. He slammed the doors closed, counting on the paramedics to get them away safely. He turned on Stanwood, almost disappointed to see two policemen had drawn their weapons and were ordering him to cooperate.

Daniel knew he wouldn't.

"Put it down," he added his voice to the chorus of those giving orders. He held out his hands. "You don't want to do this, man. It's over."

As Daniel had hoped, Stanwood fixed on him, the long, black barrel of the gun tracking his movements away from the ambulance.

"Think it through." Daniel drew his attention when Stanwood fidgeted in search of Shannon. "Take it easy." He watched as the chief and others moved the crowd back as they flanked Stanwood. Another few seconds and they could have him under control. "Don't make this worse, man."

"Worse?" Stanwood shrieked. "I'm ruined!" he screamed. He waved the gun wildly. "She ruined me! I'm not going to prison. Not for any of it."

Not if he kept ignoring the orders to stand down,

Daniel thought. "You have teams of lawyers. Think this through," he said again.

The ambulance hiding Shannon and Aiden eased forward, away from the danger. With another desperate scream Stanwood opened fire, breaking into a run. Daniel braced, holding his ground against the man's rush, determined to keep Shannon and Aiden safe from every threat.

Daniel heard more gunshots and a crack and hiss. He spun around to check on Shannon and Aiden and realized a bullet had hit one of the emergency lights on the back of the escaping ambulance. Inside, they would be fine.

He turned back to see Stanwood stumble and crumple in a strange disjointed manner. His arm was sluggish as he tried to pull the trigger again, aiming for Daniel. Then he went limp and as the police closed in, Daniel realized Stanwood was dead.

Daniel swiveled in time to see the ambulance disappear around the corner. Grateful Shannon and Aiden hadn't seen Stanwood's demise, he jogged over to the chief.

"Go," the chief said before Daniel could ask. "I'll radio for them to wait for you at the end of the street."

With a hearty thank-you, Daniel broke into a run to catch up with the ambulance.

Shannon pleaded with the driver to stop, to go back, to wait and he'd refused. The paramedic in the back with them, a man named Carson, offered her reassurances that rang hollow.

Daniel had covered her and Aiden and turned to face her crazy ex. She could appreciate the gesture and still be furious that he'd ushered her out of danger.

She'd finally discovered true love. Heart, mind and soul were all in agreement on that point. Daniel was the real deal. She wasn't confused or worried about her intuition when it came to him. Her time with him had restored that sense of wonder and hope. He'd unearthed her inherent belief in happiness that she'd buried after Bradley.

If her ex-husband destroyed that hope, if he managed to hurt a single hair on Daniel's head, she would not stop until he was behind bars for life.

"Mommy?"

"Hmm?" Her gaze was on the rear window, while her ears strained to make sense of the voices crossing on the radio.

"Are you mad at Daniel?"

"What?" She gave her son her full attention. "No. No, sweetie." How could she explain without scarring her son? "I'm mad at the man who shot the gun."

"He's a bad guy, right?"

"Yes, he is." She pulled him onto her lap now that he wasn't on the oxygen anymore. "The good guys will take care of him."

"Good guys like Daniel?"

"That's exactly right," she said with more confidence than she felt. She hugged her baby close and said a prayer the man she loved was still in one piece.

As they approached the neighborhood entrance, the ambulance slowed down. "What now?"

"Picking up a passenger," Carson said.

The rear doors opened and her fury at her ex evaporated when she saw Daniel's face. "Chief said I could ride along with you to the hospital."

"You beat the bad guy!" Aiden bounced out of her lap and into Daniel's arms. Shannon wasn't far behind.

"I'll just move up front." Carson hopped out, slapping Daniel on the shoulder as he gave them a little room for the embraces. Once they were back in the ambulance, Carson shut the doors and moved up front for the ride to the hospital.

His arms felt so right around her and she couldn't stop touching him in kind. He was really safe. Aiden, caught between them, squirmed and giggled until they broke apart when he started coughing.

"Are you hurt?" she asked.

"Not a scratch. Well, not any new ones," Daniel amended.

"I worried," she confessed, feeling guilty for it.

"She was mad," Aiden added, mimicking his mother's angry face.

Shannon felt her cheeks heat, but she didn't care. "Not mad at you," she explained.

Daniel chuckled, holding them steady as they turned a corner. "Admit it, you were a little mad at me."

"I'm over it. Mostly. You're a firefighter, not a cop. You weren't even armed." She forced another wave of worst-case scenarios from her mind. "He's out of his mind."

"He *was*. He won't bother anyone again," Daniel said.

She caught the full meaning of that statement in his eyes and felt no shame in the relief coursing through her.

"How'd you win without a gun?" Aiden asked.

Shannon winced. He'd seen too much violence in recent days and she had to hope that those memories would fade with time and examples of better, more honorable behavior. Examples she hoped Daniel would enjoy providing.

"Same way I saved *you* with only a brick." He kissed

Aiden's head. "I had the best weapon ever made on my side," Daniel replied.

"A laser gun?" Aiden asked, peeking under the open panels of Daniel's coat.

"No." He tapped Aiden's nose and rubbed a hand over his hair, his gaze locked with hers. "Love."

Shannon's heart stuttered in her chest.

Aiden didn't seem too impressed. "How's that beat bad guys with guns?"

"Love gives you an edge over the bad guys every time."

Aiden leaned forward. "How?"

"Love is right here." He tapped his heart, then Aiden's. "It gives you something to fight for, a special reason to win no matter what happens. And when someone loves you back, it's better than any laser gun."

"You did beat him fast."

"I had some help out there," he allowed. "It's a team effort. But we were fast. Know why?"

Aiden shook his head.

"Because I have two people, you and your mom, to love and fight for. It's like a power boost."

Aiden's eyes were wide as his gaze traveled from Daniel to her and back. "You love me, too?"

"With all my heart, Aiden."

"With us loving you, you'll always beat the bad guys." Aiden climbed into Daniel's lap and burrowed under the coat while Shannon swiped at the happy tears spilling down her cheeks.

The hospital exams were a formality and the doctors quickly confirmed none of them needed to be admitted for treatment. The late hour was catching up with Aiden and he was half asleep on Daniel's shoulder as they went upstairs to visit Matthew. The doctors were holding him for observation due to a concussion and a broken rib.

Tess waved them in. "You're all well?"

"Absolutely," Shannon said, giving her a hug. "You're well here, too?"

She nodded. "I'm glad you came by. He's been insisting on speaking to you tonight."

"Dad," Daniel began with a sigh. "Whatever it is can wait until tomorrow. We need to get this little guy home to bed."

Shannon shot him a look. Until now, she hadn't let herself think about where to go, where she could go. With her ex out of the picture, they could all go back to her place without worry. Would Daniel want that too? Aiden could sleep in his own bed again. Of course the prized truck collection was lost. As was the blue rabbit. But those were problems easily remedied.

"Not you," Matthew snapped. "Shannon." He waved her over and adjusted the bed to sit up.

She bit back the admonishment that he should rest. If he needed to finish their earlier conversation, she'd deal with it.

"Thank you." To her surprise, he clasped her hand between his. "They didn't have to tell me I would've been in far worse shape without your quick thinking with the wet coat."

She leaned down and kissed his forehead. "Thank you for getting Aiden out of harm's way."

He snorted and looked over to Daniel. "They know it's arson, right? No other answer for it."

"Dad, it's under control." He swayed side to side with the sleeping boy on his shoulder. "The investigators think it's the same arsonist for hire who set the warehouse fire at the pier. They'll find him."

"Good. You're back on a full-time firefighter schedule right?"

"Yes, sir."

"And I'm outta commission for a few days at least." He looked up at Shannon. "Tess keeps telling me to dial it back more. I'm inclined to start agreeing with her."

"That's good news." Shannon squeezed his hand.

"This trouble of yours, is it over?"

"Dad…" Daniel's voice had dropped to a warning, but Shannon halted any argument with a raised finger.

"It's a fair question." She glanced back, confirmed Aiden was asleep. "I'm told my ex-husband is dead, thanks to Daniel and police at the scene of the fire. There is no reason for anyone else who knew him to come after me."

"Good news all around." Matthew sat up a little straighter. "With that cleared up, I'm offering you Daniel's job at Jennings Construction."

Those weren't the words she'd expected to hear. At all. "I beg your pardon?"

"Someone has to run things. Someone reliable who will protect what I've built. Full time, steady hours and benefits that were good enough to raise our two boys."

She floundered for the right words. "You should sleep on this decision. You can't mean—"

"I'm not handing you a construction business and walking away. I'm asking you to manage it, to help all of us make a better transition. Your mind, your skills are what our company needs. We'll draw it up legal and take into account what should happen if Daniel or his brother want to change their roles. No one will have the right to kick you out of the boss's seat because of a last name."

"You have a concussion." She sent Tess a pleading look. "This should wait."

"Take the job, Shannon." Tess beamed at her. "Aiden will be in school soon and you both need the stability. None of the crews will have a problem answering to you."

"There are more senior people, more qualified people," she protested.

"And not one of them had an eye on this job," Tess said. "They all know we're a family company and Matthew always planned to keep it that way."

She was tempted, so tempted. The stability, the salary, the challenge were dangling right there within her reach. She'd been making ends meet as part of the crew, but this…it was too much. She clapped a hand to her mouth, remembering she didn't even need the money after what Gary had done for them.

Turning toward Daniel, she braced herself for his reaction. He couldn't be happy about his dad making this move, yet she knew how much the firehouse meant to him. If he convinced her he was okay with this, she'd consider it.

"Look at me." Holding Aiden in one arm, he tipped up her chin with the other. "Is this what you want?"

"It's your family business. It should be about what you want, too."

"That's an excuse, not an answer. And I want a lot of things," he said. He stroked a thumb along her cheekbone and the tenderness swamped her. "If nothing else was mixed in and you got this job offer, would you take it?"

She nodded, lips clamped together so she couldn't add excuses or conditions. Already her mind raced along, eager to discover and learn what would be required to manage a company of this size.

"That's one issue out of the way." He lifted his chin toward his dad. "Give him your answer."

With happiness thrumming through her, she laced her fingers with Daniel's and accepted Matthew's offer. "Good. Now go on so I can rest. I'll start the contracts when I'm out of here."

Daniel gave her hand a little tug and caught her attention. "I know it's been crazy and my timing could be better. I have a question for you as well. One that shouldn't wait."

She watched, fascinated, as he went down on one knee with Aiden snoring softly on his shoulder.

"I love you, Shannon. More than anything I want to be your husband and Aiden's dad. Will you marry me?"

"For Pete's sake. There are more romantic settings," Matthew muttered.

Tess hushed him.

Overcome, Shannon's voice failed her when she tried to say yes.

"What was that?" Daniel asked.

She dropped to her knees, too, wrapping her arms around Daniel and her son. "Yes. You're the best thing that's happened to me since Aiden. I'd be honored to be your wife and I know he wants to call you Daddy. I love you, Daniel. We love you so much."

"That settles the nonsense of keeping the business in the family, I suppose," Matthew said with a bit of a sniffle.

They said their goodbyes to his parents and headed home. *Home.* The word resonated in her heart. Home and a family complete at last with Daniel.

When Aiden was clean and settled in his bed, she

stepped out on her porch and looked up at the stars. All those wishes she'd been afraid to make had come true.

"What are you doing?" Daniel asked, wrapping his arms around her from behind.

"Just what you taught me best." She leaned back into his strong and warm embrace. "Believing."

* * * * *

Don't miss other books in Regan Black's
ESCAPE CLUB HEROES *series*

A STRANGER SHE CAN TRUST
SAFE IN HIS SIGHT

Available now from Harlequin Romantic Suspense!

And look out for Regan Black's novella,
"Special Agent Cowboy" in the
KILLER COLTON CHRISTMAS *anthology,*
available December 2017!

COMING NEXT MONTH FROM

◆ HARLEQUIN®
™

ROMANTIC suspense

Available December 5, 2017

#1971 KILLER COLTON CHRISTMAS
The Coltons of Shadow Creek
by Regan Black and Lara Lacombe

In these two holiday novellas, the Ortega brothers each find love in Shadow Creek, Texas, amid murder, death threats and computer hacking. Will they finally be able to defeat Livia Colton once and for all?

#1972 WYOMING UNDERCOVER
by Karen Whiddon

Private investigator Jack Moreno infiltrates a remote cult to locate his clients' missing son. There, he finds more than he bargained for when beautiful but naive Sophia Hannah—whose parents are pushing her into an arranged marriage with the cult's leader—needs saving, too.

#1973 OPERATION NOTORIOUS
Cutter's Code • by Justine Davis

Opposites attract when trusting librarian Katie Moore is forced to turn to high-powered defense attorney Gavin de Marco to clear her father of murder charges. Gavin doesn't trust anyone, but can he manage to open his heart to Katie?

#1974 BLACK OPS WARRIOR
Man on a Mission • by Amelia Autin

Black ops soldier Niall Jones's assignment? Prevent Dr. Savannah Whitman from revealing the top secret military defense information she possesses to the enemy...by whatever means necessary. But when Savannah is the one in danger, Niall has to do whatever it takes to protect her and convince her that despite his original assignment, they're meant to be.

She was a quick learner and from the couch, Scrabble gave a soft woof.

"Thanks, sweetie," Marie said to the dog, breaking the lesson to go rub Scrabble's ears.

He stared at the two of them. "Choke hold."

Marie's eyebrows arched high as she gave him her attention. "Really?"

He caught her hands and put them on his throat, immediately regretting the contact. There was a warmth in her touch that left him craving her hands on other parts of his body. To save his sanity, he made her grip stronger. "Hold on. First, keep your head."

"All right." Her eyes locked on his mouth and she licked her lips.

A bolt of desire shot through his system. "Raise your arms overhead and clasp your hands." He demonstrated and her gaze drifted up his arms to his hands and back down to his biceps.

This was a bad idea. "Now sweep down and twist to one side." Gently, in slow motion, he showed her how to escape the hold.

"And run," she said for him when he was free of her.

"Your turn." He moved in front of her. "Ready?"

She gave an uncertain nod.

He wrapped his hands lightly around her throat, the blood in her veins fluttering under his hands. "This is practice," he reminded her as her eyes went wide and distant. Her hair was soft as silk against his knuckles. "Marie." He flexed his fingers, just enough to get her attention. "Keep your head."

He struggled to heed his own advice since everything inside him clamored to pull her into a much different embrace and discover if her lips were as soft as they looked.

"Uh-huh." Her arms came up, her hands clasped and she executed the motion perfectly, breaking his hold and dancing out of his reach.

"Well-done." He straightened his shirt and tucked it back into place.

"Thank you, Emiliano." She perched on the couch next to his dog. "That helps me feel better already."

Good news for one of them. Edgier than ever, he needed an escape. "I'll be in the study." He glanced at Scrabble, but she didn't budge from her place by Marie.

He left the room without another word. Her determination to be prepared and take care of herself made him want to lower his defenses and care for her. He couldn't afford that kind of mistake. His team was counting on him to do his part for the investigation and he would not let them down.

Don't miss "Special Agent Cowboy"
by Regan Black in KILLER COLTON CHRISTMAS,
available December 2017 wherever
Harlequin® Romantic Suspense books and ebooks are sold.

www.Harlequin.com

LOVE
Harlequin
romance?

Join our Harlequin community to share your thoughts and connect with other romance readers!

Be the first to find out about promotions, news, and exclusive content!

Sign up for the Harlequin e-newsletter and download a free book from any series at
www.TryHarlequin.com

CONNECT WITH US AT:

Harlequin.com/Community

Facebook.com/HarlequinBooks

Twitter.com/HarlequinBooks

Instagram.com/HarlequinBooks

Pinterest.com/HarlequinBooks

ReaderService.com

HARLEQUIN®

**ROMANCE WHEN
YOU NEED IT**

HSOCIAL2017